Crew

Hockey Royalty

Victoria Denault

Editing: Brandi Zelenka at My Notes in the Margin

Cover: Winona Randall Designs

Proofing: OCA Proof Reading

Reader Advisory

This book contains mention of physical assault. My FMC has been the victim of an attack (not sexual) and although it happens off-page it may be triggering for some. Reader discretion is advised.

HOCKEY ROYALTY
Garrison Family Tree

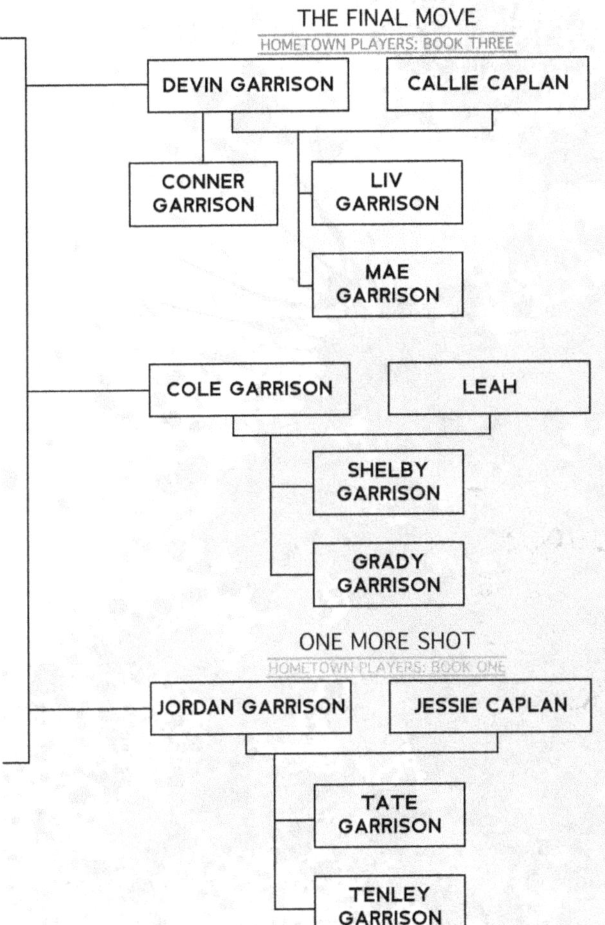

HOCKEY ROYALTY
Westwood Family Tree

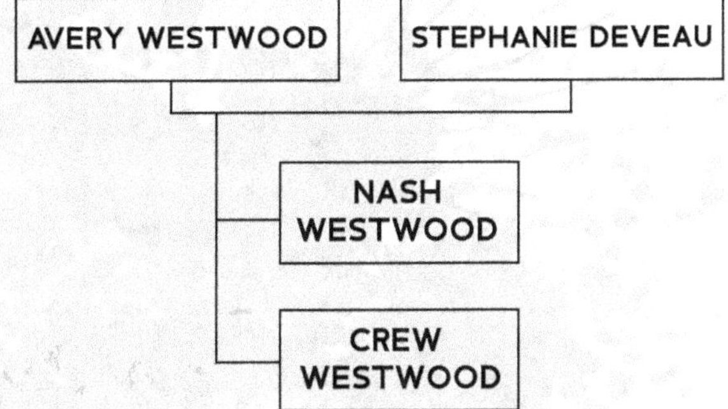

Chapter 1

Liv

I just stare at my hands. I can't stop. They're twisted together in my lap, motionless, but my nails are digging into the flesh. I think I can feel it. I mean, no. I can't. Not the way I should. But the dulled pain I feel is welcome because I'm here to feel it. I'm here. Alive. Unharmed, mostly.

"Olivia," a gentle voice says. I look up to find a nurse's head poking through the ajar door. "You're cousin—"

And then the door is pushed all the way open and the nurse barks out a complaint but Tenley shoves her out of the way anyway. "Liv. Oh my God. Liv."

She is charging toward me at the speed of light. I flinch and hold up my hands, palms out, as my eyes snap shut. Her sneakers squeak on the white tile floor she stops so abruptly. "I'm fine. I swear."

I am *so* not fine. Not mentally. But physically, on paper, I am and that's important. It's everything. I have to focus on that.

"Ma'am I told you to wait in the hall until she gave consent."

"I give consent," I say and my voice is oddly horse. Oh right, I screamed when he tried to... do whatever he tried to do.

The nurse hesitates but closes the door and Tenley squats in front of me, a foot from the edge of the medical bed I'm perched on. She looks up at me, her fearless blue eyes are... fearful, and that's when my own tears overtake me. Fuck. I've scared the one unflappable, brave, fearless person I know. Fuck. Fuck. FUCK.

"Liv. Oh, God." Tenley is crying now too. I can't see it, because my eyes are swimming in tears, but I can hear it. "Oh my God, I am going to fucking murder this guy. I am going to rip his throat out with my bare hands. Oh my God."

"I'm fine," I repeat because eventually I should believe it, right? Manifest it or some shit. "He didn't. I wasn't."

"You weren't?" Tenley questions, and we don't have to say the words. We're women. We both know exactly what we're talking about. "He didn't?"

"He tried. I mean I think he was trying," I swallow and wipe at my cheeks, willing the tears to fucking stop. "Maybe he was just going to rob me, but the police think... I stopped him from maybe doing both."

Tenley raises to her full height and I watch her walk to the little bathroom attached to the private room they put me in off the emergency waiting room. She comes back with a paper towel in her hands. "Can I touch you?"

I nod and she leans forward and wipes the paper towel gently across my cheek. I'm shocked when it's pinkish-red. "You have blood on your hands and you wiped it across your face."

I look down. My nails sliced my flesh. There're three bleeding half-moons on the flesh of my palm. I press them into my jeans. The door opens and we both turn. I jump though because I'm still freaking out inside.

The doctor looks at me with a small reassuring smile. "Your CT came back clear. You don't even have a concussion."

"Thank god," Tenley sighs out. "Can you look at her hands please?"

The doctor's eyes flit down and his eyebrows pinch for a

second but he smiles again and puts his tablet on the bed beside me as he asks me to flip over my hands. He sees the marks. "I'll get a nurse to clean that up and I'm going to prescribe you some Ativan. I want you to take one before you leave. And another tomorrow morning and then, as required."

"I don't need drugs."

"You do," he insists. "Just for a couple of days. And you also need counseling. I am going to give you some pamphlets."

"I don't," I argue. "Nothing happened to me."

"Miss Garrison, just because you didn't experience the worst-case scenario doesn't mean you didn't experience valid trauma," he tells me like I'm some silly little kid who doesn't know how the world works. I kind of feel like that so I'm not offended. "And I'm still going to advise you to let us call your parents."

"No. Never. NO!" Did I just yell that last no? Judging by the way the doctor stiffens and Tenley jumps, I guess I did. I try to take a deep breath but I can't. "Are my ribs broken? Bruised. I can't... I can't take a deep breath."

"That's what the Ativan is for," he explains as he picks up his tablet. "It will help with the shock and panic. So will the therapy. And the support of your family. Parents."

Tenley's hand gently touches my shoulder. "I'm her cousin. She lives with me. I'll take good care of her."

He looks less concerned after Tenley reveals that but still a little worried. He nods and hands Tenley some pamphlets from his lab coat pocket. "The nurse will be here in a second with the prescription and to clean your hands. Take care, Olivia. You're a warrior. Remember how strong you were tonight."

He leaves the room and Tenley runs a hand on top of my head and looks at the bruise I know is forming on my cheek. She forces her eyes to mine. "He's right. You *are* a warrior and I'm so proud of you."

She tucks the pamphlets into the back pocket of her jeans and goes back to smoothing my hair. It's nice, and that feeling of comfort starts to seep in. My mom used to smooth my hair after I had nightmares when I was little. My mom... oh God... if I was just more like my mom maybe I wouldn't be this shaken. Maybe the asshole wouldn't have seen me as a target. She's the only person I know who is as fearless, strong, and tough as Tenley.

My eyes start to well up again but the nurse comes in and I focus on her, and her instructions, and I take the little tablet she gives me and let it melt under my tongue as instructed. Honestly, I feel like I'm listening to her talk but not truly hearing a word she says. And then the drug starts to work before I can even stand up. I need Tenley to guide me slowly out of the hospital and to her waiting car.

All I remember for the rest of the night is waking up in different places. The car. The outdoor courtyard of our apartment building where I was being carried by my cousin Tate, Tenley's brother. My bedroom. Tate's girlfriend Mallory was sitting on one side of my bed, and Tenley on the other.

Every time I woke I only said one thing. "Don't tell my parents."

And they all promised not to tell.

* * *

When I finally wake up and actually feel awake, the room is dark. I'm not in the clothes I'd been wearing when it happened. I'm in my favorite pajamas. I guess Tenley, or maybe Mallory, changed me. I stretch. My hands ache a little. My head feels like someone has stuffed it with cotton, and my neck's stiff, but I remember everything.

I remember walking on Hilgard Avenue, the street that skirts the University campus. I remember seeing the bus stop on

Sunset and starting to dig in my pocket for my bus pass. I remember the feel of big, cold, clammy hands on my throat. The harsh way he yanked me. The feel of my left shoulder being crushed into the grass next to the sidewalk. I don't remember clawing his face. I do remember the punch, seeing his hand coming for my face and the pain radiating up into my skull like a lightning bolt, but I don't remember slamming the butt of my hand into his nose. I remember his weight being gone from my body as the blow caused him to topple backwards, off of me. I remember scrambling to my feet. I think I screamed?

I swallow now and my throat is desperately sore. Yeah. I screamed. I remember a woman yelling. A man my dad's age appeared out of nowhere. He jumped on the guy who attacked me. I don't know who he was or what happened next. I don't think I blacked out. I don't know though. I just remember being in an ambulance and then the little room at the hospital.

I sit up and slowly get out of bed. My door is pulled but not tightly closed, and I can hear voices in the living room just down the hall. As I walk on shaky legs to take my robe off the hook on the back of the door, I eavesdrop.

"It's not your fault, Ten," Tate says firmly. "You need to stop with that. Now."

"But I took the car. I knew she had an evening class. I was just meeting friends for dinner. I should have Ubered." Tenley sounds distraught.

"If Liv hears you, she'll waste all her energy making you feel better when she should be concentrating on herself.." Tate warns his little sister and he's not wrong. I feel guilty hearing the anguish in Tenley's voice.

I never mind when Tenley takes the car. I mean, we share the car. She usually uses it less than me but, I've been trying to lessen my carbon footprint. Los Angeles has a fairly decent transit system that nobody uses. I was being responsible. Even if

Tenley had left me the car I might not have taken it to school that evening. There have been times when she's home and the car is available but I still walk or take the bus. I won't anymore, but I did.

"He's right, Ten," Mallory says. I worry that Tate's girlfriend is here and knows about everything. The more people who know the harder it will be to keep it from my parents. My family is large and a bit of a sieve. All the grains of news and drama eventually slip through. "Let's all just concentrate on the fact that she kicked that dude's ass. He's in jail and she's okay, more or less anyway."

"I'm so proud of her."

"Thank fucking god she knows how to fight," Tate adds. "And she found the courage to do it. And he wasn't armed. And that couple came out of their home."

I open the door and make my way down the hall. My legs are shaky like they're weaker than they were just twenty-four hours ago. The living room curtains on our two big windows are pulled back and the room is bathed in light. It feels like the sun is extra bright. Everything feels... Extra.

Mallory sees me first and gets to her feet. She's on the floor by the coffee table with Dylan, Tate's son. Mallory's eyes are soft, her smile tentative. "Hey. You okay?"

"Yeah." My voice is thick. I clear my throat as Tenley jumps out of her chair and spins to face me and Tate leans forward from his position on the couch. "Hungry. I think."

"I'll get you something," Mallory says and hands Tate the truck she's holding. Dylan gets to his feet and reaches for it.

Mallory passes me on her way to the kitchen and shoots me another gentle smile. I think I smile back. "I feel... numb."

"That's probably normal," Tate surmises and slides over to the other end of the couch. "Come sit."

I walk toward him. Dylan looks up at me. "Wivvy!"

I look down at him and my heart starts to feel warm, and my body starts to wake up. He's the best. The addition our family had no idea we needed. This time last year Tate had no idea Dylan existed. Now, our big family couldn't imagine life without him.

He, like Tate, Mallory, and the rest of us, has spent the summer in Maine with our extended family. It was a great summer where we celebrated Tate's Stanley Cup win, Dylan's first birthday, his first steps, and his first words. One of which was Wivvy (his version of Livvy) because I spent every moment I could with him.

Tenley is now in her senior year at UCLA and I should have graduated last year but I switched majors and now I have another year of classes, and an internship, in order to graduate with a degree in Art Education.

"Shouldn't you be at practice or something?" I ask as I take a seat next to Tate and Dylan waves at me with the enthusiasm only a toddler has.

"Season hasn't started yet, Liv," Tate reminds me gently. Right. It's only September. Hockey starts in early October which is... almost two weeks away. "I told the coach I had a family thing. It's fine if I miss a practice or two right now."

I start to panic. "You didn't tell him details, right? Did you tell anyone else? Please say no."

He raises both hands and his aquamarine eyes get wide. "I swear I didn't tell anyone. He probably thinks it's Dylan-related. I understand this is personal, Liv. I am not telling anyone anything. But I think you should talk to Uncle Devin and Aunt Callie."

My parents. My anxiety ratchets up so quickly at the thought I shudder. Tate touches my shoulder. I shudder again. He pulls his hand back. "Liv, you know they'll support you."

"I know. I don't want them to, though," I reply and, as if he senses my stress, Dylan discards the truck Tate gave him and starts to try and climb my legs, tugging on the leg of my pajamas. I pull him into my lap and he immediately snuggles into me.

"I felt the same way when I found out about Dylan. I didn't want to tell any of you because I didn't want help. But I was wrong," Tate replies and runs a hand over Dylan's head. His blond hair is almost white thanks to a summer at the lake. "I should have told them immediately."

"He should have," Tenley agrees. She's been watching me quiet as a mouse, hugging her knees to her chest in the chair.

"The difference is Dylan is here forever," I explain and it's tough trying to put my feelings into words. "This isn't forever. I don't want this to be forever. It was a thing that happened. It sucks. I'm fine. I don't want to have to keep talking about it forever. I don't want Dad to be stressed about me living here. I don't want Mom to ask me if I'm okay until the end of time."

"I get that but..." Tenley sighs. "I'm worried about you."

"Please don't be. I'm going to be okay. I swear," I say firmly.

Tate and Tenley exchange pessimistic glances. I frown as Dylan squirms a little in my lap. "I'm serious. I refuse to not be okay."

Mallory comes back into the living room carrying a glass of orange juice in one hand and a sandwich on a plate in the other. "BLT with avocado. I made them earlier for the rest of us and left some extra ingredients in case you woke up."

"Thank you. I need coffee too." I put the plate down and lift Dylan into Tate's lap, but Tenley pops up from her chair like a backyard firework going off.

"I'll make it for you!" She disappears into the kitchen.

Mallory takes Tenley's vacated seat and I take a bite of the sandwich. It's delicious, but they're all watching me like I'm a baby panda at a zoo or something. I swallow and smile. "Thanks. It's perfect."

"You're welcome." Mallory smiles. "How else can we help? I've been through a bit of a different kind of trauma so I know that people's idea of what you might need and what you really need can be two different things."

A stricken look flashes over Tate's face for a heartbeat. Mallory was in a car crash last year with her best friend—Dylan's mom—who didn't survive. I swallow another bite of the sandwich. "I need to..."

Be smarter. Be stronger. Have less to lose.

"I need something to look forward to," I say as something blooms in my memory. Something Tenley said last week. I turn my head toward the kitchen door, which is one of those swinging ones from the sixties. It's propped open right now. "Ten! Are you still going to Vegas next week?"

"I can cancel!" she calls out and appears in the doorway with a coffee mug in her hands. "Tate and Mallory won't care."

"I don't want you to cancel," I tell her and take the cup. "I want to go with you."

"What?" Tate looks shocked.

"I know. It's not my jam, but I need a distraction," I explain. "And it will be fun, right?"

Tate, Tenley, and Mallory all exchange glances. I start to get annoyed. I mean, yeah, it's not something I would have ever wanted to do before. But what I wanted to do, who I was, and the choices I made, led to me getting randomly attacked by a stranger who wanted to either mug me or rape me or kill me, or all three. So I think now is as good a time as any to do something that isn't what I always do.

"I can go somewhere else, by myself, if you guys don't have room or don't want me there," I announce and put the sandwich down, ready to head back into my room.

Tate wraps an arm around my shoulder and gently pulls me

against his big, hulking frame. "You are always welcome to come, Livvy. Right, Ten?"

"Yes. Of course." Tenley nods emphatically. "We have a suite booked. Plenty of room."

"Cool." I reach for the sandwich and try not to shake as I bring it to my mouth.

This is what I need. I'm not going to sit here and be the same lame duck that got me targeted to begin with. And I'm going to make sure that if God forbid, this ever happens again, I have one less thing to worry about.

I'm going to go to Vegas and I'm going to lose my virginity.

Chapter 2

Crew

Nash is seething, which is hard to do while also panting as heavy as a cow in labor. I don't even try to bite back my smile. "Fuck you. I'm still recovering from surgery."

"Are you still seriously going to milk that?' I question with a judgy arch of my eyebrow. "Coach Braddock isn't going to put up with that, you know? And neither is Dad. Dad had both wrists operated on one off-season and still beat his own goals record in the first two months back on the ice."

Nash gets off his treadmill, bends, and puts his hands on his thighs, glaring at me. It's the type of glare that actually makes me feel like he's trying to incinerate me and might actually succeed. "You're a fucking dick."

"And you're still out of shape," I reply, unperturbed by his insult. I sip from my water bottle and walk over to the stretching area. I drop down on the mats and reach for my ankles. "You need to work double-time, Nash. I'm sorry but you know it's true. We wanna repeat, don't we? If we can win the Cup back-to-back we've done something dad hasn't."

Our father, Avery Westwood, has won the Stanley Cup a whopping four times, but never back-to-back. It's not easy to find something he hasn't done in hockey, so of course this is my new obsession. It should be Nash's too. He wants to get out of our dad's shadow as much as I do.

"The season hasn't even started yet. We're supposed to be here to chill out before it starts, so chill the fuck out, bro," Nash grumbles. He has been super-pissy since… well forever. I don't know what's up his ass. I've been trying to give him space but it's starting to annoy me too much. If he keeps it up, I'm gonna confront him.

I watch him grab his towel and water bottle and walk towards the gym doors with a slight limp. "You need to stretch."

"I need ice for this fucking leg," Nash snaps. "I'll stretch in the suite, with ice."

He disappears, leaving me alone in this big, fancy hotel gym. I sigh and continue to stretch. Nash and I used to be so close. We were the best of friends and the quintessential twins. We finished each other's sentences, we had inside jokes and could find each other without even looking on the ice. We were two peas in a pod.

I have to admit that started to unravel when I married Anne-Marie. Nash liked her when we were in high school and I first started dating her. Hell, even my parents liked her. But all three grew concerned when I popped the question at such a young age.

Nash and I spent our first year on the Los Angeles Quake living together, with Anne-Marie who unofficially moved in. I was fine with it. It irked Nash and my dad who said it looked bad. Yeah, live-in girlfriends were fine for other players but not for me. The son of hockey's golden child. So I proposed. I was in love, I don't deny it. I loved that woman with every fiber of my being. My very young, very naive, and very immature being. And once we were married, I would do anything to make it work. I did anything and everything, which is why it was so easy for her to rip my heart to shreds.

The distinct beep of a pass card at the door pulls me from my mental walk down Heinous Memory Lane. The door to the gym swishes open and this hot dude walks in. He's taller and fairer than I usually like, but he's built like a male fitness model. Lithe but with all the right ropey muscle in all the right places. He's not that tall. Probably just under my six feet, but he's got nice lips and a nice smile, which he's aiming at me.

"Hey."

"Hey."

"Hope you don't mind some company," he says as he walks past me to one of the bikes lining the back wall.

I check out his ass. "Nah. The more the merrier. I'm just finishing up anyway."

"That's too bad."

Okay, he's not dancing around things. I smile and he catches it in the mirror and smiles back, adding a wink as he climbs onto the Peloton. Yeah, he's interested. But I don't know who he is, or where he's from, or if he knows who I am. All of this has to be established before I hook up with anyone—male or female—which is why so far my male hook-ups have just been hockey players or those working in the NHL, like trainers or equipment managers.

"What brings you to Sin City?" he asks, and I push the heels of my feet together and lean over them to stretch out my groin.

"Partying with some friends from work," I say vaguely. "You?"

"Medical conference."

My eyebrows lift. "You're a doctor?"

"Anesthesiologist."

"You put people to sleep," I say and he chuckles, our eyes meeting in the mirror again.

"Only when I have to, I promise," he replies and his grin deepens as his pace on the bike picks up a little. "I am pretty good at keeping the right guy awake too."

Shit. Is it Vegas that's making him hit on me so brazenly or is this just his M.O.? Or is he fishing for something because he's a reporter or fan who wants a story or a reel that gets him famous? Fuck, my dad has made me so fucking paranoid.

There's another beep before I can figure out how to respond to the guy. In walks a woman. She's young. Like my age, or younger. She's got the most incredible body I have seen in a long time. On a woman. It's wrapped in a white and pink cropped lycra top and matching capri leggings. Her brown hair, which isn't very long, is separated into two little ponytails at the base of her neck. Her skin is pale and dusted with freckles. Her eyes are wide and brown and there's not a lick of make-up decorating them, but they sparkle.

She stops short upon entry. Looks at the guy on the bike. Look at me. I shoot her a smile. She looks at her feet before she can catch it though. I swear she's about to turn right around and leave. But she takes a deep breath, shoves her earbuds into her ears, and marches past me. There's a boxing station in the corner of the gym and she goes right over there.

I watch her as I move into the downward dog yoga pose, to stretch some more. She starts putting on the gloves as she reads the instructions for the machine on the wall. It reminds me of a giant Simon Says game. There are large pads in different colors. You are supposed to hit the one that lights up. The machine gives you a different sequence to punch depending on the workout you select. She's reading the instructions with a furrowed brow like she's really concentrating. She's even hotter in profile with a long, elegant neck and sharp cheekbones.

"You said you're here for work?"

Right. Hot guy is still here. I turn to look at him again. He's lifted his butt off the seat and is cycling hard now but he's barely out of breath. "I'm here with co-workers, but not for work. We are blowing off some steam before we... head into another long hard quarter."

He nods slowly. "Long and hard, huh?"

I nod and can literally feel the heat in his gaze like it's the sun hitting my face on a cloudless day. I stand up and his eyes trail down my body, over my shorts and my tank that is clinging to me thanks to sweat. My dick twitches but my eyes move to the gorgeous girl as she punches the flashing blue pad, hard. Then she slams her gloved fist into the yellow one. She's tiny almost to the point of looking frail but all her muscles tense as she punches and the power behind it is shocking. And also hot. My dick twitches again.

I pull my phone out of my pocket to check the time. I'm supposed to meet a bunch of the guys in the casino for some blackjack before we head to some fancy sushi place for dinner and then a club. "Are you pulling that out to get my number?"

"Do you want me to get your number?"

"Yeah," he replies, slowing his cycling to a stop. His dirty blond hair is damp and he's breathing a little bit heavily, finally. I can imagine all the other ways I can make him do that—pant and sweat. "I'm here until Tuesday. You?"

"A day or two. Playing it by ear. We're only a drive away. From California." I act like I don't know, but I know. We're here until tomorrow afternoon. And we didn't drive. We flew. But I don't really want to get into that with him. In case he is fishing for a story or worse.

"Okay well..." He's walking toward me now. Towel draped

around his sweaty neck, hand extended toward me and my phone. I don't hand it to him though. Instead, I extend my hand and shake his. That has him grinning in that "oh, so we're gonna play coy, are we? I'm game" sort of way. "Jason."

"Hi, Jason." I don't offer my name. It's too distinct. But now he's staring at me like I'm an asshole so I smile and lie. "West."

Yeah because that's less unique you fucking idiot, my brain scolds. But it's my standard fake name because I'm not creative and West is the only acceptable pseudonym for Crew Avery Westwood. Obviously using Wood as a name on Grindr or in gay bars would be too on-point.

"Hey, West." Jason smiles. "Fourteen forty-four."

"What?"

"My room number," he explains with a shrug. "Obviously we're both staying here so if you wanna hang out, grab a drink, or more call the front desk and ask for room fourteen forty-four. I'm staying alone."

"I'm with my friends," I say. "Two per room."

Not a lie. Nash and I are staying together but in a two-bedroom suite. I could sneak this guy into my room, fuck him until he screams my fake name, and get him out the door without Nash ever knowing. And I might. But probably not... my eyes move to the woman beating the shit out of the boxing machine.

I clear my throat and turn back to Jason. "Nice to meet you."

"Hope to see you soon."

I leave the gym and head up to my suite. The entire time I'm in the elevator I think about the woman pummeling the boxing machine like it had personally wronged her. But I still punch Jason's room number into my notes app, just in case.

As I'm walking down the hall to my room my phone rings. "Hey, Dad."

"How's Vegas?" he asks.

"Wild. Insane. Have you seen *The Hangover*? It's like that," I say, rolling my eyes. "Only with fewer babies and more tigers. Do you know a good lawyer? I probably need one. The internet's not forever, right? I mean I can get Mark Zuckerberg to delete the video that topless girl posted. The one wearing my underwear. You know Zuck, right? Will he do you a favor?"

"Even your mother doesn't have this level of sarcasm," Dad replies, his tone flat with annoyance. "But I'm sure it's from her side of the family."

"Probably get it from Uncle Seb," I say, and he chuckles. "Anyway, we've only been here a couple of hours and I've spent most of it in the gym. Happy?"

"Delighted," he replies. "But I do want you guys to have fun. Careful, well thought out fun."

"Yeah. Sounds like a blast." I'm giving him a hard time because I can. In reality, as much as it sometimes eats away my last nerve, I know he's right. We have to be cautious. Nash and I were already endorsement darlings thanks to our dad being Avery Westwood, Canada's King of Hockey and the NHL's beloved former Golden Boy. But now we're also Stanley Cup winners and about-to-be official co-captains of the best team in the league. Our deals got bigger, which means our images, if tarnished, don't just affect the family legacy. It affects the team and the trophy.

"How's Nash's injury?"

He's asking me probably because he asked Nash and he got growly. "He's struggling but won't admit it. I'm worried he won't be ready for the season."

"I am too." Dad groans into the phone. "I'm gonna get Doc Forsberg to fly out when you guys are back in L.A. Don't tell him that though."

"Okay." Nash will be as angry as a bear that sat on a porcupine if he finds out Dad's personal orthopedic surgeon is making a trip out to California from New York, but I agree with my dad. Better safe than sorry. "Your secret is safe with me. You and Mom still set on coming to the banner ceremony?"

They raise the Stanley Cup winning banner in our arena the first home game of the season, and they'll award Nash and me the C. Coach Braddock told us he wanted us to share the Captain's position—a rare move to give it to two people—last week. I think Dad was happier than we were.

"Of course. Your mom has everything booked already."

"You can stay with me," I remind him.

"She wants to stay at a hotel," Dad replies. "Give her boys their space. Keep me from nagging you too much, I think. And the Beverly Wilshire is slightly better than that townhouse you moved into."

"This from the guy who lived in a shack at the beach just so he could flirt with a girl." My dad bought a teardown semi-detached house so that he could live next to my mom when he was playing in San Diego.

They have since bought both sides of the place and turned it into one, gorgeous home. We grew up there until we were twelve and Dad retired. Then we moved back to Canada and only spent summers there. Now he and Mom spend winters there, to avoid the snow in Canada so they can pop in and watch our games whenever they want.

"Dad, what are the chances the media know the Quake is here?" I ask him.

"In Vegas?" Dad replies. "Pretty high. I mean at least the hockey blogs and stuff. Why?"

"I just... I just met someone and it felt... too easy."

There's a pause and I wait outside the suite door for him to respond. I'm holding my breath. I really tend to not talk to my dad or mom about my personal life. That changed when I went temporarily insane because of the split with Anne-Marie. Mom and Dad showed up to fix the mess I'd made, and I confessed my darkest secret to them. That I'm bisexual. They told me they loved me unconditionally. Always. So I guess now I'm making a bigger effort to open up to them.

"Trust your gut, Crew," Dad replies. "Even if it's hyperactive because of the Anne-Marie drama. It might just mean you're not ready to meet someone new."

"Oh, I'm not," I promise. "I am not settling down ever again. This is just... I mean I want some fun, but this guy felt like he... I don't know. He came on strong."

"He?" Dad repeats and I hold my breath. "Crew, I don't know... he could just be confident and know what he wants and it's Vegas so he's you know, just letting it all out there. Or he could be a reporter for a blog or TMZ Sports or some shit. You never know. But if it feels off, it's best to trust your instincts."

"Yeah. Okay."

"And for the record, you will get serious about someone again one day," he tells me. "And I want you to. And if it's a guy, I don't want you to think you have to hide that. You don't. And I will have your back."

"Thanks, Dad." I smile and pull my key card from my pocket. "But you don't have to worry about that. I'm not getting serious about anyone. Ever."

"Crew... then she wins." I know he's referring to my ex.

"Nope. I win," I reply as I swing open the door and find Tate Garrison and Duke Hendrix standing at the bar in our living room pouring tequila into a blender filled with fruit. "Gotta go. Boys are here."

"Okay. Have fun! Make good choices! Or bad ones with no consequences!"

"Okay, Dad."

I hang up. Tate grins at me over the blender. "Heard you

went to the gym, nerd. Thought we'd make you a fruit smoothie."

"Vegas style!" Duke yells.

Tate turns on the blender and my laugh is drowned out. I walk over and happily take the drink from Tate after he pours it.

"Let the games begin!"

Chapter 3

Liv

"You look hot," Tenley insists and swats at my hand as I tug on the top of this scandalously skimpy strapless dress. It's hers and I have no idea why I let her talk me into wearing it. "Stop fussing and drink your drink."

I put the chocolate espresso martini to my lips and sip. Tenley has already finished one and is on her second. She's wearing an equally teeny dress but in a loud fluorescent pink color. Her long thick blonde hair is slicked up into a high, lush ponytail. Her makeup looks like a fairy barfed glitter all over her but in a good way. She glows. She looks like a supermodel. I'm pretty sure I look like her little sister playing dress-up. I feel like it. And I keep wanting to rub my eyes but that will smear all the black liner Mallory spent half an hour applying on me.

I sip the martini again. It's dangerously delicious. I'm not a big drinker. I stick to wine and beer normally because when I was seventeen Tenley and my other cousin Harlow snuck a pitcher of spicy margaritas off the outdoor bar at the family Fourth of July barbecue and I got drunk for the first time and barfed for three hours. Spicy margarita out the nose? Zero stars. Do not recommend.

"So, like, are you sure you're good?" Tenley asks over the din of the music. "Because I'm cool with heading back to the room, ordering room service, and—"

"No you aren't," I interrupt and swallow down the anger I feel bubbling up toward my nearest and dearest relative. "You've been looking forward to this trip since Tate mentioned it at the beginning of the summer. You invited yourself, without even asking him. You had a bucket list of things to do on this trip. Dance till dawn, pool shenanigans, find an Elvis impersonator, and possibly get a tattoo."

"I know, but like, now that we're here—"

"Ten. Stop!" It comes out as forcefully as I feel it but not at all how I wanted it to come out. I hate being angry at her. I hate being angry at everything, which I am. Ever since the attempted mugging, or whatever the hell that was, I have been furious with myself and everything around me.

Her big blue eyes are wide and her face has gone so slack that her dimples, which are always visible because she's always got some version of a smile on her drop-dead-gorgeous face, are gone. I take another sip of the drink, bigger this time, and collect my thoughts. "I will feel worse about everything if I ruin this trip for you. So please, just be Tenley, my overbearing, terrifyingly bold favorite cousin, and let me figure out what I need to be or do on my own, okay?"

She seems skeptical but nods and then clinks her glass to mine. She turns back to survey the bodies bumping and grinding on the other side of the velvet rope that has us sectioned off in a VIP area. Well, one of the VIP areas. This club is gigantic with multiple levels and VIP areas. So many that we have yet to find Tate. He went for a guys' dinner and was going to meet us here, but we gave up trying to shove our way through the masses and slid into this space for drinks.

"Look! There's Tater Tot!" Tenley points into the crowd.

Despite the mass of humanity, I pick out Tate right away. He's with two of his teammates. They're all dressed in ridiculous Hawaiian shirts. Tate's is red and pink and it's the least ugly one of the bunch. I think they look like idiots but I'm also appreciative of it because I can find them in crowds easier. I know none of them know me because I don't go to games or help out at Quake charity events like Tenley does, but if I get lost tonight and see someone with one of those shirts I know I can say "I'm Devin Garrison's daughter. Tate's cousin." And no matter how drunk each one of his teammates will help me out.

There are about ten Quake players who came on the trip. Word seems to have gotten out that the Stanley Cup champs are in Sin City because as Tate and his teammates cut their way through the crowd, a lot of very pretty women stare and point. I see one lean in and say something to Tate, her hand on his shoulder. He nods and smiles but keeps walking.

I look over at Mallory who is sipping her cocktail on the other side of Tenley. She glances at me with a smile. "I trust him."

"You guys have something real. Something strong."

"Yeah." Mallory smiles. "Tate's it for me."

Her eyes are clear and bright. Her smile genuine and filled with confidence. Tenley groans. "Do not placate her fantasies."

"What are her fantasies?" Mallory asks.

"That she's going to find Prince Charming right out of the gate." Tenley turns so her back is to me, like she and Mallory are having this conversation in a room I'm not even in. "She doesn't want to kiss a toad in case it's the wrong toad. I've been trying to tell her for years that you gotta kiss a couple frogs on this quest of hers to find Prince Charming. And that sometimes the frogs can be fun."

Mallory laughs. "Are you saying Liv hasn't had a boyfriend? Like ever? Are you... have you been kissed?"

Mallory is staring at me like I'm an Amish girl off the farm for the first time. I roll my eyes and give Tenley a little shove. "Yes. I've been kissed. I've had boyfriends."

"Two. And you never went past third base."

"Ten!"

"Really?" Mallory is genuinely shocked, reaffirming the fact I've been living with —an almost twenty-three-year-old virgin is unheard of.

"I don't want to talk about it," I snap and swallow half the martini in one gulp. "Next round's on me."

I turn and head to the bar.

* * *

Three hours and two more martinis later, I'm on the dance floor. Me. Little timid Liv Garrison is shaking my ass to some song by someone other than Taylor Swift, who is my go-to. I think this is Swift-adjacent though as it might be Ed Sheeran? I am too tipsy to figure it out. Tenley is watching me with wide eyes and a laugh on her lips. Even drunk I know it's a positive laugh, not a negative one. She's in awe. So is Tate, I think, as he's over at the railing of the VIP area staring at me too. His eyes as wide as his sister's but he's not smiling. He looks rather concerned. Probably about the guy who is plastered to my backside.

I think he said his name is Gavin. Maybe? It was hard to hear over the music. But he's cute and he has a nice smile. I feel his hand on my hip now and I fight the urge to stiffen. I keep swinging my hips. This is what I want. This is why I came here. Tenley spins in front of me, arms in the air. Gavin's friend is beside her dancing away. He's touching her too and Tenley isn't stressed about it. Tate also isn't watching his sister like a hawk, just me.

"Hey!" I hear in my ear and turn my head a little to lock eyes with Gavin. His eyes are brown, rich, and deep. They seem kind. Please let them be kind. "Wanna grab a drink at the bar upstairs? Away from that giant dude who is trying to dismember me with his eyeballs."

I glance up at Tate and glare at him momentarily before turning my back on him to face my new friend. "That would be lovely."

"What?" he shouts back because the music is deafening.

I take his hand in mine, alcohol making me much bolder than I am. "Let's go!"

We don't make it more than five steps when I feel a hand on my shoulder. It's not Tate's though, which surprises me. It's Tenley. "Where ya going?" she asks casually, but her tone isn't light.

"For a drink somewhere more private." Oh God, that sounds so mature and racy. I mean, probably not to other people, but coming out of my virginal mouth, yeah. It's shocking. Tenley's blue eyes widen and I know I'm right. I lean closer to her. "Tate is freaking him out."

"I know you don't come out with us much, but girl code is no one leaves alone," Tenley announces.

"I'm not alone. I'm with Gavin," I tell her. "And I'm not leaving. Just going upstairs. Away from my ridiculously over-protective cousin. Or is it cousins, plural?"

"Dude, Tate Garrison is your cousin?" the guy behind Tenley interjects. He literally has cartoon stars in his eyes he is so star-struck. "He was incredible in the playoffs this year. I don't think the Quake would have won a Cup without him."

"Yeah he's a total hockey rockstar," Tenley says, her flat tone and the roll of her eyes indicating her sarcasm. "I'm coming with you, Liv."

"Third wheel, much?"

I'm annoyed but deep down in the depths of my soul, the

part I'm currently trying to kill with alcohol and bad decisions, that part of me sighs in relief at her declaration.

"Do you know him too?" the guy with Tenley asks. "Could you introduce me?"

"Do you want to possibly get lucky tonight? Or do you want to meet Tater Tot Garrison?" Tenley asks. "You don't get both."

Thankfully the guy doesn't hesitate. "Let's go."

Gavin starts leading me through the crowds, off the dance floor, and to a small staircase in the corner. The upstairs of the club is walled off with plexiglass. It has chairs and couches, like the VIP area, but bigger as it runs the whole back wall of the club and is just as packed as the dance floor but less noisy.

I let him guide me to a corner by the bar. I jump up onto a bar stool and hope it looks graceful or at the very least cute. My feet are killing me and I just want to sit down. Tenley slips into the spot between me and the next stool, leaning on the bar. "You okay?"

"Yes," I whisper back. "Why?"

"Because you aren't acting like yourself," Tenley explains what I already know. "Liv doesn't get tipsy and dance with strangers and try to sneak off with them."

"I'm not sneaking anywhere," I argue. "I told you where I was going. And I'm a grown adult, Ten. Older than you. Maybe it's time everyone started letting me grow up."

Tenley blinks and her eyes shift to Gavin who is talking to the guy who followed Tenley up here, Tate's fanboy. They're waiting for the bartender to notice them and take their order. She looks back down at me. She's taller than me by an inch or two but tonight she's wearing heels that are two inches taller than mine. She's a freaking skyscraper. "No one wants to stop you from growing up Liv. In fact, no one thinks of you as not grown up. What's going on?"

"I'm just living." I shrug.

"What will it be ladies?" Gavin asks.

"Water. Sparkling," Tenley says and looks at me.

"Chocolate espresso martini."

"Liv, I—" I glare at Tenley and she immediately stops talking and looks away.

The guys order two beers, my martini, and Tenley's water. Gavin drops an arm around my shoulders. "What hotel are you at? We're at Bellagio. We each have our own rooms."

They look mighty proud of that fact. Also, I'm not so naive I don't know if it's an invitation of sorts. "What are you here for?"

"Work conference," Gavin tells me. "I'm a doctor and I'm here for a medical conference."

"Doctor?" Tenley interrupts, like she's part of the conversation. "How old are you guys?"

"I'm thirty," Gavin tells her. He takes a small but noticeable step back as his gaze ping-pongs from Tenley to me. "Why? How old are you two?"

"I'll be twenty-three next month," I volunteer. "She's almost twenty-two."

His shoulders drop and he steps into me again. His smile is gentle. "That's cool. I was worried you were underage or something. You live in Vegas?"

"Los Angeles," Tenley says for me.

"But I'm from Maine." I always feel the need to tell people that. Maybe it's because Los Angeles, even after four years of school, doesn't feel like home yet.

"Silver Bay, Maine," Tenley's guy says proudly because of course he knows where his favorite hockey player is from. He is still bursting with excitement. "So, wait, is your dad one of the famous Garrison brothers? Or the brother who didn't make the NHL? Or are you from his mom's side of the family?"

"Both," I volunteer even though Tenley looks like she'd rather we were talking about anything else. "My dad is Devin

Garrison, Tate's dad's oldest brother. My mom is also Tate's mom's sister."

I can literally see the dude trying to build the family tree in his brain. Tenley sighs as the bartender places the drinks on the bar top. "It sounds incestuous but it's not. Can we talk about something interesting now?"

Tenley grabs my drink off the bar, leaving me with her sparkling water. I glare at her. She ignores me. The guy is not giving up. "Wait, you're a Garrison too?"

"Yep," Tenley replies and sips my drink. She ignores him and turns to me. "I'm going back down to the VIP area. Come with me or give me your phone."

My phone? I look at Gavin. He seems nice. And I like that he's not a drunken frat boy. I don't know what kind of doctor he is, but I'm sure he's very aware of how the body works, how STDs are transmitted, and the best way to have safe sex, right? I want this kind of responsibility in a sex partner. Yeah, he's the one, I guess.

"What are you going to do with my phone," I ask as I reach into my purse because I've made the decision to stay. To go back to Gavin's room with him and hopefully have an enjoyable time, while also dumping this stupid v-card.

Tenley looks shocked that I'm handing over my phone. She doesn't reach for it at first, but then she sighs in resignation and plucks it from my hand. She flashes it at me to get the face ID to work, and then she starts doing something. I'm not worried. There's sadly nothing to hide on my phone. I make the occasional Instagram post, call my parents, and partake in the family WhatsApp chats. That's it. Oh, and read books on my Kindle app.

She hands back my phone. "I'm tracking you. So if you don't make it back to me, or back to the hotel in the next hour I am—"

"Calling the police?"

"Worse," Tenley replies. "Your dad, mom, and all the cousins. Group Chat Amber Alert."

"Jesus Ten, chill," I hiss and Gavin and his buddy both look mildly amused.

"Hey, I'll kidnap her myself for a chance to meet the entire Garrison family," the friend jokes. At least I hope it's a joke.

"Dude, not funny," Gavin warns his buddy.

Tenley ignores them both. "I mean it, Liv. Love you. Make good choices."

"You sound like my mother," I quip. Mom does say that to Conner and Mae but not to me. She realizes I'm too chicken to make any choice other than the smart one. Well, not tonight.

Tenley turns and leaves with my martini without another word. I have to fight the very strong urge to chase after her and retreat to the safe space that is the VIP area with my cousins and friends. But I'm not getting laid if I do that, so I stay glued to the bar stool with Gavin smiling down at me on one side and his friend looking like a kicked puppy on the other.

"She really just bailed on me?" his friend says, stunned.

"I don't know much when it comes to dating but I do know, as a Garrison woman, the fastest way to lose our interest is to be more excited about our hockey-playing siblings than us," I tell him and take a sip of Tenley's water. The water is refreshing and probably what I physically need right now, but it's not going to do anything for my waning confidence.

How do women do this? I feel like I'm at the front of my high school auditorium in the middle of graduation, naked. I lean over and order a shot of Fireball from the bartender. As I drop back down onto my stool, and Gavin consoles his friend about Tenley shunning him, I notice a guy a few feet away at the bar. He's staring right at me with a smirk. It's a fetching smirk, to say the least. The kind that is warm and filled with mischief. He looks away to wave the bartender over. The smirky dude has dirty blond, almost brown hair longer and tousled on top but short on the sides. His frame is very broad and toned. His eyes aren't dark but not light. It's the best description I can muster in the low light from this distance.

He's got tattoos decorating every inch of both his arms. I can't make out any of them because of the lighting and they're all black ink. They're pretty though. He looks... like a Hollywood version of some kind of anti-hero hero. The bad guy that the good girl reforms because his heart was never as dark as he, or the viewer, thought.

I'm staring so I blink and look away when I realize Hollywood Anti-Hero is watching me again. Gavin's friend is walking away now. The bartender plunks a full shot of Fireball in front of me and I reach for my wallet but she waves me off. "Paid for."

"Oh." I smile, and she struts off to make the next drink. I lift the shot glass to Gavin. "Thank you."

I gulp it, shiver, and purse my lips. Gavin chuckles. "Don't thank me. I didn't buy it. I mean, I would have, but I didn't."

I shiver again. "Well, who then?"

He leans into me. He smells like pine trees and tobacco but not because he smokes. It must be in his cologne. His breath is minty. "I don't know who bought it, but I think I should stake a claim before we find out."

The next thing I know Gavin's lips are on mine. It's not an awful kiss. It's not aggressive or sloppy. I should be enjoying this. But I feel instantly uncomfortable. Angry, even. My whole body tenses, like it did that night when I was suddenly thrown to the ground. I even smell the wet grass from that night in my nostrils somehow. I swear to God every muscle in my body is stone. I can't even move my lips. I'm so fucking angry, not at Gavin. He's just shooting his shot on someone who acted like they were a willing target.

I am! I am a willing target! My head screams at my angry

heart and terrified soul. I am willing! I want this. He's the perfect candidate. Why am I freaking out? I slip off the stool, which brings me closer to Gavin who moves a hand around my back and that's when I feel the flight part of my rollercoaster of emotions wash over me. Nothing is stone anymore. Every muscle is moving—away from him.

"Bathroom!" I call out way too loud and then I'm blindly pushing through the crowd away from the bar, away from Gavin.

I stumble down the stairs, almost tripping, clutching the railing with white knuckles. I see the hallway where the washrooms are located to the left of the staircase and I march toward them as fast as I can without running. My vision blurs and I wipe away the tears tumbling out of my eyes and ruining the make-up Mallory helped me apply.

I am a few feet from the women's restroom sign, and of course, there's a line so I panic and turn the other way. I'm just going to leave the club, maybe even Las Vegas. I never should have come. I...

Smash! My entire body hits a wall. A warm, but hard wall.

Chapter 4

Liv

Hands drop to my shoulders, gently. "Whoa. Fireball. Where's the fire?"

"I..." I see the tattoos first. Then the smirk. Then the eyes. Hazel. They're hazel. "I... I just..."

"Didn't want to be kissed by him," the stranger finishes for me. Is he a stranger? He looks familiar for some reason. His smirk is fading but his expression remains soft. Kind. "Don't worry. He didn't read the signs. He's not offended. He's still up there waiting for you to come back."

"I... I will."

"Nah. You won't."

"I should."

"You shouldn't," he counters calmly. "Because you don't really want to."

He's right. How is he right? I don't even know him. "I had a plan."

"To kiss a guy who makes you look like your puppy just died?" he asks me, the smirk reappearing. "That's an awful plan."

"I did NOT look like a puppy had been murdered!" I

realize his hands are still on my shoulders, so I take a step back, even though his touch doesn't bother me.

"Murdered? Whoa Fireball, I didn't say this was a *Dateline* episode. Maybe the puppy died by accident. Like it got hit by a car." He laughs softly, but it's deep and has bass to it, and I find myself biting back a smile. I like it. I like this whole thing with this stranger. This is drunk, I guess, liking ridiculous conversations with tattooed strangers.

"Manslaughter," I reply. "That's puppy manslaughter."

"Are you a law student or an animal rights activist?" He tilts his handsome head as he studies me.

"Neither. I mean, I love puppies, I'm not a serial killer. But I'm an Art Education major," I reply. His smile drops in shock. "Surprise, Inky! I'm not some shot-slurping bimbo. And who I kiss, and if I like it or not, is none of your business."

He steps back like I slapped him, but his smile returns with an intensity I wasn't expecting. "Okay. All valid points. But for the record, I didn't think you were a... shot slurping bimbo. I don't even know what that is, and I would never shit on any woman for kissing anyone, even if they didn't like it."

"Oh." I blink and my tipsy little mouth won't shut up. "I'm not degrading women either. It's a valid life choice, being sexually liberated and liking shots. I just... I'm just not good at it, I guess."

"Just admit you didn't like him," Hottie Mc Stranger says. "Give me that. Also, what's Inky?"

"You" I point to his arms covered in tatts, but my depth perception is off and I end up poking his forearm.

As soon as my finger touches his skin I feel a snap of electricity between us, like static electricity but stronger and deeper and much more enjoyable. My finger stays there like it's stuck to his warm, smooth skin and I trace one of the lines on his arm, the stem of a rose. It's nice.

His eyes drop and watch my finger move. There's something hot about it. Something intimate, which is weird. Right? I mean what do I know? Nothing and that's why I'm here. To change that. "I should get back to what's his face."

"The guy you don't like kissing?"

I frown and our eyes meet again. Man, he's fucking something. "You're gorgeous."

"Thanks," he says easily. This is not news to him. He doesn't need to hear it. Oh to be that self-assured. "You're beautiful."

A blush blooms on my skin. I look away and concentrate on tracing another tattoo. Until he puts a finger under my chin and tips my head up toward his. "Now admit you didn't like kissing him."

"Why do you care? You don't even know me."

"I know you're staying at the Wynn. I know you like to punch things." Okay... maybe that's a red flag. Maybe this is a sign there's danger. He smiles that sweet yet confident smile at me again. "I was in the gym this afternoon when you walked in. I'm staying there too. I'll try not to take it personally you didn't notice me."

"Oh." So that's why he looks familiar. I remember there being men in the gym, but only vaguely. Because I almost turned around and left when I saw them. But how the hell am I forgetting what this specimen looks like in workout wear? Tenley wouldn't. Hell, even my book nerd of a little sister Mae wouldn't have missed him. I think I'm broken.

"You gonna say it now, Fireball?"

"I didn't like kissing him," I blurt out and it feels good, which I wasn't anticipating. I ignore his victorious smirk and look him dead in the eye. "But I do like kissing. So I should have liked it with him. I blame me, not him."

"Bullshit." His voice is so strong and confident it's contagious and I start to feel it too. "Chemistry isn't easy. You didn't have it with him, maybe because I stole it."

I blink. He chuckles. "You looked over at me before you kissed him and you felt it. Just like I did. We have chemistry."

"You're not my type, Inky." It's the truth but it's also kind of cruel. I hope he realizes I don't mean it that way. I'm too shy to look up at him to gauge his reaction so I go back to sliding one of my manicured nails over his ink, this time a skull with a flower crown.

"Right. Because your type is people you're not attracted to?"

Okay, now I look up. He's smirking. I feel it in my underwear. I swallow and bite my lip. He reaches up and presses his thumb just below my lip, pulling it from between my teeth. "If someone is going to bite that, it's going to be me."

"Okay."

Yeah. I said okay, all nonchalant and unbothered like I was agreeing to a pizza topping. Even he is shocked, his eyebrows raising sharply. But he recovers fast and then his head is bending and I'm tilting my chin—which he's still kind of holding —and...

I'm kissing this ink-covered stranger.

It's soft, at first. He's testing the waters. His lips gentle but not timid. He's still got my chin in his big hand, and he angles my mouth to the side, his tongue ghosting the edge of my lip.

It feels so good. Like really good. Like oh my God, I finally get why everyone is so horny all the time type of good. Not a single part of me tenses or freezes or turns to stone. My fight-or-flight instincts have left the building. I could stay here, kissing this guy, for years.

I grab his ass as I open my mouth and his tongue finds mine. Sparks fly and they clear my head for a second. Just long enough that I register the feel of his ass under my palms. His very hard, very round, very muscular ass. There is one specific type of man that has that specific kind of ass.

I pull away like the sparks flying from the kiss are actually electrocuting me. His eyes fly open and he looks equal parts startled and confused. "What happened? You were into that."

"I was," I admit as I wipe my mouth. "But you play hockey."

He blinks. "You recognize me?"

I shake my head. "Do you recognize me?"

He frowns, confused. "Why would I recognize you? And how would you know I play hockey if you don't recognize me?"

"Are you... a Quake?"

"Yeah."

"Fuck no."

I bolt. Like a fawn in the forest after the startling boom of a gunshot. I make my way out of the club and through the casino it's attached to without incident. I'm on the famous Las Vegas Boulevard gulping fresh, warm air and trying to get my bearings when I feel a hand on my shoulder.

Of course, he followed. The lights of the strip give me a much better view of his face, which is even more ruggedly handsome than I thought. Chiseled jaw, high cheekbones, and eyes... they're the real masterpiece. A shade that could be described a thousand ways, because it's not just one color, it's a vortex of many. I see moss and amber and chocolate and storm cloud.

"So hockey players are a no-go? Why?" he asks. "And why would I recognize you? You said you were an Art History student. How would a professional hockey player know a—"

"Art Education. I teach kids about art and music. Well, I will when I graduate." I sigh and shake my head, trying to clear what's left of the alcohol from my body. "Which one are you and why aren't you wearing one of those stupid shirts?"

He stares. Hard. Like he's searching his brain for a reason I'm this crazy. He'll never find it. I'm the Garrison no one knows about. I hide easily and gratefully in the giant shadows of my relatives. I avoid hockey games, and when I do have to go because someone in my family is being awarded something or winning something, I duck cameras and leave early.

"Westwood."

Westwood? Is he a Westwood? I smile and then I laugh, because of course he's a Westwood. I see it now. I've met both his parents on multiple occasions. I've even seen him before, although we never officially met. The cheeks are his dad's, the hair is his mom's color, the eyes a mix of both. "Which one? Crew or Nash?"

"Crew, and to answer your earlier question I'm not wearing the shirt because there was a fuck-up with the order and mine came in a small" he replies. "Nothing about me is small."

A bubble of laughter explodes from my mouth. "Nothing about you is subtle either, apparently."

"I just had my tongue in your mouth, and you liked it, so I figured we could be candid." Crew shrugs. "If you hate hockey players, why do you know our names?"

"I don't hate hockey players," I reply. "I love them. But I know them so I avoid kissing them. Thanks though. That was great. Really. Five Stars."

I start down the street. He hooks my left arm and spins me to face him before I even realize what's happening. "The Wynn is that way."

He points in the other direction from where I was walking. So much for a strong finish to this weird failure of a night.

"Oh." I could pull my arm back, but I don't. I love how his skin feels on mine. How he holds me with gentle force. I feel safe but nervous when he touches me, and I like that chaotic blend. Who knew?

"You were heading home, right?" he questions. "Or do you

have another club to go to where you mind fuck another poor hockey player?"

"All the hockey players are in this club."

"You are equal parts intriguing and confusing."

"Thanks."

We're still chest-to-chest. His hand is still around my bicep. We're within kissing distance and the thought of doing it again crosses my mind, but that would be crazy, right?

But didn't I come here for crazy?

"What did you mean when you said you *know* hockey players?" Crew wants to know. "How? Why did you ask if I recognized you?"

"Because I'm drunk and confused. You confuse me," I babble and then answer the first question with some vague lies. "I follow TMZ Sports. I know the Quake won the Stanley Cup and are here to party hard. I'm not into partying hard or wild nights and random hook-ups. No judgment, but I don't fit. So best to avoid me, so you're not disappointed."

"There was absolutely nothing disappointing about that kiss."

He's right.

A warm breeze wanders through my hair, sending a piece across my face where it sticks to what's left of my lip gloss. Before I can brush it away, Crew does. It's such a simple, gentle gesture but it births butterflies the size of pterodactyls in my belly. Whoa, this man is reeling me in like a fish on a hook. I'm not at all used to this. But isn't that the point?

"I'm not going to lie, I'm not a relationship guy, and we, as a team, are definitely here to party. But why are you in Vegas, letting dudes you don't know kiss you if you're not looking for something meaningless too?" Crew just took a proverbial hammer and nailed it.

I *am* here looking for some random guy to rid me of my virginity because that near-mugging-slash-more proves if I don't make the decision, someone may make it for me. And what would be safer than hooking up with Crew Westwood? I know for a fact that hockey players get regular STD tests and that they don't want a baby as much as I don't. They always have protection on them. And they're usually incredible in bed. At least, that's why I hear.

"Fireball, that wasn't a tough question for a smart woman like you," Crew reminds me. His eyes sparkle. His smile is somehow equal parts cocky and kind.

"Wanna go back to the hotel with me?"

My heart gallops as soon as the question leaves my lips. See, Mom, I do have some of your DNA. He doesn't say a word. He just wraps his arm lazily over my shoulder and we start to walk together.

* * *

On the short stumbling walk back to the hotel, I make a mental list of everything I know about Crew Westwood, which isn't much. I know my cousin Tate talks about him a lot and considers him a friend, which is good. It means he's a nice guy. Tate doesn't suffer fools. I know he's the son of Avery Westwood who was the league's poster boy when he played. He was a child phenom from Canada who was drafted number one when he was eighteen and an avalanche of trophies, Cups, and endorsement deals followed. Avery made the most money of any player in the league in his day. I know Crew is a twin. I know his mom is the sister of one of Avery's old teammates so his bloodline is double hockey, like ours. My mom's dad was also a professional hockey player. I know he had a significant other at some point because I remember Tenley coming home from a party she went to with Tate and complaining that "Crew Westwood had just gone through a horrible break-up."

So as we approach the lobby I decide to be direct. "Do you have a girlfriend? Because I don't do one-night stands with guys who cheat."

"Fair policy," Crew replies. "I'm single. Entirely unattached in every possible way."

I nod and he holds open the door to the Wynn for me. As we cross the lobby, his hand pressing gently against my lower back, I feel like every set of eyes in the place is on us. I'm probably paranoid, mostly. I mean Wynn employees know there's a slew of hockey players in their hotel, but no one cares about the women they bring up to their rooms... probably.

"And for the record," his head dips so his breath glances off my cheek, causing me to fight a shiver, "I have the same policy. I don't fuck with people's relationships."

"I've been single since last October," I reply, and he gives me a small nod as he punches the button on the elevator panel.

The doors slide open and he ushers me inside. He stares at the panel of floor numbers. I watch him carefully. The elevator is filled with flight. Crew looks even more handsome than in the dimly lit club and shady street. His skin is dewy and smooth, a tan making the lighter grays and greens in his eyes pop. He's so damn big. I've been around hockey bodies my whole life, but I've been related to all of them so I've never really looked at them. There's a lot to admire. Broad shoulders, bulky biceps, taut, trim tummy, the bubble butt. Yeah, I get why women like that now. It felt really nice to grab onto.

"Your place or mine, Fireball?" he asks as the elevator doors slide closed but we don't go anywhere. He pulls his room key from his back pocket. "Full disclosure I'm in a two-bed suite on the second to last floor. It's nice. Has a private hot tub on the balcony, but it also has the thief of joy in the other bedroom."

"Who?"

"My brother. He's what would happen if Squidward and Eeyore fucked without protection." He says it without an ounce of jest or sarcasm in his voice and the absurdity makes me smile. "He's likely home from the club already and muttering to himself about the room being too cold or the club being too loud, and how he never should have come."

"Oh. Well then my place it is." I take my keycard out of my tiny little purse and swipe it over the reader before punching the button for the top floor. My head tilts back and I look at him. "Since we're being brutally honest, I'm in a three-bedroom suite with three other people, but they definitely aren't home and they definitely won't bother us when they do come home. If you're still there."

"I'll still be there and I'll be completely indisposed." His tone is confident and smooth. I'm not sure if it's a promise or a warning, but it warms me from the inside out.

"For the record, I only use protection. Lots of it," I blurt out. "No Squidward-Eeyore offspring in my future. I'm on the pill and you are wrapping it up. Got it?"

"Yes ma'am." Crew grins down at me and my abnormally blunt mouth. His hand moves to my lower back again but slides down to casually cup the round of my ass. "For the record, my offspring would be more of a cross between Prince Eric and He-man."

I smile. He's taking away my nerves without even knowing it. I'm going to do this. With Crew Westwood. "Okay, so we agree protection is non-negotiable."

"Not a worry Fireball." He winks at me. "I have a couple condoms in my front pocket. You are more than welcome to go fishing for them... see what else you might find. I've been hard since I set eyes on you."

Whoa. The casual way he tosses that out there has me flustered, but it also reinforces my desire to do this. I'm going to get rid of my virginity and Crew Westwood is going to help me. This is what I've been hoping for since I stepped off the plane.

Chapter 5

Crew

There is something about this girl that's different. I mean I could list a bunch of superficial stuff like how skittish her body language is, but how ballsy her brain is. She says stuff that a lot of puck bunnies wouldn't dare, even though they think it, yet she's kept her hands to herself since our kiss and her eyes constantly dart to the exits, first in the lobby, and now in the hallway as we step off the elevator. She definitely knows who I am, and knows hockey, but isn't a bunny. Yet she's taking me to her hotel room.

I'm so confused. But I'm also trusting my instincts, like my dad told me to earlier, and I don't feel like she's a risk. She's something... But it ain't a threat.

I'm about to ask her if she's sure about this because honestly, I am *so* not about persuading a partner. They have to be all in on their own. But then she reaches out and takes my hand. I lace our fingers and it makes the corners of her mouth perk up a bit.

A room service guy passes us in the hall pushing a cart of empty dishes and he smiles fleetingly. We look like a couple stumbling home after a night out in Sin City. I can tell by the way his smile is sweet and not snarky. We don't look like a debaucherous one-night stand, but that's what we are. I have to admit I don't usually hold hands with hookups but this feels right.

She pulls her room key out again and stops at the last door in the hallway. Instead of swiping the key card, she presses her ear to the door. I smirk. "Making sure my… suite mates aren't home yet."

"Pretty sure Vegas is big on the soundproofing."

"Because of all the mafia hits that used to happen here?"

I blink and a gust of laughter huffs out of my lungs. "No. Because of privacy and the whole what happens in Vegas stays in Vegas thing. Your mind is dark, Fireball."

"I've been gently reminded recently that the world is dark," she mutters, and before I can ask what the hell that means she swipes her key card and pushes the door open.

The only light in the suite is what filters in from the strip below the floor-to-ceiling windows that line the wall in the living room.

There are four doors, two on the right and one on the left. She leads me to the one on the left, opens it, and tugs us inside, closing and locking it immediately. There are no lights on and the curtains are pulled tight so it's dark. I use my free hand to grope for the light switch. I find it and the room lights up. There's a queen-size bed, and in the corner of the room, under the window, is an open suitcase. Beside it, in a pile, I see the workout gear she was in earlier at the hotel gym.

I let go of her hand, turn to face her, and cup her cheek. She looks up at me with big, petrified chocolate brown eyes. My heart skips in my chest. "Hey. Are you okay?"

She nods.

My heart stutters again and I drop my hand. "You know there's no gun to your head and as much as that kiss was incredible, and I know anything else would be too, I am okay with calling this a night."

She blinks and swallows so hard I can almost hear it. Why is she so afraid? "No. I want to have sex. With you."

Whoa. Okay. I guess? That glimmer of uncertainty in those beautiful eyes is throwing me off. "What's your name?"

"Never mind that," she says, shaking her head and then stepping toward me.

I gently palm her shoulder to keep space between us. "I mean I know this is a one-and-done type of night but I should at least have a first name, right?"

"Wrong."

"You know my name."

"Half the world knows your name. And your dad's. And your brother's and your uncle's for that matter."

Oh. So she doesn't just know hockey. She *knows* hockey. The world might know I'm Avery Westwood's son and have a twin brother I play with, but you have to dig deeper into the sport to know that my mom's brother, Seb Deveau, was also a pro.

"Are you a closet puck bunny, Fireball?" I flash her a smirk so she knows I'm teasing.

"I am probably the farthest thing you can get from that," she replies with a sheepish smile. "I avoid hockey like the plague but... well I have..."

"Let me guess," I interrupt because I've heard this before. "You have brothers or uncles or your dad who are hockey fans?"

"All of the above."

She looks away. Suddenly she seems skittish again. "I make you nervous."

She shrugs a little and looks around the room, but I don't know why. I think she's just trying to avoid eye contact. "Everything makes me nervous. I'm horrible that way."

"I'm sorry. Anxiety sucks," I tell her. "I've had some incredibly intense bouts of it in my life. I wouldn't wish it on anyone."

She finally lifts her gaze to me. "You? Mr. Cocky Confidence? Son of the King? Born with blades strapped to your feet and athletic excellence in your bloodstream? So hot that you probably dehydrate any woman that looks at you too long?"

"I'm sorry, are you my new PR person? Because you should be." I smile at her. She's stroking my ego and I have to admit it's almost as appealing as if she was stroking something else.

She gives me the cheekiest grin while rolling her eyes at the same time. Her hands go to her tiny hips as she tilts her head. "Tell me more."

"Well, first off I wasn't born with skates strapped to my feet." I walk toward the bed. I can feel her eyes track me. "Although technically they did put very tiny knitted booties made to look like skates on our feet for our newborn photoshoot. And that was released to the media so they keep posting it and I will never live it down."

"I meant tell me more about the anxiety."

I quirk my lip. "I knew what you meant."

I sit on the bed. I can see her tense up. She is not ready for this. "Well... there was a time in my life when I... made some wrong choices and instead of admitting defeat I doubled down and went the fake-it-till-you-make-it route. And spoiler alert: sometimes you do not, in fact, make it. But you develop a shit ton of stress and anxiety trying."

"Huh."

"Do you know enough about hockey and my family to know I was once married?"

"Married? Wow. ." She cocks her head again and folds her arms across her chest, not in a defensive way, but a protective one. ""And a failing marriage gave you anxiety."

I lean back on my arms, my spread fingers sliding easily

across the five-star sheets. "Actually giving up was the least stressful thing about my marriage. The holding on was the anxiety part."

She nods slowly. I have no idea why I'm word-vomiting my failed marriage to a stranger I'm just supposed to be getting naked with. But the more I share the less tense she looks. And I've got an idea on how to make us both less tense.

"Got any alcohol?"

"It's a suite in a luxury hotel. Duh."

"Grab some of those fancy liquors off the bar. I promise to pay for them." I use my index finger to make a cross over my heart.

She hesitates a half-second but then walks over to the minibar in the corner of the room and surveys the selection. She walks back over to stand in front of me at the foot of the bed and presents the stash.

Spiced rum. Premium gin and.... Fireball.

I grin. "Good girl."

I gently sweep the bottles out of her open palm. I tilt my head to find her gazing down at me, looking almost sad. "I am so sick of being a good girl."

"Then let's play a game, Fireball," I suggest and pat the bed beside me. "Ease you into your bad girl era."

She slowly turns and lowers her cute behind onto the edge of the mattress beside me. Her bare thigh brushes mine and a warm tingle settles in my lower abdomen. I crack the seal on the bottle of Fireball. "Two truths and a lie. Know it?"

"Yeah."

"Well, we're gonna play two lies and one truth. Similar premise. If we guess the wrong thing as the truth, we drink."

"Okay..." She's skeptical but she's willing. I'm down with that. I may not get laid tonight but I am going to have some fun.

This girl intrigues me and I'm enjoying just hanging with her, to be honest. "You go first."

I smile. "I once got caught having sex by my coach. I have a pierced cock. I once turned orange."

She blinks those deep, delicious brown eyes before letting them drop directly to my cock. I wiggle my eyebrows when she looks back up. "You... pierced it?"

"Is that your guess?"

"Umm... yeah. Sure."

I hand her the Fireball. "Drink."

She looks so relieved I laugh. "I thought about getting it pierced. They say the pleasure is off-the-charts, even made an appointment once but chickened out because my brother Nash kept sending me stories about infections and one dude had to have his penis amputated."

"One dude out of millions has an extreme issue and you chicken out?" She looks adorably judgy right now.

"One amputated dick is one too many, Fireball," I say in a deadly serious tone that has her bursting into giggles. The sound makes my cock jump. It's hot. She is hot. So fucking hot. "The truth is my skin once turned a very pale orange color because of a natural supplement I was taking. It lasted over a month and I was only fifteen and wanted to die."

Her giggles subside. "Fifteen is a tough time to be orange. I'm sorry."

"Your turn," I say and wait as she thinks way too hard about what she's going to say. "How about throwing some names out?"

I don't know why I want to know her name so badly. I've slept with people whose names I never got before. It's not ideal but it's not a deal breaker. She stares at the half-empty mini bottle of booze in her hand. Her nails aren't painted, which is different. They're perfectly shaped and glossy like they have clear polish on them, but most girls I pick up in bars have brightly painted nails. Some of the dudes too. Her fingers are long and narrow like a piano player and she doesn't have a single visible tattoo—even in the short dress she's got on. I'm still hoping I get to discover if there are hidden ones.

She nibbles her bottom lip again, but then tucks her dark silky hair behind her ears and steadies her gaze on me. "My name is Olivia. My name is JoAnne. My name is Callie."

I study her. What does she look like? I rule out JoAnne almost immediately. It's too old soul for her. She's too skittish to be an old soul. Callie is nice and more modern but... she doesn't feel like a Callie.

"This is doing nothing to curb my anxiety," she whispers, and I see her cheeks are pink under my scrutinizing gaze. It is a bit ridiculous I'm putting this much effort into it. There are no real clues.

"Olivia."

Her startled expression morphs into a pout. "No fair. You got it right. How did you know?"

"Shot in the dark," I tell her with a cheeky grin. "I have a lot of dumb luck."

She makes an incoherent noise and flops backward on the bed. "So now what? I lost so do I have to drink again? Fair warning I am not a big drinker. Already had more than my fair share tonight so I'm going to have to forfeit the game."

"That isn't what happens when you lose a round." I slide back, lowering myself and turning so I'm beside her on the bed, elbow bent, head resting on my hand as I stare at her. "If you lose a round, I get to kiss you."

Her eyelashes flutter as I lean in, and she wraps an arm around my neck, which I take as the go-ahead. The kiss is heavy and hot, right out of the gate. She's kissing me back with the same horny energy I am kissing her with and so I slide over, moving my body so a leg is over hers and my torso is pressed into her side. She keeps kissing me, her tongue dancing with mine. I slide the rest of my body on top of hers, and she doesn't stop me. In fact, she loops her other arm around my neck and keeps me in place.

"Well that hardly feels like losing," she whispers when our lips finally break apart.

I wink at her. "I'm glad I know your name."

"Why?"

"Because I know what to moan later."

"Oh god would've done just fine."

"Goddess," I correct.

"Sexist," she all but pants as I nip at her earlobe and brazenly grab a handful of her perfect ass in my palm.

"Nah. I'm okay with gods too," I reply and wait... for the muscle tension of shock I expect that announcement to bring.

But there isn't any. I watch her face. She's focused on the tip of my only chest tattoo. I have the first two buttons of my shirt undone and gravity must have it gaping so she can see that over my heart are two crossed hockey sticks with initials in each quarter made by the crossed sticks. Well, except for one.

I lie flatter on her so that she can't stare into my shirt and when her eyes meet mine, she repeats my words. "Gods?"

I don't always tell one-night stands I'm bi. In fact, I used to never tell anyone. It was my dirty little secret. Now... since my marriage imploded, it's not so much a secret as a fact that I am soft-launching to the world.

Nothing tenses. Not a single part of her body. Instead, she slides her lips to my ear and sucks so gently and sweetly on the lobe it sends surges of warmth zipping through my veins. This isn't the usual one-night stand behavior, and that's kind of cool. This woman is an enigma and I didn't realize how much of a turn-on that is.

"Gods. Goddess. You'll call me anything, won't you?"

Okay, so the subtle meaning flew right over her head. So much for soft-launching my sexuality. And I'm enjoying her lips on me too much to derail this moment to make a statement. I'll never see her after tonight anyway, so might as well stay on topic. And the topic is pleasure.

"I'll call you Olivia," I murmur, my hands in her hair. "After I make you come so hard you forget your name."

"Oh Jesus, this is happening..." she whispers. I stare at her and she bites her bottom lip as she gazes right back at me from under her thick, dark lashes that don't look like they've got a lick of mascara on them. Natural beauty this one.

"It's only happening if you want it to happen. Do you?"

"Yes." She says it with confidence as her hands slide down my back. "You. Just you. Tonight. Just tonight."

I really like the confidence in her voice. She's choosing me and I know that's important. She's fucking gorgeous and charismatic. She could have brought that other guy to her hotel room tonight. Hell, I doubt there is a single straight or bi man in Vegas who wouldn't want to be here. But she wants me and that feels great. I kiss her again. The taste of cinnamon from the Fireball is still on her tongue.

I roll my hips, gently, slowly. Normally I'm not this casual with hook-ups. There's usually a sense of urgency on both our parts. We know what we're here for and we're ready to get to business. But Olivia isn't rushing so neither am I.

Her hands land on my ass and she squeezes. I respond appropriately by rolling my hips again. Her legs have spread to either side of my hips and there's a short, sharp intake of breath as my very hard cock ruts up against her very soft center.

"Fireball, I'm gonna need to loosen my pants or take a cold shower," I confess against her cheek. "Your call."

And that's when I feel her hands slip around my waist and start unbuttoning my fly.

Chapter 6

Liv

I think my hands are shaking a little as I pop his button on the fly to his shorts. If he notices, I'll blame it on desire. I mean I think that's a factor because, under all my jitters, I really do want this. I'm not just convincing myself I do like I have been all night. Now... with Crew's warm, welcoming body on mine and his lips kissing me senseless, I am totally on board.

He kisses my neck and lifts himself off me. As he kneels at the end of the bed and finishes undoing his fly, I move to the top of the bed. Resting my back against the headboard, I watch him. I'm grateful the light is dim so he doesn't see the look on my face too clearly. I'm sure it's a mix of awe and trepidation.

Crew stands at the foot of the bed now, so his shorts slip right to the ground. He keeps his eyes on me as he reaches for the hem of his shirt and pulls it up over his head, ignoring the buttons. Now I may be a virgin but I'm not dead inside. Crew Westwood in nothing but his underwear in front of me is a gift. "You look like someone graffitied a marble sculpture of a Greek god."

He chuckles, his hand cupping and adjusting his very big, very bulging package. "Fireball, do you just say whatever pops into your head? Not that I'm complaining. You are great for the ego."

I give him a tiny shrug as he kicks his shorts off his ankles. "Actually I usually don't say anything I think or feel. I'm branching out tonight."

"Interesting." He bends. I can be hyper-critical of hockey and its players but I will never fault the physique it gives them. Never ever. Crew stands up with a square foil thing in his hand. "I am here for whatever you need me for, Olivia."

He says my full name, the only one I've given him, slowly in a deep tone that I swear just made my panties damp. He tosses the condom and it lands squarely on the night table. He grins like an NBA player who just made a buzzer-beating three-pointer. And then he leans forward and grabs my ankles.

Before I realize what's happening I'm slipping down the mattress, flat on my back. Then he's hovering above me again, this time balancing on one hand while his other lands on my bare thigh at the hem of my dress. I look him dead in the eye while his hand begins to climb. He has the dress up to my hips in no time then. He kisses my stomach, which makes me tingle everywhere.

I tip my head back and tell myself not to freak out. I am not the completely innocent, scared virgin my family likes to pretend I am. I've had boyfriends and we've done stuff. Lots of stuff. I'm not scared of men. I'm not saving myself for marriage. I was just waiting for a feeling. But then it became a thing. I was the only virgin I knew and then it just felt like pressure. Like I had to pick the right guy and the right time or it was all for naught. So I did what I always do in situations where I have to be bold. I did nothing.

"Olivia. Look at me."

That's when I realize I was all the way up in my own head, staring blankly at the ceiling while Crew has unzipped the side zipper on my dress. I hold my breath and lower my eyes. He's staring at me curiously. "You good?"

"So good." This is exactly what I want.

"If you aren't, just say it. Say no. Say stop. Say hey Crew get the fuck out," he tells me with a soft smile. "I promise even if I've got balls bluer than the ocean I will listen."

I smile. Man, I like this guy.

"But if you don't say any of that..." He starts tugging my dress down, and as my boobs pop free I cover them with my hands. He pauses and lifts one eyebrow at my act of modesty but I lift my hips, to help him get the dress all the way off and show him I'm not changing my mind. He takes my underwear with the dress throws them over his shoulder and climbs on top of me again. His lips find my ear. "If you don't say stop, I will not stop kissing you, or sucking you, or telling you how fucking gorgeous you are, or how good you taste. I won't stop at all. Not until you come so hard I'm all you think about for weeks."

What a gift would that be? To not think about the attack or how to tell my parents or what will happen next and to only think about this beautiful, charming, sexy man. "Hey Crew," I murmur as he kisses a trail down my neck. He stops as soon as the words leave my mouth. "Call me gorgeous again."

He lifts his head, then reaches out and runs a hand through my hair from my temple to the ends which are tangled against the mattress. "Olivia. Fireball. You are beautiful. In a Vegas club full of women you were the only one I saw tonight." His hand slides up over my knee, around my hip, and as it slides down again it starts to take my underwear with it. "Something about you sparkles, baby. You may be shy and confuse the hell out of me but you shine a little bit brighter, from the inside, than anyone I've met in a long time. I am going to enjoy the hell out of this."

I can't help but open my eyes and watch as his kisses move

to below my belly button and then lower. Then... oh. Oh. Oh... yes.

I've done this before but it has never felt like this. *I've* never felt like this. Crew is deliberate. Confident. Slow and savoring. He's not rushed, trying to get to the next part, where he gets gratification. He's getting something from this too. And if I needed confirmation, the low rumbling sound he makes is it. "I was right. You do taste incredible."

Crew is doing everything right. I feel good. I feel safe. I feel adored. And just a few moments later I feel the gentle euphoric push of an orgasm fighting its way through my over-active brain. I fight it, dodging it like a fighter dodges a punch but eventually, way quicker than it should, it knocks me out. I grip the sheets and pant out his name as my back arches and my hips roll.

"Oh fuck, Olivia. You are so damn hot," he murmurs against my sensitive, quivering flesh. I swear—something I rarely do— and squirm and he chuckles and gives me one last lick.

My eyes are closed and I'm fighting for some deep, calm breaths as he crawls his way up my body, lifting the clothes I have left, my crop top and bra, and kissing his way to my breasts, which I'm no longer trying to hide. He sucks on each nipple with care, swirling his tongue and gently nipping. It has me feverish with desire again and I run my hands into his hair, which is surprisingly thick and soft, and I pull his mouth to mine and kiss him deeply. I taste myself and I don't care. I just want him so much. I have never been this turned on.

He reaches out blindly with his left arm, groping the night table, and it isn't until I see the foil packet in his hand that I realize, I'm actually about to do this. I'm nervous, but not hesitant. I boldly, at least in my opinion, pull off my shirt and bra and drop them to the floor, then I watch him roll the condom over his very hard, very thick cock.

When he's properly sheathed he leans down again, cups the back of my neck, and whispers, "Roll over."

Oh.

I don't know if I should argue. I mean, I always pictured my first-time missionary but there's no rule about it.... Right? I roll over and immediately feel his hands on my hips, pulling me up. I'm... exposed. So exposed. But I mean, I'm naked so of course I'm exposed but this just feels... more vulnerable.

Crew keeps one hand on my hip but the other moves and then I feel it and I almost jump. The tip of his cock being rubbed across my sensitive, slick center. I arch my back almost involuntarily at the shiver of pleasure. This is nice... I'm still wrapped up in knots in my head but my body has no complaints. "Crew..." I whisper his name almost sheepishly. "Can you be... gentle?"

I feel like a failure for asking. I'm on the verge of complete humiliation but he responds by leaning over my back, kissing the spot between my shoulder blades, and... oh... he's started to inch inside... I...

"Baby, I will be whatever you need," he promises as he inches more and more and in... then out a bit... then I feel his fingers against my clit, moving in slow circles. I arch my back even more. He slips in completely and there is this moment of brief but biting pain but then... wow. This feels... weird. Good but weird. I have a man inside me.

He kisses the base of my neck and his hips roll slowly but firmly as he moves in and then out just a little bit. "Olivia, how are you so impossibly tight? Jesus..."

"I'm sorry," I choke out.

"Baby do not apologize for your perfection," he scolds with a quick, light slap to the side of my right ass cheek which, between that and his fingers still on my clit, have me tingling everywhere.

He keeps moving, in and out and the pace gets faster. His

rhythm grows uneven very quickly and he curses and it sounds like it's through gritted teeth. I am overwhelmed trying to adjust to this new normal and it's not that I don't like it. I do like it. It's nice but it's also weird and I think coming beforehand made it easier but now... I have too much to process to think about coming again, even though everything he's doing feels good. Really good. But still...

"Olivia, are you close?"

He needs me to come and I want to give him that. I like Crew. He has been nothing but charming and he's gorgeous and he deserves to think he rang my bell twice so I make a noise. A small breathy moan and he growls in victory. "Yeah baby, do it. Come."

I make the sound again and arch my back a little more and he snaps his hips hard and fast and I have to brace a hand against the headboard to keep from smacking my head into it. I hear him groan so loudly I panic for a second. I hope to hell no one else is back yet. They would definitely hear that. He grips my hips so tightly I might have bruises, but I'll worry about that later. Right now I just take in the moment, the first time I've made a man come this way.

His torso collapses onto my back and the movement causes his dick to start to slide out. I watch over my shoulder as he grabs the base, including the edge of the condom, and slides out, flopping onto his back beside me.

I drop down onto my stomach, so only my ass is exposed to his gaze, which is heavy and satisfied. I satisfied him. It's a good feeling. It's all I feel actually, which surprises me. I don't feel relieved I finally had sex. I don't feel regret either. I just feel... content. And oddly proud that I put that look on such a sexy, charming, wildly attractive man's face.

He rolls onto his side. "I should clean up."

With a quick kiss, he gets off the bed and lumbers into my

attached bath. The light flicks on and the door half-closes. I love how men can just wander around buck-naked and not give a fuck. I am always in some sort of clothing. Even on the hottest night last fall when the AC in our apartment was broken, I had on boy shorts and a tank even though Tenley claimed the only way to sleep was fresh out of a cold shower, completely in the buff. Nope. Not me. Clothes are covering me at all times.

So now I take the alone time to scurry over to my suitcase and throw on fresh undies and a tank top. I pause and touch myself. I'm a little achy but it's not horrendous.

The bathroom door opens as I'm pulling back the sheets and crawling into bed. Crew walks right over to me and cups my face in his hands. "You all ready for bed? Need me to tuck you in?"

Before I can respond he kisses me, slowly and gently and it's wonderful. I let him push me back down onto the mattress and lower his naked self on top of me, even though in the back of my brain I'm panicking my relatives might come back and catch us. I locked the door, right? I think I did... but yeah, a minute or two of cuddling with Crew won't kill me.

He rolls onto his side and tucks me into him. The feel of him against my back is soothing, one of his big strong arms draped across my torso and the other under my head as a pillow. He slips a leg in between mine and I sigh. "This is nice."

"Cuddling is the second best part," he murmurs, and it's the last thing I remember because I drift off to sleep.

Chapter 7

Crew

I hear voices. They're not loud but they are filtering through the closed bedroom door. And then I feel the soft, warm naked body curled into mine tighten. The next thing I know the body is gone, and so are the sheets.

My eyes flutter open. Fireball is standing, beautifully naked in the middle of the room with her hands on her head, palms against her forehead. "Oh shit. Oh shit. Everyone's awake. Fuck."

She's whispering it to herself, I think. I sit up slowly and admire the view. Somewhere in the middle of the night, I remember we fooled around again. No sex, but kissing and touching and her clothes came off. So now when our eyes lock, and she realizes she's naked, she panics and starts grabbing clothes off the ground. She puts on my shirt from last night, wrapping it around her body like a bathrobe. "This can't be happening. They can't know you're here."

"Who are they?"

She doesn't answer. Her eyes drop to my exposed hips and my rock-hard cock currently trying to touch the ceiling. She points at it accusingly. "Stop doing that!"

"Umm... I can try but he doesn't always listen," I explain, and she shushes me like I just used a bullhorn to say that.

"Get dressed and get out," she whispers and the voices outside the door, in the living room of the suite, seem to grow. There are a lot of people in this suite.

"Who's out there?"

"The people I came with. Co-workers," she replies hastily. The glint in her brown eyes is wild like she's absolutely terrified. "And I'll lose my job if I get caught with you?"

She says it like it's a question. Weird. And wait a minute...

"I thought you were a student?"

She nods and shakes her head and then nods again. "A student with a job."

"Oh."

There's a knock at the door. She jumps at least a foot off the ground and covers her mouth to keep from squeaking. I have to admit, now I'm a little nervous. I mean, I don't want to get her in any kind of trouble.

"Livvy! We're going to brunch. Get your butt out of bed and join!" It's a female voice.

"I'm good!" Livvy calls back—or Olivia, as she said last night. "Go without me!"

"No!"

And then the person attached to the stubborn voice tries turning the handle. Luckily Olivia locked it last night because it doesn't open. So the person starts knocking, incessantly.

Olivia swears under her breath again. "Seriously! I'm hungover and want to sleep it off. Go! I'm fine!"

"Livanator, nothing cures a hangover better than the huevos rancheros in the restaurant in this hotel," a male voice assures her. "Trust me. I have it every morning I'm here. It's magic."

That voice... it's muffled but it sounds... familiar. Why? How? I climb out of bed and walk over to her. "Who is that?"

"Get dressed!" she hisses.

"Liv?" A third voice. Another female. "Come! I promise you won't regret it."

I hear mumbled talking like the group outside the door is discussing something amongst themselves. I take Olivia's arm and pull her away from the door so I can whisper without a chance of being overheard. "Why is this such a big deal. People hook up in Vegas all the time."

"Yeah but... *I* don't do this and they don't know I wanted to do this and I don't want them to," she whispers back and her pretty face is still awash with terror. I hug her because I don't know what else to do to calm her down.

"Okay. I get it. Reputation and everything." I try not to take it personally. She's not ashamed of me. It's bigger than that.

"Come on Livvy!" The first female voice is back. She's whining now. "If you don't go I'll feel bad like we broke you or something, and then I won't go."

"I'm fine Te..." She stops, puts a palm to her forehead again, closes her eyes, and sighs. "I'm fine. I promise. Please just go. I will meet you there in five minutes."

"Good. Five minutes or we come back up here. Let's go. I'm starving." That familiar male voice again. How do I know that voice? "See you soon Livanator."

The mumbling behind the closed and locked door diminishes, but Olivia, or Liv as they keep calling her, still looks petrified. I open my mouth to ask why but she rushes to me and slaps her hand over it. I grimace at the unexpected rough contact. "She's still out there."

I hear a door close, probably the main one to the suite. Our eyes connect and so do our torsos and... she jumps back and points at my still-hard dick. "I told you. That needs to disappear!"

"It's not a genie." I chuckle. "well, maybe it is, come to think of it, because if you rub it the right way…"

"Shush!"

"Livvy, let me in. I'm worried. I haven't seen you since last night." The female voice is back. "Everyone else is gone."

"I told you," Olivia mouths at me, and then she's scurrying around the room, grabbing my shoes, my socks, my underwear, and shorts and before I can do a thing about it, she's shoving everything, and me, into the closet.

It's a tight fit and I bang the back of my head on the rack. I hiss and she shushes me again. She pauses as I'm trying to pretzel myself against the back of the closet. "Promise me on all that is holy, on hockey and Wayne Gretzky and the Stanley Cup and all your dad's trophies and medals and every single one you still have coming to you that no matter what you hear you will not… will not come out of here until exactly five minutes after you hear us leave."

"Wow. You mean business."

"I do. I'm all business. I'm more serious than a heart attack," she whispers and our eyes lock. "Please?"

"I promise, Olivia," I say her full name. She smiles. It's fleeting and soft but my heart thumps harder in my chest. She's something else.

She starts to close the door but pauses. "And thank you. For last night. That was… I'm glad we did that."

"Me too." Before I can offer to do it again, if she wants, at a date to be determined later, she shuts me in the closet.

I hear nothing for almost thirty seconds and then there's another bang on the door and Olivia yells. "I'm coming. Calm your tits!"

There's a bark of laughter that sounds pretty loud so I think Olivia opened the door and let the relentless female friend into the room. "Oh my god, who are you and what have you done with my demure little cousin?"

"First of all, I'm older than you so I'm not your little cousin," Olivia reminds the woman as my muscles burn trying to keep myself motionless in this ridiculously small closet. "Second of all, I had too much to drink last night and unlike the rest of you, I'm not a pro at that. I need to sleep it off. But since you won't let me do that, let's eat."

"Yay for drunk Liv! And I promise my dear brother is right. The huevos rancheros here is fire," the girl says happily.

So this is a family gathering? Interesting. Why did she lie and say it was co-workers? I always wanted a big family but I didn't get one. It's just me, my twin, and my parents. No cousins as my aunts and uncles didn't procreate. I likely won't either so the Westwood family will grow even tinier.

"Anyway I'm so glad it was just booze," the cousin says and even in the cramped darkness of the closet I can hear the relief in her voice. "I thought maybe it was a panic attack that had you locked in here. You know, from the—"

"Let's go!" Liv cuts her off and I'm left wondering what the end of that sentence would have been.

"Where did you get that shirt?"

"Thrifted it."

"It's too big."

"I like big."

"That's what she said." Giggles and then a thump, like a door closing.

I wait an excruciating five minutes after that, as promised. Eventually, I pull myself out of the closet, tripping on a fallen hanger and landing in a heap at the foot of the bed. I hiss out an expletive and lift myself up off the carpet. I put on the clothes that tumbled out with me, but of course, my shirt walked out the door with Olivia.

I'm standing there, naked from the waist up, when I see her open suitcase. There's a hoodie in the pile next to it. The kind with a zipper opening, not the over-the-head kind. I walk over and pluck it off the ground. It's charcoal gray and I start to put it on.

To say it doesn't fit is an understatement. The arms, which I'm sure are full-length on her, are barely past my elbow. And I can't get it done up at all. But if she can steal my shirt, I can steal her hoodie. Of course not forever, I hope. I am going to leave my phone number for her so she can call to get it back.

I glance around the room. It's still dark in here since she closed the door again when she left, but there's some hotel stationary and a pen on the night table. I walk over and grab it, jot down my number, but I don't leave my name or any other note. She'll know. Olivia is a smart cookie.

I crack the door to the rest of the suite. It's deadly silent. They're all definitely gone so I make a beeline for the main door. I open that one slowly too, peering out the crack to make sure I can't see anyone in the hall. There's a housekeeping cart a few doors down but that's it. I slip out of the suite and down the hall to the elevators. The housekeeper comes out of one of the rooms with her arms filled with dirty sheets and she does a bit of a double take at my hulking torso squeezed into the too-small hoodie. I smile and wink.

She ignores me completely and goes back to her job. As a housekeeper in Vegas, I'm sure she's seen much worse than a professional hockey player in a woman's sweatshirt. The elevator opens and... I'm face-to-face with Tate.

Oh well. I've been caught in worse situations by people I know.

"Hey!" he says with a smile that falters when he sees my attire. "Did they shrink your clothes at the dry cleaner? Is this another wardrobe malfunction like the Hawaiian shirt last night?"

I grin. "Not exactly."

He glances past me down the corridor and then to the left where the hotel hallway stretches out in a different direction. He's clearly trying to figure out where I came from. The color drains from his face fairly quickly. "Please dear God do not say you hooked up with Tenley."

"What? No! Of course not. Team rules," I reply and make a face like hooking up with his sister is the most horrendous thing I can think of. It's not, honestly. Tenley is hot as all hell. I mean she's no Olivia, but she's stunning.

But a bunch of core guys on the team made a pact one night. Granted we were all drunk but we promised each other that family was off-limits. Too many teammates fall out and create drama for the entire team when they date a sibling of their teammate. And to be honest, as pretty as Tenley is, she's also hell on wheels. Not at all unlikable, but feisty and wild and the type of girl you say you would never marry and then wake up one day on your fifteenth wedding anniversary, four kids in, madly in love, and trying to figure out how the hell that happened. I am not looking for that on any level.

"Why on earth would you jump to that conclusion?" I ask.

"Because..." He scans my outfit again. "That's a woman's hoodie and this is our floor."

"You and Tenley?" I ask. "You're sharing a room with your sister and your girlfriend? I'm not here to judge but I'm judging."

The housekeeper and her cart wander by as Tate smirks at me and my comment. "No dipshit. I'm sharing a *suite* with my sister, my girlfriend, and my cousin. I mean technically. And I thought I heard Tenley sneaking someone out of her room early this morning."

"Obviously not me, because we made a pact." I raise my hands. "Also, I'm sneaking out now, not in the wee hours."

"Right." Tate nods and then he smiles again, relieved. "I gotta go. I forgot my phone but we're downstairs having breakfast if you want to join."

"Nah thanks. I need some sleep. I didn't get much last night." I grin, and he gives me a congratulatory slap on the shoulder. I hit the elevator button again because it closed behind him. He takes a couple steps and then something he said earlier echoes in my brain. *Cousin.* I turn as he walks down the hall. The wing I just sauntered down, not the other one. "Tate! Who all are you here with again?"

"Ten, Mal, and Liv."

Oh fuck.

He stares at me and I stare back. My only thought is do not let your jaw drop. Do not react at all. "Liv is..."

"Conner's sister. My uncle Devin and Aunt Callie's oldest daughter," Tate explains. "She lives with Ten and they go to UCLA."

My expression must be as blank as my mind because my brain has literally short-circuited. That's why the male voice was familiar. It was Tate's. My mystery lay. My sexy stranger. My Olivia. Is my teammate's cousin. The one he protects at all costs. The one he says is shy and sensitive and stays out of the hockey limelight. And... is a virgin.

"You said Liv doesn't do hockey stuff."

"She doesn't. And she doesn't do much of anything like this for sure," Tate agrees and stops in front of the door I just exited. My heart beats faster. His green eyes stay on me as he pulls his key card from his pocket. "She's been through some stuff lately and she's... well she's trying new things. Anyway, she went home from the club early last night so maybe she's not as ready as she thinks she is for a new lifestyle. See you later?"

"Yeah. Later!" I nod and slip into the elevator just as the doors are starting to close again.

It's me. I'm the new thing Olivia Garrison is trying.

Did I just take her virginity?

Oh fuckity fuck fuck.

Chapter 8

Liv

"You're smiling," Harlow notes, which means everyone turns and stares at me, ignoring Jake Gyllenhaal kicking ass on the screen in front of us.

"No. I'm... enjoying the movie."

I'm not not enjoying the movie. I mean I'm sure this remake of *Road House* is as good as the guys in our family say it is, but I haven't been able to focus for more than a few minutes at a time. Every time I see a muscle bulge or an abdomen flex, I think of Crew Westwood and then my mind drifts to that night and the sex. I've had sex. With a hot, sought-after, gorgeous man.

"That quirky, sweet kid's store just went up in smoke." Tenley lifts a sculpted blonde eyebrow as she points at the fiery scene on the television. "And that made you smile?"

"No of course not. I'm smiling at... The fact that Jake Gyllenhaal will swoop in and save the day." I've been telling so many little white lies lately that I swear to God I should teach a class on how to deceive your relatives and convince yourself it's a good thing.

"Something is going on with her," Tenley tells our cousins.

Harlow and our other cousin Shelby pause the movie on the

screen to join the conversation. Harlow and Shelby both live in Silver Bay, our hometown in Maine, but they're here for a long weekend. Shelby is a nurse. Harlow runs our Uncle Cole's bar and has been working out like mother-fucker judging by how sculpted she looks in the cropped tank and leggings.

But my focus isn't on Harlow's buff physique. It's on Tenley and her big mouth. She better not tell them about the attack. I love Shelby and Harlow and would have easily confided in them if they had been here when it happened, but they weren't. I've learned that in our family the more people who know, the shorter the amount of time until your secret is a group chat topic.

Like the time Conner got drafted to the Barons and thirteen-year-old Theo thought it would be an epic tribute to painting the light posts around the parking lot at Last Call, Uncle Cole's bar, in Barons colors. He snuck out and did it in the middle of the night and woke up to a town scandal. Because the light posts were town property, not property of the bar, so the Mayor and city council were furious.

They had no idea who did it and didn't connect the colors to Conner's first NHL team. Theo confided in Grady, who helped him paint them back to white in the middle of the next night. But Grady also told Harlow, who whispered it to Tenley who told God knows which other cousin, and the next thing Theo knew, even though the light posts were white again, he was grounded for two entire months.

I did not want my mom or dad or even my brother and sister hearing a word about this incident through the Garrison family grapevine. It will be so much worse than if I told them. And I *will* tell them, just not until it's over. The police called last week and said they are awaiting a trial date and my attacker has not made his bail, but he might and they will keep me informed if he does and is released.

Tenley blinks her impossibly long, natural eyelashes and seems to mentally clue into the worried look on my face. She gives her head the teeniest barely visible shake to let me know she isn't about to share that secret.

"So spill it, Livvy," Shelby urges. "What's going on?"

"Nothing," I promise. "I do nothing but go to class, go to my internship, sleep, eat, repeat."

"You went to Vegas," Tenley reminds everyone. "That was not classic Liv."

"Did you get lucky in Vegas?" Harlow wants to know. "Win some money or lose your virginity?"

"Finally!" Shelby joins in and I'm offended now.

"Not you too! You were always my ally," I complain. "No sex is the safest sex. There is nothing wrong with a slow pace in life and all that."

Shelby reaches out and lays a hand on my forearm from her position in the bean bag chair by the window. "I promise I am still pro-abstinence. But I assume if you did it, it was because you wanted to and were ready and I'm all for that too."

"I wish I'd never told any of you about my lack of sexual escapades."

"You didn't have to *tell* us," Tenley reminds me. "We grew up in Silver Bay. The town is the size of a postage stamp. Everybody knows what everyone else is doing, and who they're doing, and when they're doing it. Do you think I wanted everyone to know my first time was with Andrew Howlett? I didn't but word got around anyway."

"He didn't want everyone to know either," Harlow says with a smile. "Because he proceeded to get body checked by every male teenage Garrison for, like, a month after that. On the ice and off."

"Right, Theo checked him into the lockers in the hallway at school," Shelby laughs.

"That was after Tate, Conner, and Grady had him eating the boards every time he stepped foot on the ice for months," Harlow adds.

"It's also why I didn't have sex again until we left for college," Tenley sighs.

"So is there a boy?" Harlow asks and leans closer to me from her position snuggled into the crux of the L-shaped couch. Her hazel eyes soften. "Someone serious?"

"No one serious." I roll my eyes and reach for a handful of the cheddar popcorn in a bright pink bucket on the coffee table. "God why are you all so hyper-focused on my dating life or lack thereof. You guys are all single too, you know."

"By choice," Tenley announces.

"Not by choice," Shelby adds and sighs, shoving a piece of her gorgeous red hair behind her ear. "The dating pool in Silver Bay is puddle-deep, girlies. Do not come home without a prospect or you'll end up alone for life."

"You're not even thirty. Relax." Harlow waves a hand at Shelby like she's dispersing something foul in the air. "I don't have time for a dude right now. I'm drowning with work."

"And your new fitness regimen?" I ask because Harlow is seriously ripped. Like I think she's got less body fat than her hockey-playing brother, Theo, at this point.

"I'm working out more... for stress management," Harlow replies and averts her eyes and waves her hand again. Tenley cocks an eyebrow but doesn't say anything. "Now you said no one *serious*, but that doesn't mean no one. Is there an unserious guy?"

"Must be someone from school." Tenley furrows her brow and taps her chin with her index finger as she thinks. Her big green eyes light up and land on me. "Oh! Is it that cute guy I saw when I dropped you off at the junior high?"

"Carlos? No. I mean yeah he is cute and nice, but no." I

shake my head adamantly because I know my family—they need things loud and clear. "We work together. This internship is super imperative to my program and I need to be hyper-focused. So does he."

Harlow sags in disappointment. "Ugh, I was hoping someone was getting some butterflies in their ovaries."

"I thought I had butterflies last week," Shelby tells us and sighs. "It was bad Chinese food."

I laugh. "Can we watch the movie now?"

"Fine, but something is up with you." Tenley points at me sternly, and she is so channeling my mom right now.

Tenley acts so much like my mom and not hers. Genetics are weird that way. I'm still trying to figure out where my shy, timid, reclusive gene came from. Although my mom once told me my auntie Rose was 'so much like me' when she was a kid. Genetics were pretty straightforward when it comes to physicality. I am a mirror image of my mom, dark hair, eyes like melted milk chocolate, skin like porcelain with a dusting of freckles across my nose if you look hard enough. But I have a dimple in my chin which is all Garrison, but I'm the shortest Garrison girl, even my baby sister Mayhem towers over me. The lack of height is all Caplan, my mom's side. I think of Crew and how I can see both his parents in him. How he and Nash, who are fraternal twins, share so many similarities from eye color to hair color but are nowhere near identical. Crew is bulkier and slightly less fair in coloring and Nash has sharper features. I may have spent a couple of hours googling pictures of Crew... because I was bored. No other reason.

"Should we have invited Mallory?" Shelby asks a minute later.

"I did, but I knew she would say no." Tenley pauses to toss some popcorn into the air and effortlessly catches it in her mouth. "Mom and Dad went back to the Bay for a few weeks and their regular nanny quit last week so she's got her hands full with Dylan and going back to school."

"She could have brought Dyllie Bear," Harlow replies. "I love that little cuddle muffin."

"He's a lot right now. He has Tate's energy and really needs that backyard they have to burn it off. He's been here before but he almost hurled himself off our balcony," Tenley explained.

"Have they hired a new nanny yet?" Tenley turns to me and shakes her head. "Because I'd be interested."

"Really? How? Why?" Harlow looks confused. "You're still taking classes and you have the internship and you don't exactly need the spending money."

She's right about all of that. I'm overloaded as it is, but I also can't seem to shut off my brain. When I do have spare time all I think about is that guy tackling me or... that night with Crew. One is a bad memory I don't want to think about and the other is a good one I don't want to think about too much because then I'll develop a crush on a guy I can't be involved with. Not for real. And if I crush too hard I will use that number he left on my night table. And what good will that do me? Crew doesn't know how we're connected and I want to keep it that way.

I shrug. "I think it will look good on a resume, especially because I want to get a job at one of those fancy performing arts schools when I'm done."

That part is true too. It will look good on my resume if I can be a private nanny for a professional athlete. Harlow stretches. "I know Tater Tot would love having you watch Dylan. Make sure he pays you fairly. No family discount."

"He always pays well," I assure her because I watched Dylan a lot this summer and Tate compensated me even when I told him I didn't want money. One time my sister Mae stayed home with me too while I watched Dylan and Tate paid us both, even though she wasn't technically watching him.

"I just texted Mal and told her you want to watch him." Tenley holds up her phone before dropping it on the pillow next to her. "I'm sure she'll reach out. Do yourself a favor and walk him down by the beach. There are a ton of hot men who mack all over you when you have a baby and no wedding ring."

"Like men even bother to look for a ring." Shelby rolls her eyes. She is the most jaded of all of us when it comes to love, which I've never understood. She hasn't had any really horrible break-ups that I know of. In fact, Harlow had her relationship implode hours before her wedding and she's less jaded than Shelby.

"Well I'm demanding you come to the game tomorrow night," Harlow announces and I immediately shake my head. She pretends she doesn't notice. "You and I have both sworn off hockey players so we can keep each other company while they ogle asses and stuff."

"Hockey players are fine if you only fuck them once," Tenley tells us. "Anyway, Harlow is right. You have to come. I hardly ever see you and I live with you."

I think of Crew. Skating hard across the ice. Brow furrowed with exertion, legs pumping. Then I think of him naked, sweaty, hips pumping.

"Are you... blushing?" Tenley sounds horrified.

I stand up and walk to the window. "No. I'm hot. It's Los Angeles in September. It's the devil's armpit."

I punch the AC unit up a couple degrees. Now they're all looking at me like I'm a complete weirdo. So I say the one thing that will distract them. "Fine. I'll go to the game."

* * *

This isn't a big deal, I tell myself as we filter in through the turnstile, flashing our passes, on lanyards around our necks, at the security guard. "Do we really have to go down there?"

"Yeah," replies Tenley. "I said we would meet Mallory down there. Plus candy bar."

I swear to God Tenley's entire diet is candy. She loves sweet stuff. Always has. Her parents have a framed photo of her at their house taken the first time she tried ice cream. Her eyes are wide, and her toothless smile takes up her entire chubby face, which is covered in chocolate. It's honestly the cutest thing I've ever seen. I wasn't a pudgy adorable baby like Tenley. I was skinny and weird-looking if you ask me.

"Oh shit. There's Nash," Tenley grumbles and her step falters as we make our way past another security guard at the bottom of the stairs that lead to the corridor that winds around to the VIP lounge.

I look up and see Nash Westwood in a Quake tracksuit, dirty blond head tipped downward focused on his phone. He's wearing dark-framed glasses, which makes me wonder if Crew has glasses. "You hung out with him just fine in Vegas," I remind my cousin.

"I was drunk," she mutters. "I do a lot of stupid things when I'm drunk. By the way, I'm doing dry September. And probably October."

"Is that a thing? I thought it was January," Harlow asks.

"Apparently Tenley doesn't want to accidentally party with hot but nerdy hockey players anymore," Shelby says and smirks. "Because Tenley is an idiot."

Nash looks up before anyone can say another word and his hazel eyes lock on Tenley and he looks... annoyed. "Can I talk to you?"

He doesn't even acknowledge the rest of us, which seems weird. I've heard he's quite the good guy, all manners and best behavior. "I'd love to, but I want to stay awake during the game and you always put me to sleep."

"Ouch!" Harlow stage whispers.

Shelby pretends not to be listening, her big blue eyes darting around the hallway for something, anything, to focus on besides Tenley and her mean-girl attitude. Nash's stubbled cheeks start to redden.

"Hey Nash. I'm Liv," I say and now they're all staring at me in awe because, I admit, I'm not the one to jump into a tense situation. Or any situation. I shove out my hand despite the mild panic that's started pumping through my veins along with my blood. "I'm Tenley's cousin. Tate's too. I'm Conner Garrison's sister. Anyway hi. I hope you guys have another great season."

"I know who you are," He extends his hand and his smile is tight but friendly. He yanks his eyes from Tenley. "I'm happy to finally meet you. Your family adores you and I can see why. Unlike your cousin here, you seem to be nice and normal. And thanks about the season. I guess I should be going."

"No need. We're going," Tenley says and starts storming down the hall. I scurry after her.

Shelby and Harlow wave at Nash as they bustle past. "Jesus, Ten. Did he piss in your Corn Flakes or something? I mean, I get the whole ice princess mean girl thing works for you, but that was a little much. He's a family friend."

"He and Crew never came to any of our summer hockey gatherings," Tenley retorts. She's right. When their dad retired they moved back to his hometown in Canada and the twins were in hockey camps all summer long. "And for the record, he was an absolute dick to me in Vegas. He's not at all the sweet, adorkable guy he pretends to be."

Oh. Well... this is news. She hasn't brought it up.

"What did he do?"

"I don't want to get into it. But I've warned you all." Tenley has her eyes glued to the ground and is fussing with her hair. Everything about her right now is self-conscious and out of character. "He's a dick. Now let's talk about something else. Hey! Tater Tot!"

She yells her brother's nickname and we all look down the hall to see him wandering over in the same tracksuit Nash was wearing.

"You have to stop calling me that in public." Tate rolls his big aquamarine eyes and frowns at his sister. Tenley grins in return and spins so he can see the back of her Quake jersey. Harlow moves to stand shoulder-to-shoulder with Tenley and turns as well so he can see that they both have his number. But across the shoulders where his last name would normally be stitched, Tenley has the word Tater and Harlow has the word Tot.

His eyes get wider and his frown gets deeper. His eyes move to me and Shelby and the Quake logo on the front of our jerseys. "Please tell me you two didn't participate in my sister's slanderous prank."

"Guilty." Shelby turns so he can see the Tater on her shoulders. She grabs my arm and spins me too.

"Sorry! I told them we shouldn't do it," I tell Tate and he sighs.

"I am never giving you guys tickets again. Traitors."

"It's a cute nickname, Tater Tot," Mallory says as she walks out of the VIP lounge doors across the hall. "Right Dyllie Bear? Tell Dada his nickname is cute."

"Dada! Dada Dada!" Dylan claps and kicks his feet on Mallory's hip. She beams and Tate's frown melts. They both love this kid so much.

Tate reaches out and plucks his son from Mallory, giving him a big kiss on the cheek as he squeals in delight. No one had Tate producing the first grandchild on their bingo card, but honestly, it couldn't be more perfect. He needed something to tether him and he also needed Mallory Echolls. She needed him too. They're a perfect pair and she is the perfect second mom to Dylan.

"Dyllie Bear!" I walk over and he immediately extends his arms.

"I can't tell you how amazing it is to know he's going to be with you four days a week," Tate says as he hands his son to me. "He loves that little guitar you got him this summer. Never puts it down."

"There's a ton of other musical instruments I can get him," I say. "All specially made for kids."

"Make an Amazon Wishlist and I will buy them," Tate promises. "I have to get into the locker room and get ready. Take those ridiculous shirts off."

"Never!" Tenley announces loudly as Tate kisses Mallory, waves goodbye to his son, and disappears into the locker room, which is the first door on the left side of the hallway almost directly across from the VIP lounge.

"Come. I need candy," Tenley announces and marches off to the lounge. Shelby and Harlow follow immediately but I hang back with Mallory and Dylan who has grabbed the end of one of my short braids and is trying to stuff it into his mouth.

"I told you Dylan, no eating hair!" Mallory says firmly as she gently takes his little pudgy fist and pulls my hair free. He makes a disgruntled sound but doesn't pitch a fit, even when Mallory takes him from me.

"Are you sure you can handle four days with your school schedule and your internship?" Mallory asks and I nod.

"The way the hours are now, yes. I'm at your place three to nine three days and one weekend day from noon to six. That's fine. I don't have school or the internship on weekends and all my classes are over by three," I promise.

"You'll miss all of Tate's games." Mallory looks disappointed.

"Spoiler alert, I would miss them all anyway like I did last year and every year," I remind her with a sheepish grin.

"I just thought, since you went to the Vegas party and you seemed to enjoy yourself that maybe you would want to do more things with us," Mallory replies and the disappointment in her voice is apparent. I feel instantly guilty, the way Mae and Conner used to make me feel when I didn't want to spend my free time at the rink when we all lived at home and the two of them were playing local hockey.

Mallory must see the turmoil her words have created on my face. I've never had a poker face. She immediately tries to explain better. "It's just I'm more of an introvert like you, but being a player's girlfriend, I have to go to these things now, and Dyllie loves them. So anyway I just... it would be nice to have someone around who is mellow, like me. Ten, when she comes, is full throttle, like she is everywhere with everything and the other wives and girlfriends are more intense too. You bring this Zen quality I love."

Awe... she's so sweet. And I love hanging out with her and maybe I would consider attending more games but... my thoughts are interrupted when the *but* walks by.

Crew Westwood is in the same Quake track bottoms as Tate and Nash, but he's wearing a plain ribbed black tank on top. His inked, muscled biceps and forearms on full display. He sees Mallory and Dylan first and a friendly smile covers his wide mouth. A twinkle enters his eye as he takes in Dylan and gives the toddler a cute little wave.

But then his eyes meet mine and my ovaries, which had started to dance at the sight of him, start to do what feels like an Olympic-worthy rhythmic gymnastics routine. Good God, he is hotter than an LA August.

"Mal, Dyllie," he says to them and leans in to hug Mallory and ruffle Dylan's hair. His eyes stay locked with me though and then he turns that work of art he calls a body to face me. He doesn't look shocked. He knows who I am.

"Olivia. Hi." I wonder when and how he figured it out? Did he know all along?

Mallory lifts her eyebrows toward the fluorescent lighting about our heads. I am instantly nervous. "Hey. Hi. Crew, right?"

I stick out my hand abruptly and awkwardly. He stares at it for a moment but doesn't leave me hanging. I feel the same electric jolt I felt in Vegas as our skin connects. "Are you here for the game?"

"Yep. Some cousins are in town. Doing a girls' weekend and Tenley wanted to harass her bother," I explain, my words rushing out of my mouth for some reason. "Anyway, I should go. Bye."

I turn and walk toward the stairs at the other end of the hall. I force my pace to be slow and casual even though my legs are itching to run. "Tell everyone I've gone up to the seats."

I don't wait for Mallory to respond, I just keep walking.

I make it all the way to the foot of the stairs before I feel his warm, large, strong hand on my shoulder. "Olivia."

I turn around and keep my eyes level with his chest. His glorious, broad, firm, toned chest. All I can think is, I've kissed the nipples under that fabric. "Don't call me that. No one calls me that. And you aren't even supposed to really know me. Act like it. I haven't told anyone about that... thing... and I don't want you to, okay? Please say you haven't said anything to anyone."

My desperation sends my gaze upward and our eyes meet. Why does he have to be so handsome? Why did I spend the first few days home from Vegas googling him and checking out almost every interview he's ever done? Studying every picture he's ever taken? Stalking his social media? Why?

"I told you before I realized you were my best friend and teammate's relative that I wouldn't tell anyone, and that still holds," Crew replies, his voice low but still deep and smooth like butter. "Why didn't you tell me who you were?"

"Because you wouldn't have wanted to..." I let my sentence trail off knowing he'll know what I'm talking about. "It would have complicated things. A one-night stand is supposed to be uncomplicated, right?"

Yeah, I'm asking because what the fuck do I know?

"Oh I still would have wanted to," he replies, pausing while his eyes dart around to make sure no one is overhearing. The security guard is the closest person to us and he's ignoring us. Crew's eyes find mine again as he confesses, "I want to right now. But I wouldn't have because you're right, it does complicate things. The team has an unofficial pact. Relatives are off limits."

"I didn't know that. Tate has never mentioned it."

Crew sighs and keeps staring at me. I can't read his expression but I could get lost in those hazel eyes if I let myself. And I can't. This is still a one-night stand situation. I take a step back. "Look, we never have to talk about this, or tell anyone. You did what I wanted you to do and we don't have to make it weird if we happen to run into each other again."

"I did what you wanted me to do?" Crew repeats and the way he says it, with indignation, makes me realize I offended him. I didn't mean to so of course I feel bad, but I'm so beyond new at this and what the hell do you say to a one-night stand after the fact? Ugh. I should have googled it or something.

"I won't come to any more games so don't worry about that," I tell him. "I'm sorry."

"For what?"

"I don't know but I feel like I should say it."

He sighs again and runs a hand through that thick ash blond hair that I know feels like silky fur. When he doesn't speak I decide to go. But he loops his fingers around my wrist. He stares right into my eyes. "Were you...? Was that your first time?"

Fuck. How does he know that?

Like I said earlier, I have no poker face so as soon as the words leave his mouth he sees the answer on my face. The shock. The embarrassment. It all screams *yes*. Now his handsome face is filled with horror and tinged with... empathy. He feels bad and now I'm humiliated.

"Please just forget it ever happened. I will too."

I yank my wrist free, blow past the security guard, and take the stairs two at a time. I make it to the main concourse level and beeline for the first women's bathroom I see.

I lock myself in a stall and let the hot tears poking my eyes fall. I made such a huge mistake sleeping with Crew. And now I get to add that to the pile of stuff haunting me right now. Great.

Chapter 9

——————

Crew

"We won!" Duke Hendrix reminds me as he gives my shoulder a shove with his as we make our way back to the locker room.

"I know. It's great!"

"Then maybe tell your face," Duke replies with a cheeky grin. "Because it looks like someone just took back your Stanley Cup ring."

"Sorry." I decide to lie. "My wrist is tweaking a little bit. And it was just pre-season. I don't wanna overreact."

I had a small fracture during the playoffs last year which, thankfully, is all healed up, but blaming my growly face on it is easier than explaining to my teammate that I accidentally took the virginity of my best friend's cousin. And that it's got me all vexed that she doesn't think it's a big deal and that she ran from me like I was contagious or something. And basically said it was something she would like to forget.

"You should go see the doc about that before it gets worse," Duke advises, looking serious now. "We need you full throttle for the season."

I nod and walk over to my locker area, then start peeling out

89

of my gear. Because it's pre-season there isn't much media coverage and the reporters who are here are talking to guys in the tunnel, not the locker room. I opted out of interviews. Yeah, they usually want to hear from the team leaders, which I've been even while not officially the co-captain yet. But Nash can handle that. He loves it and I never have. This 'injury' is also a good excuse for that because I know Coach Braddock will give me shit for not fielding media if I don't have an excuse.

I don't reach for my towel like the other guys. I tug on my track pants and tank from before the game, shove my feet into my blue rubber slides, an arena must, and make my way into the hall. I go straight to the VIP lounge. It's still filled with friends and family and smells like sugar from the candy station and leather from the fancy furniture. I immediately spot Tenley by the long mahogany bar. She's talking with the redhead from earlier. A cousin, but I don't know which one. She's got a dimple in her chin and the same willowy build as Tenley.

"Hey," I say as I stand about a foot away. I haven't showered yet and she doesn't need to smell that. "I was wondering if you'd..."

I can't ask if she's seen Olivia. It will set off alarm bells. Nobody thinks I even really know her. Tenley and the redhead are staring at me blankly, waiting for my mouth to keep saying words. "Uhh... I was..."

I did not think this through.

"You were wondering if I would... what?" Tenley asks as she lifts a glass of wine to her lips and the redhead reaches for the other one on the bar.

"If you would intro... introduce me," I croak out like a very petrified teenager at his first high school dance. Not at all the vibe I want to give off, ever, let alone with Olivia's relatives. "I haven't... met everyone in Tate's family yet."

My eyes move from Tenley to the redhead and back to

Tenley who is definitely taking this the wrong way judging by the smile on her face. "Crew Westwood, this is Shelby Garrison. She's my Uncle Cole and Aunt Leah's kid."

"Hi." I give her a wave and then change my mind and extend my hand like a gentleman because I'm not a complete asshole. At least not always. Her grip is firm and her smile is friendly. She's a very pretty woman but all I can think about is Olivia. "Hey. Tate's my best friend."

Am I suddenly a twelve-year-old? Is this a *Freaky Friday* or a time-travel situation? Why am I acting like a prepubescent boy with zero game? Because you aren't trying to pick up this woman, butt head, I scold myself.

"Hi."

And then it hits me. I try not to look horrified as I ask, "Is your brother Grady Garrison?"

"Yep!" She smiles proudly.

Oh fuck. Well, this just got even more awkward. I need to get the hell out of here. "Hell of a goalie. Anyway, nice meeting you. Have you seen Mallory? Tate was looking for her."

Another lie. One that I could get caught in. Why am I like this?

"I thought he was doing press." Tenley scrunches up her perfect little nose. "Anyway, Mallory is walking Liv and Dyllie Bear to the car. She'll be back in a minute."

"And hopefully she can hang for a bit," Shelby adds. "Parents' night out!"

"Liv is taking Dylan home. He's exhausted and getting over a cold and Liv never parties anyway so this way Mal and Tater don't have to rush home," Tenley explains.

"Home to her place or Tate's place?"

"Tate's," Tenley replies and blinks. "That's your old house, right? I've wanted to ask you why you would give that place up. It's amazing."

"Too big for a bachelor," I reply quickly. "I should go shower. Nice meeting you Shelby."

"You too, Crew."

I dodge people as quickly as possible and make my way back to the locker room without stopping for anyone else. Not even my brother who is at the end of the hall surrounded by reporters. He glares at me for a millisecond, something only a twin would notice. I ignore it, rush through my shower, and am out the door and in my car heading to Venice before Nash has even taken off his pads I'd bet.

I'm hellbent on having another conversation with Olivia but to what end? I mean she's right. She was a one-night stand. That night has come and gone. The deal is done. But the thing is, I wasn't clear on the details of that night and I don't think that's fair.

The streets are clogged like they always are in Los Angeles, but because it's a Tuesday it's not unbearable. I'm also grateful I can avoid the freeways and take regular streets from the arena downtown to the beach community where my former home, and my current home, are located. The only thing I really detest about California is the freeways.

I expect the call from Nash that lights up the screen in the dash of my Tesla. And I ignore it. I can drive to Tate's house on autopilot because I lived there for years. I never wanted to live there, though. My ex Anne-Marie picked it out one day, from a real estate site, and insisted we go to the open house. I didn't even know we were looking to buy. I mean... I wasn't.

I'm slightly superstitious and I was in the first couple years of my first NHL contract. I didn't want to jinx anything by getting too comfortable. Tons of guys get dropped down to the farm team or traded away before their first contract ends. Committing to a house seemed like jinxing myself. But yet somehow I was signing an offer on the Tuscan-style McMansion on the Venice Canals by the end of the day. I would have done anything to make Anne-Marie happy. I loved her that much. But it was a trick because nothing I did could or would ever make her happy.

I push Anne-Marie out of my head as I turn down the narrow street I know so well and slide the car into the driveway behind Mallory's car. I get out of mine and walk swiftly up the path that leads to the front door, located midway down the side of the house.

I'm glad this place is working out for Tate. He and Mallory have decided to buy it off me and we're just waiting for the lawyers to finalize everything. However, I'm not buying his townhouse that I've been living in since we decided to swap homes at the end of last season. In fact, I'm in the process of trying to find a new place to buy. I honestly can't decide where or what I want.

I ring the bell, a sound I always hated, and then knock on the door for good measure. Anne-Marie bought some custom bell that sounded like seagulls however it was a stupid idea because there are seagulls everywhere in Venice California. It's a beach community. I could never tell the doorbell from the birds outside, hence the additional knock.

I'm left there waiting so long, with nothing but the sound of the canal lapping gently against the cement borders of the walking paths that skirt the house, that I contemplate knocking again. Harder. But the outside light comes on suddenly and through the still-closed door I hear "Hello?"

It's Olivia, but her voice is abnormally low like she's trying to sound like a man. I smirk. "Hey. No human trafficker or serial killer here. Just the only guy you've seen naked."

The lock turns, the door opens, and she's standing there, still in the same clothes she wore to the game. Her gaze is hard and she shushes me. "Never say that out loud again.

Also, you are not the only guy I've seen naked. Get over yourself."

Okay so me and my stupid mouth just made a bad situation worse. Nifty. What is it about her that brings out the stupid in me?

I swallow down the urge to turn and run and just leave her alone forever. "Can I come in?"

She lets go of the open door and steps aside, her non-verbal yes. I step over the threshold and am shocked at how I barely recognize the place. It's not like Tate and Mallory have changed anything structurally on my old house. All the walls, windows, and doors are still in the same place. Hell, some of the furniture is still the same, but it *feels* different. They painted the living room a soft, smoky blue and the couch is in a different place, swung around to have views of the fenced yard and the wide-screen TV. And it smells like cookies and ocean air. But it's not those small changes that make it foreign either. It's hard to explain but it doesn't just look lived in, it looks loved. When Anne-Marie and I lived here it looked pretentious and stiff and... unloved.

"What?" Olivia says, and I realize I'm staring off at the contents of the open-concept first floor and not at her.

"Sorry. I used to live here and it's weird sometimes to be back." I give my head an actual shake and focus on her. She looks uncomfortable. Her hands are tucked up into the sleeves of her hockey jersey and her cheeks are a little pink. She isn't looking me in the eye but instead studying the very expensive travertine tile Anne-Marie insisted we install. "I'm also sorry about... that night in Vegas. I came on strong and went in hard and fast and I... had I known I would have—"

"Not done it," she interrupts. "Not done me. You would have looked at me like you did in the arena hallway. Like I'm a freak. A loser. And you would have bolted."

"No."

She looks up now, briefly, and then turns and walks into the living room. I follow. I don't see Dylan anywhere. She must have put him to bed already. "You say no because you think it makes you a bad guy to admit the truth. But your eyes gave it all away earlier."

"I was shocked, okay? That you're Tate's relative. He's my best friend and teammate and like I said we had a pact. Also, I was a little confused as to why you didn't mention you were related to him." She looks me in the eye only long enough to glare and then turns and walks to the bi-fold doors that lead to the small yard that backs onto the canal. "It might not have stopped me. I mean... I definitely wouldn't have wanted to stop or leave. If anything stopped me it would have been the pact, not the virginity thing."

She looks skeptical when I say that so I keep talking and pray I don't stick another foot in my mouth. "I don't have a kink for virgins or anything. But I'm not phobic over the whole thing either. I truly believe that it's not a big deal either way, which I guess you believe too since you, like, just..."

"Fucked you?" The word fucked coming out of her mouth is somehow super-hot. So is that cocked eyebrow of hers. Olivia is sexy AF in every mood. At least my dick seems to think so.

"Why me?"

She shrugs. "Why not?'

Wow, she is great at deflating any ego I might have. "Okay. Then why that trip, that weekend? You're... twenty... four?"

"Twenty-three, shortly. Tate and I are three weeks apart," Olivia corrects. The baby monitor on the kitchen island lights up and we both fall silent as we listen to Dylan make some noises that only babies make.

I follow her gaze to the monitor where we both watch him roll over and fall silent again. I move over to the bright yellow chaise in the corner by the windows. This isn't something I left behind. Mallory must have bought it because Tate isn't cultured enough to know a velvet yellow chaise goes perfectly with the smoky blue walls. I drop down onto it. Shit, it's comfy and curved in all the right places to support my aching back. I make a mental note to ask Mallory where she got it and then it hits me. "Wait. Tate's birthday was two weeks ago right after we got back from Vegas."

"Look at you, Sherlock Holmes!"

"And you're three weeks after him so..." I lean forward. "Your birthday is next week."

"Oh look, he does math too," she quips and shoots me a gentle smile that says even she thinks her snark level is high at the moment. It's adorable. Everything about her is adorable at the moment including that slightly too-big jersey, which for some reason, I wish had my name on the back.

"I've got skills you do not even know about," I tell her with a saucy wink that makes her blush. And then it hits me. I don't know if she enjoyed it. "So, like... I know this is awkward but let's be honest, that's kind of our thing at this point, so can you just tell me if you came or not that night. I assumed you did, but first times are notoriously bad for women."

"Are we really going to talk about this? Like it's a debrief after a work assignment or something?" Olivia goes from pink to red and she starts moving again, toward the bifold.

She yanks them open and once the wall is basically gone, she steps out into the small fenced garden. I can call it that now, legitimately because Mallory and Tate have a ton of potted plants and even a small vegetable plot behind Dylan's toys. Olivia won't look at me. Instead, she's got her back to me and is staring out past the wrought iron fence at the Canals. There's a bright yellow pedal boat bobbing directly in front of the house. I guess Tate and Mallory bought it. I always thought to do that but never actually did.

This house is nothing but a giant concrete ode to 'coulda, shoulda, woulda' for me. Ironic because standing here in the backyard is a woman who has become the exact same thing. I rub my stubbled chin. "I would have been different if you'd told me. I'm not saying you should have. That's your choice, and I don't know why you decided not to tell me. But now that I know, I wish I'd known then. I would have been..."

"Charitable?" Olivia offers, and I'm immediately horrified. "Sympathetic. Do me a favor? No, thank you. And no thank you for the sympathy now. It's embarrassing. Can you just go?"

She turns away from me and marches back into the house. I panic. Every step sends a shot of adrenaline through my veins. I'm getting angry with how stupid this has all become. I'm not being clear. She's taking everything the wrong way and I blame myself. I've never been a great communicator. Ask Anne-Marie.

So I do what I do best. Act. She stops to glance at the baby monitor screen and I come up behind her and slide my arms around her waist. Every part of her thin, toned body tenses as I hold her close, her back pressed into my chest. I dip my head and whisper in her ear. "The only charity work I do is for the Quake. You were never, and never could be, a pity fuck, Olivia. I don't fuck people that don't make me as hard as the ice under my skates."

"Oh." It's a breathy soft response that makes me very, very hard. I gently push my hips into her soft, round ass. She lets out a small gasp but doesn't move and doesn't push me away or protest.

"Now don't be embarrassed or shy. Remember I've seen you naked. I've had my dick inside you. I'm the only one you share this bond with right now, so no holds barred, Fireball. Be honest," I demand, my voice soft but my tone firm. My hands slide around her hips to her abdomen. I slip them under the hem of the jersey. "Did you come when I fucked you?"

"N-No. Not during," she whispers back and a brief strong wave of disappointment hits me. "I came from your... your tongue before, though."

I can feel her skin heat everywhere from that confession. My fingers have danced their way up under the jersey and are currently against the soft skin just above her belly button. Why am I so turned on by her modesty? Also, thank Christ I made her come once.

"A lot of women can't from... you know..."

"You can. With me," I promise, and she tenses again. "If you want to."

"What?" She starts to turn in my arms and I loosen my grip so we can be face-to-face. Her cheeks are still pink and her dark eyes wide, with fear or arousal or maybe both. God, I hope it's at least a little of both. "It was a one-night stand."

"Yeah but you were on a mission and you handed me an assignment without letting me in on the details," I explain. "The mission isn't complete. I'm a perfectionist and I didn't do a perfect job. Gimme another chance."

She bites her bottom lip. I thread a hand through her hair and cup the back of her neck. Her head tips back and our lips are a few, very small inches apart. "I'm... I'm..."

I kiss her. She responds, her tongue meeting mine. She tastes sugary and sweet, like cotton candy and Jolly Ranchers and all those other treats the VIPs get in the lounge. When I pull back her eyes stay closed, eyelashes fluttering. "Let's have a second first time, Fireball."

There's a sound—the front door opening—and voices. *Lots* of voices. We both jump back, away from each other, like the guilty parties we are. Olivia storms right past the group as they file into the living room, each face with varying shocked looks as they see me there.

"Crew? What are you doing here?" Tate's tone is confused and there's a tinge of protectiveness in there. Because it's weird I'm at his house when he isn't and I obviously knew he wasn't here.

"I can't find my tax statements from last year and my accountant needs them to get my mortgage pre-approved," I tell him. "He's on my ass like you would not believe and I keep forgetting to ask you if they're here."

"You could have asked me at the rink dude." He states the very, very obvious.

Tenley is watching Olivia basically run upstairs and when she turns to me her expression is filled with curiosity. I don't know her all that well but I know enough about her to know that a curious Tenley Garrison is a lethal Tenley Garrison. I purposely ignore her.

Shelby flashes me a stunning, flirty smile and then calls after her cousin. "Liv! Where the hell are you going?"

"Dyllie was fussing on the monitor, just checking on him," Liv calls back.

Mallory immediately follows her up the stairs, obviously worried about Dylan. I turn back to Tate. "I didn't think of it until I was in the car. See? I'm really bad at this, which is why I drove right here. If I waited, I would forget again."

Tate nods but the casual look on his face is slightly less casual than I would like. His light eyes are hyper-focused on me like he's not totally buying what I'm selling. I swallow. "I figured you would be going out so I thought I would just swing by here and look myself. I heard Olivia was here with the kiddo so... I think they might be in the office. They may have fallen behind the filing cabinet I left for you guys.

Tate groans. "We were going to go out but you disappeared

and your brother was in a mood so we opted to come home and order in. I would have gone out if I knew you'd want me to move furniture."

"I can do it," I pause. "I mean I did do it, and they weren't there. Anyway, I should get home."

"Nash's mood, you should know, was caused by you rushing out of there without doing press and without saying a word," Tate informs me as I move through the cavernous living room and dining room to the hallway with the front door. "Coach was even kinda shocked you took off but then he heard something about your wrist bothering you."

"Yeah, I wanted to get home and ice it and do some of the exercises the trainer gave me at the end of last year," I lie again. Gee, I am so good at this. Kind of impressing myself and embarrassing myself at the same time. "Anyway, I should go do that. Nice meeting all your relatives and I'll see you at practice tomorrow."

"Yeah. Sure. As long as that wrist is okay," Tate says, genuinely concerned, which makes this worse. I can sleep fine when I lie if it's to protect myself or others. But when people believe it so easily well, that doesn't sit so easy. "Don't overdo it. Tell Coach if you think it's not ready for ice time. Better you sit out some pre-season games now than later when we need you the most."

"I'm sure it's fine." I smile and give him a wave as I make my way to my car, forcing myself not to look back.

I do however look up at the house when I get to the drive and I swear I see Olivia looking down at me from Dylan's bedroom window. But the curtain snaps back into place before I can be sure.

I drive home ignoring another call from Nash and wondering what would have happened if the Garrison clan hadn't interrupted me and Olivia.

Chapter 10

Liv

I'm staring at the number on the Vegas hotel stationary when there's a knock at my bedroom door. I know it's only a matter of moments until Tenley opens the door and I can't even be mad at her. She's going to be carrying my favorite Sprinkles cupcake with a candle in it. She's been waking me up on my birthday like this since we moved to Los Angeles together years ago. I don't hate it.

I tuck Crew's phone number under my pillow and smile as there's one more quick knock and the handle turns as soon as I call. "Come in!"

She starts singing immediately. It's god-awful. Tenley is so many things—smart, sassy, stunning—but she has the voice of a cat caught in a car wash. Hopelessly tone deaf. "Happy birthday dear Livvvveeeeee." She finishes moving the hand she was using to shield the candle on the cupcake from the motion of her walking to my bed. "Happy birthday to youuuuuuu!"

I grin. "Thank you."

"One salted caramel custard cupcake for the bestest cousin in the world." Tenley smiles. "Don't tell the others I said that. Now make a wish! And make it good."

My mind instantly fills with Crew's handsome face propositioning me right before Tate and the others barged in. But I don't wish for a second time with Crew because that's not something that seems unreachable like a wish should be. All I have to do is call the number I have under my pillow.

"Oh Liv, please stop overthinking it." Tenley urges softly.

I smile back guiltily. My eyes drift to my phone charging on the night table. There's a voicemail on there from the police. Officer Morales, who was in charge of my case, left it last night but I haven't checked it yet.

"Seriously Livvy I love you but you're letting wax ruin all that expensive icing," Tenley says and I close my eyes.

I wish that six months from now I'm happier than I've ever been in my life and every worry I have right now is gone.

I blow out the candle. Tenley lets out a cheer and hands me my treat. She crawls up and sits next to me on the bed. "So what's the plan for today?"

"Mom got me a massage at the Beverly Wilshire Spa," I explain. "So I have class and then I was going to go there and get that. I think I'll even splurge on a facial. And then I'm meeting you guys at Marmont for dinner."

"It's going to be so great." Tenley sighs with a broad grin. "I freaking love that place. So old-timey Hollywood and yet infested with young Hollywood at the same time."

"Yeah last time I was there I saw Robert Pattinson at the bar," I remind her and she gives me the same jealous glare she's been tossing my way since I first told her this story months ago.

"I still do not forgive you for not slipping him my number," Tenley replies with a pout. "Now he's in a happy relationship with a baby and shit."

"Sorry I failed you," I snark and she flips me the bird.

"That could have been me."

"Do you want that?" I ask because it's never come up

between us, oddly. Tenley is all about dating. She's always got some guy falling all over himself to be close to her, but she's never settled down. She never talks about finding the one, like I hope to do one day.

"Hell yeah. I want what my parents have. True love and babies," she announces. "After I win an Emmy and an Oscar for Best Documentary."

"Weren't you meeting with some Amazon Prime guy soon?"

She nods. "Amazon Prime's assistant to the assistant of programming. Yeah. I honestly think he just wants to get in my pants, but I hope he'll be willing to actually listen."

"He will," I say, but it's more of a prayer than a confirmation. I know all about the casting couch and how it likely seeps into things like putting out documentaries too. "But your idea is solid and compelling and different. No one has covered the darker side of sports before. Not with the perspective you have."

Tenley nods. "Right? I agree. I hope he does."

"When do you meet him?"

"Next week," she says, and I hug her.

"You've got this!" She laughs and hugs me back tightly. Tenley gives the best hugs.

"It's your birthday. Don't worry about me." I feel her phone buzz in the kangaroo pocket of her hoodie, which is against my belly. She lets go of me and pulls it out and I almost gasp at the name on the screen.

"Nash-hole?" I say the name out loud. "Is that Nash Westwood? Calling you? *Why?*"

"Because he is a Nash-hole and doesn't care or realize that I hate him," she mutters and then sighs. "Probably Quake charity stuff or something. I should take this. Have a great day and see you later."

She hops off my bed and heads out of my room, closing the door behind her. I bite into my cupcake holding it with one hand while I dig under my pillow for that hotel stationery. I stare at Crew's number.

I made the wrong wish.

I should have wished for the courage to call him.

* * *

* * *

"How are you feeling Ms. Garrison?" the masseuse asks as she greets me outside the room with a cup of water infused with orange blossom.

I smile but I know it looks loopy. I always feel half drunk when I come out of a spectacular massage and that's what this is. "Wonderful. Thank you."

I sip the water, which is delicious. I'm not going to lie, I feel blessed. This whole day is extravagant and I get to experience it makes me beyond lucky. "I'll lead you to the facial room and settle you in there."

I follow her down the lush, dimly lit hallway to another private room. She helps me into this crazy state-of-the-art chair that hugs my body like a glove and covers me with a warm blanket before tipping me back so I'm almost lying flat. "Esmeralda will be with you in a moment."

She leaves me alone in the room. I pull my phone out of the pocket of my complimentary robe and scroll through the fourteen messages in our family group chat.

Mom: Happy birthday gorgeous girl. I love you. Enjoy the massage!

Dad: We'll call you later. Have a great day. I love you!

Auntie R: Happy birthday Livvy!

Uncle J: Ditto from Jessie and me kiddo! Enjoy!

Grady: Have an awesome day Liv!

Tate: Happy birthday Livanator! See you tonight for your party!

Shelby: There's a party? Livvy I would have flown out for a party!

Tenley: Not a real party. Just dinner at Marmont.

Theo: You bougie Hollywood brats. Anyway, have a great day Liv!

Tate: Not our fault you didn't get drafted by the best team in the league in a cool city. Enjoying Siberia?

Uncle Luc: Happy Liv Day sweetheart. And Tate, it's Canada, not Siberia.

Tate: Same difference. Is it snowing yet?

Theo: F.U.

Harlow: HAPPY BIRTHDAY LIVVY. Ignore them.

Another four messages, well wishes from Uncle Cole, Auntie Leah, Conner, and Mae all flood in as I'm reading but I can't respond because my phone rings and it makes my stomach drop. It's Detective Morales. I never listened to his message or called him back.

"Hello," I say and before he can respond I add, "It's my birthday and I really do not want to deal with this today."

"I'm sorry Olivia," he says sympathetically. "I didn't know. Happy birthday."

"Thanks."

"Unfortunately though, I have a job to do and part of that is informing you of the trial date," he explains. "We got one. End of next month. On the twenty-ninth."

"Okay. Thanks." I swallow but my mouth is dry. I try to get out of the chair so I can get the water my masseuse placed on the side table next to an aroma therapy candle. I can't get out without tipping over so I just lie back and sigh. "Do I have to be there?"

"Yes. You have to testify. It's very important. Mr. And Mrs. Jackson will also be doing so," he explains. They are the couple that saved me.

"Okay." I don't want to. I don't want to look at him. I don't want to relive it. I just want to forget it. But I also don't want him to go free and do this again. Whatever this was. I'm still not sure. "Did he... has he ever said what the hell he was thinking?"

"He isn't saying anything. He pleaded innocent."

"That's bullshit. Excuse me."

"No excusing needed. It is bullshit," he replies candidly. "He has no case. He's just prolonging the inevitable. He's going to blame drugs or something, like it wasn't his fault. He's an addict. But don't worry, no one walks with that. But we definitely need to hear your side."

"Okay." What else can I say? He gives me the details of the time I need to be at the Santa Monica courthouse. I thank him and hang up. I'm adding the details to my calendar when Esmeralda walks in with a friendly smile.

I lie back and try not to let this ruin the rest of my day. But it kind of does. By the time I'm walking up the stairs to my apartment, I'm despondent. How am I going to get up there and face this guy? What if his lawyer rips me apart like they do on those legal shows on TV? Makes it my fault? Because I wasn't paying enough attention. I was walking alone. I was...

My mother would kick my ass if she heard me blaming myself. Maybe it's time I called her. Maybe I need her advice. Maybe I can't get through this on my own.

I stop dead at the end of the hall. There's the biggest bouquet of flowers I have ever seen in front of my door. My eyes dart everywhere, over the railing and down at the courtyard. No one is around. Not another tenant. Not the landlord. Not a delivery person. I walk slowly to the door, my eyes taking in the colorful roses. They're so freaking many of them and they're in so many colors. I keep staring at them, amazed, and then sniff. Even from a standing position, with the massive vase at my feet, I can smell their rich, luxurious scent.

They're fluffy roses. I don't know how else to explain them. The petals are all wide and delicate and... velvety looking. There are... twelve white ones, twelve pink ones, twelve yellow ones, twelve red ones. I crouch down and pluck the card from the center.

These have got to be for Tenley. Maybe it's the Amazon guy? I mean with Tenley it could be anyone. But as I turn it over, the name on the front of the card is mine. Mine. "Oh my God," I whisper. I mean, was there an error? Sure someone in my family might send me flowers but not this many!

I tear open the envelope and read the card, expecting it to be Harlow or Shelby or even Mallory's name signed at the bottom. But there isn't a name. Just an initial. C.

And the note... oh the note...

Olivia,

Happy birthday. Go easy on the Fireball tonight. Or don't and give me a call.

Whatever you do, enjoy it.

All my best, C

I realize I'm grinning when my cheeks start to ache. He did not. Except... he did. I unlock the front door and carefully lift the vase. Damn, forty-eight roses are heavy!

I carry them directly into my room, kicking the door closed behind me, and plunk them down on my dresser. They are magnificent. And they're for me. Oh my God. Well, now I have to call him. It would be rude not to.

I sit down on the edge of the bed, open the nightside table, and glance at the hotel stationary with his number scrawled on it. I carefully punch it into my phone. I'm jumpy and nervous and there's a flock of butterflies bouncing around my insides.

"Hello?"

"Thank you for the flowers. You shouldn't have."

"Of course, I should have. It's not every day your one-night stand turns twenty-three," He replies and I can hear the cheeky smile in his voice. "Happy birthday Fireball."

"Thank you. They honestly made my day."

"I thought the massage at a five-star hotel spa would have done that," Crew replies. "This was just icing on the cake sorta speak."

"How did you know I was getting a massage?"

"Your cousin has loose lips," he says and I remember he and Tate just got back from a pre-season road trip this morning. "I never used to listen when he babbled about one of the hundred Garrisons, but now I do. It's much more interesting when you've seen one of them naked."

"You see Tate naked every day."

"True. I'll rephrase. It's much more interesting when you've seen one you're attracted to naked," Crew replies.

I grin. My eyes go to the flowers again. My whole room already smells like heaven. "So what are you doing?"

"At home. Fully clothed and alone," he says and my smile deepens even though it shouldn't. I shouldn't care if he's clothed or alone. "Trying to psych myself up to meet Leigh later."

"Who is Leigh?" And why do I hate her?

"My real estate agent," Crew explains. "Tate bought my old place but I'm not buying his and since Nash and I signed contract extensions this summer, and we're here for another three years, I should find somewhere to live."

"Where are you looking?"

"Manhattan Beach, Santa Monica, Venice." His voice is lifeless.

"You sound like you're listing contagious skin conditions," I remark. "No one should sound like that when talking about their future home location."

He laughs. God, that sound makes me wet even through a phone. I need to get a grip. The point of a one-night stand is that it's once. "I'm honestly not feeling anything she's shown me so far. I just... I mean every player lives by the beach because it's close to the arena and airport. But I just... I don't know, maybe I'll find the right place tonight."

"Well, good luck."

"Thanks." He pauses. "I've only got viewings until nine. And then I can always wander over to West Hollywood and grab a drink. You know a good place to do that? Maybe a hotel in the hills."

"Tate, Mallory, and Tenley are going to be at Chateau Marmont with me," I tell him and hide the sadness in my voice. I can't be sad! He's a one-night stand. One night stand means it happens once.

"Yeah but Tate is going home early because we have practice tomorrow, and Tenley won't catch on if we accidentally run into each other," Crew says, and I feel another flutter in my gut.

"Look, I know I'm not the expert on this subject but doesn't one and done mean once and never again?" I say even though I want to just say see ya there. "Also really hoping that you found some covert way to get my address and didn't point-blank ask Tate for it."

"You're lucky I like being your dirty little secret, Olivia," Crew rasps. "Tenley is his emergency contact on our team list and it includes her address, which is your address."

"Smart boy."

"Not just a dumb jock," he counters proudly. "Also, I told

you we weren't on the same page for our one-night stand so I should get a do-over."

"I enjoyed myself. You enjoyed yourself. Let's not ruin the memory." Why am I trying so hard to turn him down? I mean, it wouldn't be the worst thing in the world to do it again with a hot, unattached, incredibly charming guy who just bought me more roses than I will likely get ever again in my entire life.

"Liv! I'm home! Let's get this party started!"

"Shit. Ten is here. I have to go."

"It's all good. I have your number now."

That sounds ominous but in a very nice way. Oh god.

"Bye Mabel!" I say loudly as Tenley walks into my room.

"Mabel? That annoying girl from your child psychology class?" Her eyes snap up to the massive bouquet. "Holy shit! Who gave you those?"

She marches right over to the roses but luckily the card is tucked safely into the back pocket of my jeans. "A gift from the school I'm interning at. They send something for everyone's birthdays I guess."

"Shit. I can't wait to see what they do for Christmas!" She inhales. "These are Juliet garden roses. They're not cheap. This bouquet probably cost about three hundred bucks."

"Shut up."

"Dead serious."

"How do you know what kind of roses these are?" I can't help but ask.

She shrugs her slim shoulders. "I did a research project on this horticulturalist in New Zealand that tried to murder her in-laws with poisoned flowers and I learned more than anyone needs to about the different types of roses."

Tenley's second major was Criminology and she's a true crime addict. I'm lucky she takes everything I say without question because when she gets a whiff of a lie that degree kicks in and she becomes a relentless investigator. She figured out why Harlow ended her engagement while years later the rest of us still have no clue. And Tenley won't tell.

"We should get ready," I say, trying to change the subject. "Do you have any idea what I can wear that won't make me look like a librarian?"

"Absolutely nothing in your closet," Tenley replies swiftly and I frown. She laughs and grabs my hand. "But I can lend you something birthday girl. Let's go."

Chapter 11

Crew

This is an eight hundred and fifty-seven dollar gamble. Between this and the roses, I have spent more money on Olivia than I have on any bed buddy in the history of bed buddies. And she's technically not even that. I'm not complaining. I wanted her to have the flowers. I knew as soon as I walked into the florist that she would love them. And my mom once told me each rose color had a meaning. Yellow was friendship, white was innocence, pink was admiration, and red was passion. I feel like whatever this is between Olivia and me, it covers all those things so she got them all.

This though... booking a room at Chateau Marmont in hopes she texts or calls me tonight... it's a gamble. Chances are I will be spending the night in here alone. Not the end of the world. The guy at the front desk is a hockey fan and he upgraded me so I have a suite. It overlooks the patio dining. I stretch out on the sofa in the oversized living room and swirl the light beer I pulled out of the minibar. The three large windows are open so there's a constant din of table chatter filtering through the gauzy curtains and the hum of traffic from Sunset Boulevard just beyond that.

Olivia is probably out there, just below my windows, enjoying her birthday dinner. I haven't looked. It feels a little stalkerish. If she doesn't text me by eleven, I'll just turn on the TV, down another beer, and go to sleep. No harm no foul. But it will suck. I really want another shot with her.

It's mostly my ego talking, knowing that the sex didn't actually make her orgasm. I feel like I failed her and I don't like it. But it's also because, if I'm honest with myself, I really enjoyed that night in Vegas. Olivia is charming and entertaining and she catches me off-guard a lot, something that hasn't happened with a woman, or a man for that matter, in a very long time. I'm not looking for a relationship, but I could use another dose of that kind of night before I go back to my solo ways.

I tap my phone so I can see the time. Ten twenty-nine. I get up and pace the long room. My phone buzzes and I almost pounce on the coffee table like a skittish cat. But it's not Olivia.

NASH: You wanna grab breakfast with me tomorrow? Erewhon? 7:30?

I'm mulling over the commute time in my head because he means the Erewhon in Venice. Normally that's a quick seven minutes from my townhouse, but I'm in West Hollywood and the commute will be way longer.

NASH: Sorry. I just need to bounce something off you. It's important.

Nash thinks everything is important. It's probably whether he should paint his bedroom royal blue or navy blue or some such shit. He's been renovating his house since he bought it two years ago. He's slow and meticulous about everything. Still, I haven't been spending much time with him at all lately.

CREW: Yeah. Sure. I can meet up but I have a doctor's appt in the valley.

A lie, but it's harmless.

CREW: Can we do Erewhon at the Grove? 8:30?

It means he has to drive farther since his house is in Venice, but The Grove location is only about nine minutes from this hotel. His response is a thumbs up.

I'm about to set my alarm so that I get up in time to make this breakfast rendezvous when a new text pops up on my screen. This one is from Olivia.

OLIVIA: I really loved the flowers. Thank you, again.

"Fuck yes!" I grin and start pacing the room again.

CREW: You're welcome. It was my pleasure. But if you want it to be *your* pleasure, you should thank me in person.

I stop pacing and wait impatiently for her response.

OLIVIA: I'm tipsy and can't get to Venice to thank you.

CREW: Can you get to Room 314?

As I wait for her response there's a queasy feeling in my stomach. I hope it isn't that poke bowl I grabbed on my way here. I was fine, like five seconds ago. Before she texted me.

OLIVIA: Room 314 in THIS HOTEL?

CREW: Yes.

OLIVIA: Shut up.

CREW: I will if you come and make me. **314.**

Why is this so much fun? But also, why am I holding my breath? I am literally like a kid at Christmas waiting for Santa Claus. "You're an idiot, Crew," I lecture myself as I wait for her response.

It's been almost ten minutes when I start to compose a message to her. I can't decide between 'no pressure, honestly. I know you're with your friends.' And 'please let me show you what my peen can do!'

Then there's a gentle knock at the door. I cross the room so fast I almost give myself whiplash. I fling open the door. Olivia looks incredible. Her hair is loose in waves that skim her shoulders, which are bare because she's in a skimpy red cocktail dress that clings to her body like a second skin and matches the color painted on her perky, pouty mouth.

Her big brown eyes are even bigger and filled with disbelief. "I can't believe you got a room here!"

"A suite, technically," I say and step out of the way, motioning with my hand so she can see the huge living room.

"Holy crap!" She steps over the threshold and I close the door behind her. The dress looks even better from the back. Olivia has a killer ass. Round and plump and I flex my fingers as I remember the feel of it in my hands. "This is bigger than my living room!"

"It's not bad," I add.

She shoots me a look over her shoulder. It's glassy and mischievous and I know she's tipsy. She walks over to one of the windows, pushing aside the soft curtain that is blowing in the breeze, and sticking her head out the window. "I was down there tonight!"

"I figured," I reply, walking up behind her and peeking out the window. I rest a hand on the base of her back. She glances over at me. "How did you get away from your group?"

"Ten and Mallory wanted to continue drinking in the lounge downstairs after dinner. Tate said he had to get back and get some rest because of pre-season training like you said he would," she explains, stepping back and looking around the room again. "I told the girls I was going to hitch a lift with Tate. It's not unheard of. I'm not a big drinker and I already had two. No, three. So I walked out with Tate but then as we waited for the valet I told him the texts I was getting from you were classmates and they were across the street at The Den and were begging me to meet them."

"Sneaky girl."

"He got in his car I ran across the street and as soon as he drove away I ran back and... voila!" Olivia makes a flourish with her hands.

I step into her, my arm looping around her waist. She giggles almost silently and drops her purse on the floor before slipping her arms around my neck. I lean in and inhale deeply. She smells like flowers and vanilla. "Happy birthday, Fireball."

"It's my birthday but you're the one getting your wish," she whispers, and then her lips skim my neck just below my Adam's apple. My dick is startled awake by the contact.

"I promise you, honey, my wish is a gift to you," I tell her and then I bring my mouth to hers.

Olivia is shy and demure on the outside but her kisses... they tell a different story. Her kisses are passionate and needy in a way that makes me feel like a fucking king. Like I'm the air she needs to breathe. I tangle a hand in her hair, and as my tongue dances with hers, our bodies sway a little. It's like we're moving to the music of our kiss. I like it.

But then she wobbles ever so slightly. She's in sky-high heels and between the thick throw rug on the old wood floor and the three drinks she mentioned earlier—and probably this kiss— she's not steady. I move my hands lower, cup that perfect ass of hers, and lift her up. She squeals and laughs, tightening her grip around my neck. "I appreciate the extra level of hot those high heels bring to your already smokin' look, but a twisted ankle is not part of the plan for tonight."

I start walking as she hooks her ankles behind my waist to stay in place. "Where are we going?"

"The bedroom," I tell her as I exit the living room and march down the long hall to the left of the front door.

Olivia turns her head and lists the rooms we pass. "Kitchen. A full kitchen! Bedroom. Oh and a bathroom! Wait. Stop!"

I stop in front of the open bathroom door. "Is that a tub? A copper tub?"

"Yes ma'am."

"OMG. I want one of those in my big girl house one day!"

"Big girl house?"

She grins sheepishly and her cheeks grow pink. "Yeah. When I'm an adult."

"You're twenty-three."

"I know but I still feel seventeen sometimes," she confesses. "Anyway, when I'm working full-time and settled, and I buy my first place. I don't care if it's just a teeny one-bedroom apartment, I am getting a tub like that."

She tips her head and I glance over at the copper tub, which looks more like an enormous bucket to me. Girls and their bathtubs. I honestly don't get it but okay. "It's good to have dreams."

"What's one of yours?" she asks as I continue walking toward the primary bedroom.

"To make you come around my cock."

She bursts into a flutter of nervous giggles so adorable that I can't help but chuckle too, even though I'm dead serious. I cross into the bedroom and walk toward the California King. I move to the bottom of the bed and then climb onto it on my knees, lowering her to the center.

I get off the bed and stare at her. "Jesus Christ you are a work of art tonight Olivia."

Her smile gets deep and soft and she flutters those perfect dark eyelashes. "Thank you."

I take her left ankle in my hand and patiently undo the forty-seven straps on her six-inch heels. Okay, maybe not forty-seven but my dick isn't one for counting and it's annoyed by this wait. The shoe drops to the floor and I press my thumbs into the arch of her foot, where my massage therapist does. She sighs and arches her back. "Oh God, that's heaven."

I smile and rub it a little bit longer before moving to release her right foot from the killer shoes. Then I rub that foot for a long minute. Long enough that she's purring. I smile at her and... what the...

"Olivia..." Her left leg is now flat on the mattress, ankle hanging off the bottom, while I've got her right leg up at my hip level, which has her dress riding up a little and open and... "You're not wearing any underwear."

Her eyes fly open, dart to my face, down her body, and back to my face. She turns fire engine red and rocks up, trying to push the dress down to cover herself but I reach out and grab her wrist. "Don't. Let me look."

"Oh my God, I'm so embarrassed." She groans.

Her perfect, sweet, intimate self is pink and glistening and beautiful. "Baby, I've had my face there. This isn't embarrassing. It's hot as hell. Look at what you're doing to the front of my pants."

She glances at the outline of my cock which is currently squeezed uncomfortably against the zipper of my jeans. I let go of her wrist and she doesn't reach for her dress again, but she's still blushing. "I want to lick you there so badly. You look so wet and ready for my tongue."

"I am. I've been wet since you said you were here," she confesses in a dark whisper and then she lets out a rushed breath and closes her eyes. "Hell, I've been wet since I found the flowers on my doorstep."

"Note to self, send Olivia flowers again."

She giggles. I keep staring at her bare, beautiful pussy. "Crew. Are you going to fuck me again?"

"No," I tell her, and her face drops, her brown eyes clouded with confusion. I let go of her foot, after kissing the inside of her ankle, and reach for my belt. "I'm going to make love to you. The way I would have the first night if I knew it was a first."

She shudders visibly and bites that plump bottom lip. "Oh."

"You good with that plan birthday girl?"

She nods.

"Lift your dress higher." She reaches down and pulls just a little, maybe two inches. The hem is a little higher than mid-thigh now. "Higher."

She pulls it up again. The edges of her lips and the light dusting of hair above them are still covered, but just barely. *"Higher."*

My voice is firm, hard even. No, it's thick. With lust. I unzip my fly as she takes a breath, holds it, and lifts the dress all the way up so it's bunched at her hips. Thank God my pants drop to the floor and I can shove down my boxer briefs and let my cock get the room it desperately needs as it's swollen to capacity. "Why the hell were you not wearing any underwear?"

"The dress shows panty lines," she tells me, "even with a thong, and I didn't want anyone to see my underwear lines."

"So you risk them seeing that incredible pussy of yours instead?" I cock an eyebrow and she blushes harder. "The one only I've been inside?"

"Yeah well I was careful," she says. "I don't want anyone to see it but you."

That sounds way better than it should to my ears—and my ego. I stroke my cock. "Can I touch it?"

"You can touch any part of me you want, Crew."

I get onto the bed, lowering myself over her. I kiss her deeply, wildly, with all the unhinged feelings I have swirling around inside me for this woman. It's not at all normal for me to be this feral. I like sex. I'm good at it. I have had other partners that get me rock hard like I am right now, but not that make me feel so out of control. Not since... well it's been a very long while. And while I haven't been looking for this feeling—in fact,

I may have been actively avoiding it—I'm enjoying the hell out of it right now.

I'm hovering above her and she is biting that bottom lip of hers again. I lean in, and kiss her, forcing her to let the lip go. She threads her hands through my hair and parts her legs so I can settle between them.

We kiss and touch and kiss more. It's nice. It's hot, even, but it's not what I want. Not why I asked her here. I need to fuck her again, nice and slow with attention to detail this time. I'm absurdly nervous, unlike the last time, but I don't want her to know it. Olivia seems more relaxed than before, and definitely more exploratory. Her hands are everywhere, touching, gripping, squeezing.

As I sit on the side of the bed and dig the condom out of my discarded pants her hand wanders up my thigh and over my shaft. Her touch is gentle and warm and when she slowly wraps each finger around my length, I fight a shudder. I do not want to look weak but God, one touch, and I have to think about hockey drills to keep from pumping into her fist and finishing this before we've even started.

I try to bite back a groan and fail. I hold up the condom. "I've got work to do, baby. I need you to stop."

She leans forward and plucks the condom from my hand. "Allow me."

I smile. "Only if you do it naked."

Her eyes get big, her pupils widening. It's cute because I've just spent the last ten minutes staring at her most intimate part, but she's nervous about showing me her tits. After blinking for a quick second, Olivia sits up and pulls her dress up and over her head. I reward her by licking each nipple like they are the best damn ice cream cones on planet Earth. She immediately starts panting and mewing and my cock is throbbing now.

"I think I've found a sweet spot?" I ask and she nods and

pushes her shoulders back, bringing her round, small but perfect tits closer to my lips. I kiss and lick and suck her nipples before gliding my thumbs over them. My hands are a little rough from the hockey gloves and I've learned that women—and men—love the rough slide of them against their soft spots. Olivia certainly seems to agree.

"Oh my God, Crew... I could come from this alone," she confesses and I make a mental note to never forget that. I mean, I don't know why. This is supposed to be a one-and-done. Well, once again and then done, so I'll never need this info but yet... well, I mean right now, in the heat of it, I would sign up for another night. Or three. I mean I wouldn't be the first professional hockey player with a bed buddy, right?

One of her hands goes to my hair and she tugs me off her breasts. She holds up the condom with the other hand right between my mouth and those perfect tits. "I want to come a different way. You promised."

"I did." I smile. "And I never break a promise."

Except for my wedding vows, my conscience—ever the buzz-kill—reminds me. I push the thought out of my head and watch her carefully tear the foil package and pull out the condom. She gives me a silly smile. "I've only ever done this on a banana in health class. And the banana wasn't as thick."

I swallow down a laugh as she concentrates like this is rocket science. I don't want to make her feel self-conscious but this is so damn adorable. She does a good job getting it down my shaft and the sensation of someone else doing it, of *Olivia* doing it, steals my amusement and replaces it with desire. God, I am going to give this woman the fuck of her life. I want her to remember tonight until her dying breath.

I kiss her, holding her cheek and pushing her back into the mattress with my body. She's so wet it doesn't take much work to slide into her. She's still so ridiculously tight I'm thinking of hockey drills again to keep from letting my need to pound her into the mattress and find my own release take over. I start to roll my hips, with intention, like I'm being graded on technique. I want her to feel every sensation, every inch. I keep my pelvis low and flat against hers so that my skin is rubbing and sliding against hers, her knees fall open, and she bucks into me, and I know I'm rubbing her clit with my pelvic bone, which was intended.

I grab a pillow from beside us and shove it roughly under her hips. "Trust me," I whisper into another kiss and then I roll my hips again and she gasps and arches her neck so I move my lips there. It allows her to whisper obscenities and my name which is hot as fuck.

"Crew. Oh God. Crew. Yeah... I... God... that feels good. God."

I know it's hard for a lot of women to come this way. I am doing my absolute best to make her one of the few who can. However, I am not averse to switching positions if I have to. For her, not me. I could come right this second if I let myself. But I don't, and I also don't have to change positions. I can feel her getting slicker, loser, as her hips move in their own rhythm chasing what I want to give her so badly. "Olivia, you're fucking perfect. This is fucking perfect."

She makes a strangled sound in response. Her cheeks are flushed but it's not by her chronic shyness anymore. It's pleasure making her pink now. I start moving a little faster, harder, but I still make sure each thrust ends with contact with that bundle of nerves between her legs. I lift one arm and hook it behind her knee before moving my lips back to hers. Her lips are on my neck and damn, the way she's worshipping me makes my balls tighten dangerously.

I'm worried that this has become a battle I can't win. I might come before her, but then, her eyes snap shut, and her mouth falls open, and she chokes on my name as it bubbles up from her heaving chest. The way her body clenches involuntarily around my cock is magic I swear I have never experienced before. I guess this night is offering up firsts for both of us.

I only survive three seconds of watching her ride out her first orgasm by penetration when I succumb blissfully to my own. My hips roll relentlessly as I milk this out in a blind fury of lust. I forget to be careful. I forget to be gentle. I just fuck her like my life depends on it.

When I'm spent I drop down on her, gasping and sweaty. "Are you okay?"

"Are you kidding?" She pants back. "I'm perfect."

"That you are, Fireball."

Chapter 12

Liv

My eyes flutter open and for a hot second, I have no idea where the hell I am. No clue what day it is let alone what time or what country I'm in. I do know I've been sleeping like I was in a coma. I rub my eyes and turn over and that's when I feel the sensation between my legs—a small, satisfying ache—and the memories of what is now the best birthday ever come wafting back. I smile and reach for Crew. But I find nothing but cool empty sheets.

I sit up. He isn't in the bedroom at all. The door is closed. The room is dark and quiet, the curtains billowing thanks to the open window. The patio below is quiet, meaning the restaurant has closed. It's late. I'm alone. He did not just leave me here, did he? I feel a pinch of rejection squeeze my heart.

It's not rejection, Liv, I scold myself. He owes you nothing. He's not your boyfriend. He's a one-night stand... two-night stand. He did what he came for. Served his purpose. Don't make this something it's not.

But then I hear a noise. Water running. I climb out of bed. I'm still naked and the last thing I want to do is put on that tight dress. So I grab the short-sleeved waffle shirt Crew had on when

I got here. I slip it over my head. The hem hits me mid-thigh and it's loose and smells like him, all musky and sweet.

I open the door and step into the hall. There's light coming from the bathroom. I walk over there and am greeted by Crew's naked back. That butt is even more impressive bare and illuminated. Round and firm and I just want to bite it. Is that weird? It must be.

"Hey," he says and smiles, turning to face me not at all concerned about his nudity. God, I am such a prude. I could never walk around naked in front of someone like that. Although, my eyes slide down his body. I know everyone says women are the pretty ones naked, but Crew Westwood is the exception to that rule. "I thought we shouldn't leave without enjoying the tub you almost had an orgasm over."

I laugh and he moves to the side and throws out his arm in a flourish. The tub is almost filled with water warm enough to be letting off steam. Flowers are floating in it. Daisies and what might be lavender twigs?

"I doubt there's a flower shop open at four in the morning, and I didn't want to risk you waking up and thinking I'd left you here," he says and shrugs. "So I desecrated one of the bouquets in the living room."

I laugh. "They might charge you for that."

He shrugs again. "I don't know if you realize this, but hockey players make stupid amounts of money."

I feign a look of shock and he winks. I walk farther into the bathroom, the tiny black and white tiles cool under my bare feet. I lean forward and let my fingers skim the water. Crew stands behind me and his hands wrap around my waist lazily. "You have a habit of stealing my clothes. Word of warning, you can't bring this one home. I can't be seen walking out of here in your little red dress. This isn't Vegas. People will talk."

I laugh and turn so we're facing each other. "That reminds me, I owe you that shirt back."

"And I owe you a hoodie."

My eyebrows shoot up. "You have my hoodie? I thought I had left it in the hotel suite. I actually called them asking if they had it."

"I needed to wear something," Crew explains. Then his fingers move to the hem of this shirt and he lifts it over my head. I fight a blush as my naked body is revealed to him. "In the tub, Fireball. And leave space for me."

"What?" I look at the tub. "It's not big enough."

"It may take some creative positioning, but we can make it work." Crew sounds way more confident than I feel as I step into the tub.

I slip down into the water quickly so I can hide myself. Crew notices, I can tell by the slightly bemused look on his face. He walks to the other end of the tub and hauls one of the tree trunks he calls legs over the side. The water inches higher. I tuck my legs up, hugging them to my chest. By the time Crew has lowered himself into the tub completely some of the water has sloshed over the edge.

His legs slide down each side and he leans forward and kisses my hands on my knees, which are poking out of the water. "Put your legs down the middle. Just watch the family jewels."

I giggle and do as I'm told. He takes my ankles and props each of them up on his hips and then we both lean back on our respective ends of the tub. Our eyes lock and he smiles. "First bath with someone?"

"Yeah."

"I like being your first, Olivia."

"I have to say you're pretty good at it." I grin. "I'm not regretting my pick."

His fingers dance over my ankle bone, deliciously tickling

me. "Can I ask why you picked me? I mean other than the obvious that I'm a sex god and all."

I laugh, and he pretends to look offended. "I think it was just dumb luck. I mean I was hellbent on losing my virginity on the trip. It's the only reason I went."

"Why? I don't judge you for holding onto it or letting it go, but I have to wonder why you didn't have sex for so long and then suddenly wanted to give it up to anyone," Crew says. He looks curious and also slightly worried, like he doesn't want to offend me.

I shrug. I wish I could tell him the entire truth but I don't want to ruin last night and I think if I tell him about the attack, he'll get all sad or angry or sympathetic and it will ruin everything. So I skirt around the catalyst.

"I wasn't holding onto it for religious reasons or even moral ones." My fingers glide through the water and I pick up a daisy head and pluck off one of the petals. "My mother is a very sexually liberated woman. She has never made the issue taboo. She gave Conner condoms in his Christmas stocking when he was fourteen and offered birth control to both my sister Mae and me at the same age."

I pluck another petal and watch it drop into the water. "Is this a case of being contrary for the sake of being contrary? Like when I announced I was quitting hockey to become a lifeguard when I was sixteen?" I look into his hazel eyes, which have an amused shimmer, so I don't know if he's joking or telling the truth. He nods. "No lie, I quit hockey, took the lifeguard test, and got a job at our local beach in Nova Scotia."

"You were going to give it all up, your family's legacy, and ignore your talent and become... a lifeguard?" I am trying so hard not to laugh that tears blur my vision.

He laughs for me. "I may have gotten the idea after watching Zac Efron in the *Baywatch* movie."

Now there's no holding back my laughter. "Oh my God, that movie was so cheesy!"

"It was, but Efron was hot and made the job look sexy," Crew explains. I like the way he can admit another guy is hot. Some guys are too full of homophobia to do that. "Also my dad spent our whole lives telling Nash and me we didn't have to play hockey. That he wouldn't be disappointed and I guess I just wanted to test that."

"And..."

"My dad didn't complain or say a word," Crew replies with a whimsical smile that says he's thinking back fondly on the memory. "He would even come to the beach to watch me work. My brother on the other hand was furious and didn't talk to me the entire summer, but joke's on Nash, that just made me happier that I did it."

"So what happened? Why are you now a Stanley Cup-winning hockey player and not a beach god?"

"I missed it. It felt like I was missing a limb all summer long," Crew confesses. "And I was the worst at remembering sunblock, I spent the entire summer various shades of pink with screaming sore skin."

I laugh, plucking the last of the petals and flicking it off my finger into the water. He nudges the outside of my hip with one of his feet. "Sorry to interrupt, let's get back to you and your hymen."

I laugh. "I broke that years ago with a vibrator. On purpose. I didn't want to ruin my first time with a guy with pain and blood."

He looks shocked. "Wow."

"But to answer your other questions, no I wasn't just trying to be the opposite of my mom, or contrary, or whatever. I was... I *am* a romantic. I wanted some big, epic romance with someone I was madly in love with," I explain and feel so silly opening up like this, naked in a bathtub with a one-night stand. "I wanted it to be with someone I trusted and loved and thought of as my best friend but also couldn't keep my hands off of."

"And you never found that?" He sounds shocked.

"No. I didn't." I sigh and focus on a sprig of lavender as it floats towards Crew's chest. "I guess maybe I had all of that, to varying degrees, with my last boyfriend but I just didn't want to pull the trigger. Because at this point, it had become a thing. Like this entity unto itself. A member of the family. There was Liv and Liv's Virginity. Everyone knew about it and made a big deal about it so I felt like everyone would know about losing it and make a big deal about that. And I liked my last boyfriend. I even kind of loved him but I didn't feel like he was worthy of being the big deal."

He's watching me serenely, but I so badly want to know what he's thinking. I feel ridiculously self-conscious having divulged that. I've never explained myself to anyone. Not even Tenley or Harlow or my sister who, unlike me, is not a virgin. Oh wait... I'm not either. "Anyway, I realized right before the Vegas thing, that holding onto it made it an even bigger thing and that a one-night stand was the perfect way to just be done with it. That way it was all on my terms, and no one would have to know. The guy wouldn't stick around and so if it went badly or whatever, I would never have to see him again."

"And yet here we are," Crew says with a wink.

"Well, it didn't go badly."

"I'd say it went great." Crew ventures his hands up my calves. "I delivered on my promise in there."

He tips his head back toward the bedroom. I bite my lip and stifle a nervous giggle. "You did. Thank you."

"It was truly my pleasure, Fireball." He grips my calves and starts pulling me toward him. He leans in and our lips meet. The kiss is lazy but turns up the temperature in this bathtub.

"Have you ever had sex in a bathtub?" I ask him.

"Yeah. It can be a logistical nightmare. As a lifeguard I don't recommend it," he says and it makes me laugh. His eyes slide left toward the freestanding Italian-style shower against the far wall. "Now shower sex... that is something I would give a five-star rating."

"I've never..." He smiles. I blush. "Wanna be my first at that too?"

"I will never say no to being your first at anything, Olivia." Crew leans in and captures my mouth in a searing kiss. "Lucky for you I brought more than one condom."

And then he stands up and pulls me out of the tub and into the shower.

Chapter 13

Crew

I wake up to the sound of Olivia hitting the door frame and cursing. I open my eyes and the room is bathed in sunlight. There's a gentle murmur outside the open window like people are on the patio below. Olivia is clinging to the doorframe trying to shove her foot in one of her shoes. She's got that red dress on again and her hair is all over the place. It got soaked in the shower and dried wavy while she slept.

"What time is it?" I ask. "Why are you panicked?"

"Tenley texted me. She knows I didn't come home last night!" she explains, finally getting her foot in her shoe and righting herself. "She's freaking out. She messaged me but my phone was on silent so when I didn't answer she put it in the family chat. My mother has called three times in the last ten minutes and I can't answer. Tate is asking if he should skip practice this afternoon and look for me. I have to be... not here when I answer my mom. She's FaceTiming. She can't see the hotel."

"Oh shit. That's a lot." I scrub my face with my palm trying to wake up. "What time is it?"

"Almost ten."

"Ten?! In the morning?" I jump out of bed and grab my

phone off the nightstand. Yeah. It's nine-fifty-four. I have four missed calls from Nash, who I was supposed to be meeting at eight-thirty. Shit. How did I sleep so late? "Fuck. I had to be somewhere an hour and a half ago"

"We're both fucked." Olivia sighs. "I hope it works out for you."

Her phone starts ringing with the distinctive FaceTime chimes. "Fuck. I gotta get out of here."

"Okay. Good luck!"

She's already rushing down the hall and disappears out the door without another word. Not even a goodbye. I don't know what I was expecting after last night. I don't do a lot of formal goodbyes after hookups, to be honest. I usually just leave a nice note on the night table while they're still asleep. With guys, I'm even less subtle. I just say goodbye and walk out, but that's mostly because a lot of the guys I've slept with are not out of the closet so they know the drill. Olivia is the first hookup that I've had a bath with. The first one where I worried about what to say the next day. Well, thanks to her cousin, I don't get a chance to say anything.

I immediately call Nash but he lets it go to voicemail. That means he's pissed. I get dressed and check out. We have practice at one and knowing Nash, when I stood him up he just went straight to the arena for some extra time on the ice or in the gym. I head straight there.

I see his Mercedes EQS SUV in the player parking. Hard to miss because he's the only player here this early. I park right next to him hop out and head straight for the elevator, digging my pass out of my wallet.

I walk into the team gym but he isn't there so I head down the tunnel to the rink. Nash is super pissed off judging by the way he's hurling pucks at the empty net in front of him. I slow my gait and watch. He doesn't miss a single shot. I think he does for a second but no, that puck just broke through the netting. Shit, well at least he's improving his slapshot.

He catches me out of the corner of his eye as I approach the boards and lean on them. He doesn't skate over though. He just stands there in the middle of the ice glaring. I give him a guilty smile.

"I owe you one of those insanely priced smoothies from Erewhon. I'm sorry." He keeps staring. I keep talking. "I forgot to set an alarm. I didn't do it on purpose."

"I went by your house on my way here. You weren't there."

"I wasn't," I admit. "I slept elsewhere last night."

"So you overslept at your hookup's house?" Nash cocks his head and it says everything he isn't saying. He's judging me. He's also skeptical. "Since when do you even spend the night with randoms?"

"It's not a random," I reply and try not to be mad. He's just hurt I ghosted him. "It's a regular, and like I said, it was an accident. But I'm here now and ready to listen or talk or whatever you need."

"A regular?" He looks more skeptical than before. I try not to take it personally, or feel weird about calling Olivia a regular. We've had more than once, which is regular for me, I guess. So even if we never have it again, which I guess is our plan, it was regular for a second there. "So you have, what, like a... girl... a partner?"

My twin brother sounds so uncomfortable. Why? Because he had to correct himself and use the term partner? Because if I am dating, it could be a man. Is that it? Holy shit, that's it. I feel nauseated. "Who told you? Mom or Dad?"

His face gets so pale it's like the color of the ice under the skates he's balancing on. "It was Dad because he assumed you'd already told me. Because you're my twin brother and you're supposed to confide in me."

"I must have skipped that chapter in the twin handbook," I snap. I hate the way Nash has been acting since my marriage ended, and now I know why. He's found out I'm bi and he doesn't approve.

"Look, I was no fan of Anne-Marie's and I think you're better off without her but..." He pauses because I think he knows he should just shut the fuck up, but he's Nash and he never just shuts the fuck up. He swallows and starts to glide closer to the boards, to me. "You shouldn't let what she did to you turn you into..."

"Turn me into what, Nash?" I prompt through gritted teeth when his voice fades. "Are you seriously about to slut shame me?"

"No. I... look, I'm just worried about you," Nash huffs out like he's the one who should be offended here. "I don't know why you have pushed me away since this all happened. I haven't done anything to—"

"You haven't done anything. Full stop," I interrupt. He's right up against the boards now and between the higher level of the ice and the skates he's on, I've got to tilt my head up to look at him. "How long ago did Dad tell you?"

"Tell me what?"

"That I'm bi."

His eyes flare and then he starts looking around behind me, at the empty stands to make sure they are, in fact, empty. He's petrified someone heard me say that out loud. He's embarrassed he's got a bi-brother. I really do want to puke. "This past summer. Like I said, he thought you told me. And then he shut the hell up and didn't explain anything else that went on with Anne-Marie that night. He just said we should talk so I've been waiting for you to confide in me."

"And that's why you wanted to talk at your fancy fucking grocery store?" I bark and give him a floored look before I slide my sunglasses from the top of my head to my face. I really don't want him to see an ounce of the hurt I'm feeling. And besides, I'm leaving. I turn to walk away.

"Actually, I wanted to talk to you about one of *my* problems," Nash snaps. "But you were too busy getting your dick wet to care about making time for me."

"Fuck off," I tell him because he is not the victim here. I didn't prioritize Olivia over him, but I will from now on. Because my twin brother is embarrassed I'm bisexual.

"No, fuck you! You selfish prick."

"Boys!" The voice booms from the other side of the ice.

We both turn and see Coach Braddock standing at the end of the visitor's tunnel. I don't know how much of that exchange he caught but he definitely caught the part where we told each other to fuck off. "Can I ask why my future co-captains are screaming at each other like scorned lovers?"

"Just some brotherly bickering, Coach," Nash replies, the bitterness and anger evaporating from his tone. "Sorry, you had to hear it. Won't happen again."

"Good."

I give the coach a tight smile. "See you at practice, Coach. Later, bro."

I storm away without looking back.

Chapter 14

Liv

I stand outside the door of the classroom at Royce Hall, and I swear to God my whole body itches. I don't know why I'm here. I don't want to go in. Tenley mentioned it casually yesterday morning, and somehow I'm here. Outside the Trauma Survivors Support Group meeting.

Clearly, Tenley thinks I should attend or she wouldn't have mentioned it as we were both heading out the door yesterday. I was off to classes, and I guess I seemed tense. Tenley was off to shoot some additional footage with the crew she put together to pitch this documentary she's working on.

She believed me when I said I left Marmont and went to meet school friends for drinks across the street from Marmont and that I ended up crashing at Maria's, a girl from one of my classes. Then I had to text Maria and tell her I was using her as a cover because Tenley is the girl who would bring it up the next time she sees Maria. Maria happily agreed to lie for me and even sent me a high-five emoji and an eggplant because she just assumed I was with a guy. And I was. That's the first time someone has assumed I was hooking up and I actually was, which made me smile.

It's been a little over a week since my birthday and Tenley hasn't even brought it up again. The family group chat also believed my lie, because, of course, virginal shy Livvy wouldn't be doing anything else. Anyway, Tenley has stopped talking about my birthday night and started talking about the college's trauma group which is supposedly a "really positive thing. They don't dwell on what happened to people, they focus on how to move forward. A girl on my crew goes because she was held up at gunpoint. She's really grown in so many ways, not just gotten over the trauma."

It was the most unsubtle thing Tenley has ever said to me. She's really bad at subtlety it turns out. Shocked, not shocked. And I guess I'm heinously bad at ignoring her because here I am. But I'm frozen. The idea of stepping into that room makes me want to puke and scream at the same time. I'm fine. Well, I *will* be fine, but not if I keep dwelling on this... giving validation to the awful feeling I get every time I'm alone and think of that night. Especially at night. When Tenley isn't home at night I lock every single door and window and crank the AC, even if it's not that hot, just to drown out the sounds of our apartment building because they suddenly make me jumpy.

A woman brushes by me and walks into the room. She's got her head down, eyes glued to the tile floor. She's shuffling instead of walking. She looks beaten down mentally and possibly physically. She looks like a victim. I hate myself for thinking that. It feels mean and I am *not* a mean girl. But I'm also not a victim.

I was raised by the strongest woman on the entire planet, everyone in the entire Garrison family—hell everyone in all of Silver Bay, Maine, will say that. Uncle Jordan once said at a family BBQ, that it was tungsten that ran through my mom's veins instead of blood and what he got in response was a bunch of bobbing heads agreeing with him. Not a murmur of dissent in the bunch.

I was about eight or nine at the time and I sleepily asked him what tungsten was. It was late and I was curled up in my dad's lap half asleep and wrapped in one of his hoodies. "Tungsten is something they use to make steel stronger," Jordan had explained with a gentle smile.

"But steel is already strong," little Tate, who was a kid like me at the time, had argued as he roasted a marshmallow, probably his seventeenth of the night.

"Not as strong as Callie," Dad replied and my mom had stood up and waved a hand around dismissively.

"Stop flattering me you two," she'd laughed.

But it was true. I grew to learn, year after year, that my mom truly was incredible. She'd lost her own mom young, had already been abandoned by her dad, and then dumped by their grandmother. She and my aunts Rose and Jessie raised themselves from the age of early teenhood. Everyone says my mom was the fiercest. And I saw the way she protected us kids. She was the definition of a Mama Bear.

I never once saw my mother cry sad tears. She only cried happy ones, and even that was rare. And I know the whole family teases that I'm the polar opposite of the woman who gave birth to me. That I got none of her DNA. I roll my eyes at the way my mom overshares, has loud opinions on everything, and voices all her emotions, good, bad, and ugly... but the truth is, I *want* to be like her. I think if I had been more like her, this jerk wouldn't have picked me. No one would ever dare try and attack Callie Caplan. And if, God forbid they did, she would make them pay. And she would also suck it up and never be a victim. So I won't be either.

My feet start to move, and I walk out of the building, and straight to my car. That's how I find myself driving toward

Venice three hours early for my job watching Dylan. Mallory and Tate want a date night so I'm taking over from their day sitter and Mallory is going straight from her classes at USC to meet Tate at Wolfgang Puck's restaurant at the Beverly Wilshire Hotel.

The fact is I don't want to head home in case Tenley is there. She knows when this trauma group meets so she will know I ditched. I don't want to explain myself to her, or anyone, so I find myself parking in a visitor spot at Tate's old townhouse because I remember the code for the gate and they have free visitor parking. And it's only two blocks off the beach. I mean, yeah, technically it's also where Crew lives but... I mean there's no guarantee I will run into him. I'm not here to accidentally do it, but, like, if it happens, it wouldn't be a bad thing....

"Olivia?"

At the sound of his voice, as confused as it is, all my anxiety starts to melt away. I slowly turn my head to the left and see him standing on the small front porch of the unit Tate occupied for years. He's wet. Crew's hair looks darker and is kind of plastered back on his head. He's wearing a pair of sweats and nothing else, not even socks or shoes on his feet. He's holding a mug. I stare like a deer who has never seen headlights before. "I... hi. Hello. I just needed a place to park."

"Oh." His disappointment is heavy, like a layer of humidity in the already warm California air. He shoots me the most dazzling but poignant smile. "Thought maybe you were here to beg me for another orgasm. You wouldn't have to beg, by the way, just ask."

WWMD, my brain yells at me. What Would Mom Do? My mom would completely, without a second thought, jump into bed for another round with this fine specimen of a man, who also happens to be a pretty sweet, nice guy... not that my mom would care about that. She's told me before how she didn't give a rat's ass about a man's heart or soul until my dad.

I have always tried to ignore the gory details of my mom's youth but she's talked freely about it in front of us since we were in the higher end of our teen years. She was sexually liberal. She didn't want a relationship with anyone, not even my dad, at first. Everyone blames her childhood trauma. She says there is nothing to blame, she did what-slash-who she wanted and she was content with it.

Crew's standing there watching me, probably waiting for me to go on my merry way so that he can call one of the million women who would kill to get an orgasm from him. But I don't go to the beach like I'd planned. I just stand there by the gate staring at him. And that's when I notice the brace on his left wrist.

"Oh shit. Are you injured?" I walk toward him knowing full well being injured at the start of the season would totally suck for a hockey player. Especially one who wants to get back out there and both enjoy and defend his Stanley Cup win.

He glances down at his wrist and lifts it up as he looks back at me, tugging the Velcro on the brace-free. "Nope. I was last year, at the end of the season. Had a quick surgery and lots of physiotherapy over the summer."

He pauses and our eyes meet and damn I don't want to smile. But I do smile and he smiles back and this little moment passes between us and I don't know what it is. I've had boyfriends before but I've never had this level of chemical attraction to someone. Maybe because he's the only man who has ever been inside me? "Anyway," he starts, bringing me out of my dirty thoughts, "I lied and said it was still bothering me, so I could skip the pressers and schmoozing VIPs after our first preseason game a few weeks ago and go find you. So now Coach and our trainer want me to wear this off the ice. Just in case. I put it on after practice, after my shower so they would see it, and I forgot to take it off."

Me. He faked an injury and bailed on his commitments to the team to find me and try and get me to sleep with him again. There's no way to not be flattered by that. "So," he continues, "are you meeting someone? Like a date?"

"No."

"Thank God because I'd be insanely jealous."

Did he just... I lock eyes with him, and he smiles, but it's not cheeky like he was kidding, it's confident and there's a glint of a challenge in his hazel eyes. Strong 'what are you going to do about it?' vibes.

"I was going to go to the beach to watch the sunset, but I just realized I hate walking around after dark by myself and I would have to walk back here alone... so... do you want to come with?"

"Go with you? To the beach? To watch the sunset? It sounds uncomfortably romantic." He looks down at himself and back up. "Maybe I should put on a shirt to make it less awkward."

I laugh at his stupidity. Crew disappears into the townhouse. I glance in through the big living room window and notice boxes everywhere. He must be moving soon and I don't like that I don't know where he'll be going even though I don't have a right to know. He appears on the front porch again in a simple, pale blue t-shirt and slides on his feet similar to the ones every male in my entire family wears, because hockey players love slip-on shoes. The wrist brace is also gone. He shoves on some sunglasses and pulls his door closed.

"Let's go Fireball."

Is he always this confident and cool? I mean a random girl just shows up at his house and he rolls with it. I don't roll with it when Tenley invites me to brunch spontaneously. I know for a fact my mom rolls with anything so...

"You think a lot, don't you?"

"You don't think?" I counter as we walk the crumbling side-walks of Venice toward the beach.

"I think a lot too," Crew admits with a sheepish, fleeting smile. "But I don't overanalyze things. That trait went to the other twin. But thinking, yeah, I do that. I've been thinking about our night in the hotel a lot. Like all the time. Almost non-stop."

I glance up at him, but I don't know where he's looking because of the sunglasses he's wearing. I decide to throw my own on because they're big round things that will hopefully hide the hue of my skin when I inevitably blush if we keep talking about this. "It's definitely a fond memory for me."

"Fond?" he repeats as the light turns and we start across the intersection. "A fond memory is something you make over Thanksgiving with your grandparents. I don't want it to be a fond memory for you. I wanted it to be a life-changing one. Something that you think about when you're ninety-nine, on your death bed, and it still makes you wet."

I bite the inside of my cheek to keep my mouth from hanging open. My mom wouldn't be stunned by that. I fight the blush wanting to take over my complexion. I try to channel my mom and say something confident and sexy. "I guess fond was an understatement. And if I'm still lucid at ninety-nine, and remember my own name, perhaps I will remember that one crazy birthday I spent naked in a suite at Chateau Marmont. Perhaps."

He laughs. "Well, Fireball, I'm going to ask for one more night so that I can really cement the memory. I'm not liking the use of the word perhaps."

"Oh my God." I can't fight the blush now. "You really don't have anyone else to proposition?"

"Sure I do. I have tons of options. But you're the one that

showed up at my house," he reminds me as the wind takes a few strands of his drying hair and pushes them over his cheek. He shoves them back again. "I'm freshly showered, horny, and well... feels like fate. And to be honest, I think you want to do it again too. There's lots of other places to park in Venice."

I don't respond because I've been busted and there is no way to talk my way out of it. Yeah, I could have paid for parking anywhere else. Deep down I was hoping to run into him. We walk another block. The famous Venice boardwalk and the Pacific Ocean are visible now.

"You're thinking about it," he murmurs confidently.

"Yeah well, I think a lot, remember?"

"Touché."

We don't talk again until we're sitting in the sand, the famous outdoor gym and boardwalk behind us, and nothing but the blue-gray Pacific Ocean and a warm golden ball of light slipping lower and lower in front of us. That's when I find my words.

"Since you know my big secret, that I was a geriatric virgin, tell me some big secret of yours," I request and dig my fingers deeper into the warm sand as I lean back on my arms.

"I'm divorced."

"I know. You've mentioned that. Tell me something I can't Google." He looks hesitant so I add. "It's only fair and you can trust me."

"I don't trust women."

Wow. I lift my sunglasses and push them into my hair to really study his face. He lifts his too and I can see the seriousness in those stunning hazel eyes. "You seriously just said that and meant it? Like, *all* women."

He kind of shrugs. "I mean, I guess I trust my mom."

Red flag? This feels like a red flag. Huge, giant, waving red flag. Crew knows it too because he looks guilty as he runs a hand through his hair and sighs. "I know how that sounds, but my ex really fucked me over. I trusted her with everything. So I won't be doing that again."

"Harsh."

"Truthful," he replies, and we both turn to watch the sun as it dips toward the ocean and paints the sky in hues of orange and red. It's a real stunner tonight.

The silence is comfortable but heavy because his little announcement was a lot and I still don't know what to do with it. He must feel it too because he speaks again and I can feel his fingers graze mine in the sand behind us. "Also, that sad little fact is not something I've admitted to anyone else, so it counts as a secret."

"Okay..."

"I said no thank you and I don't have to say anything else!" a voice shouts suddenly and both Crew and I swivel our heads.

Behind us, on the edge of the paved boardwalk, a woman is yelling at a man. She's dressed in a cropped tank and a long flowy skirt and sandals. He's in a tank, workout shorts, and sneakers.

"Wow. I take it back. You're a cunt," the guy snarls.

Everything in me turns to lead. I'm like a human paperweight, held down in the sand by fear and anxiety and, worst of all, memories. Something way back in the attic of my brain says logically, "But he never yelled at you. He never called you names." But it doesn't register with my nervous system and I remain frozen, eyes glued to the two as the woman turns from the angry, volatile man with a bitter, "Fuck you."

She starts marching away but he repeats her words, almost in shock, and then takes menacing strides towards her. I feel a flutter beside me, sand rains onto my jeans and shirt from Crew's lightning-quick movements. I'm still frozen in my fear, helpless. I also can't seem to catch my breath. It's like I swallowed some of that ocean water in front of me even though I haven't even dipped a toe in.

I watch him step between the woman and the man and calmly intervene. "Hey, buddy. You wanna walk the other way."

"Why? Who are you?" the guy asks angrily and points to the woman who is looking over her shoulder but hasn't stopped walking away. "If you're her boyfriend, all she had to do was say she had one. I mean, fuck, all I did was say she looked pretty. She didn't have to be such a rude cunt. I wouldn't have bothered her if she was walking with you."

"I'm not her boyfriend," Crew replies. "I'm just a dude who understands women don't owe me anything just because they're pretty and walking alone. And I guess I'm here to teach you that lesson."

"What the fuck you gonna do about it?" He seethes and steps into Crew. The two would be nose-to-nose except the menacing dude is a few inches shorter than Crew. Crew isn't being aggressive, not even in his stance. His shoulders aren't back. His hands are in his pockets. He's relaxed... and shockingly, when he doesn't get a reaction, this guy backs down. Can you imagine, I think to myself both bitter and amazed, to be able to intimidate without even using body language? If I had that superpower, I wouldn't have been jumped.

"Look, women aren't out here looking for strangers to hit on them or even to compliment them," Crew goes on and the guy mutters something under his breath. "Walk it off and do better. Don't do it again because I promise you, I'm not the only man out here who will tell you to back off and some will be a lot less chill about it."

The guy stomps toward the outdoor gym. Crew starts walking back to me. The woman is nowhere to be found, having used the opportunity to get the hell away from the situation, which is exactly what I would have done.

Crew walks to me casually, like he isn't a fucking hero. I watch him. He isn't looking around for accolades from strangers watching or from the girl he saved. He didn't do it for himself. He did it because it was the right thing to do.

I realize Crew may have announced he doesn't trust women, but he's a guy who has been burned. Badly. And nothing else about Crew screams red flag. In fact, everything about him screams anchor. Safety. Warmth. He's the guy you go to when you're in trouble, which is why I think I picked him. Without realizing it. So by the time he reaches me again, I'm no longer paralyzed. I'm on my feet, dusting sand off my jeans.

"Sorry about that."

"Let's go."

"Where?"

"Back to your place," I tell him and it feels like the boldest thing I've ever done. I keep walking toward the boardwalk, and the road, without looking back so I don't lose my nerve. Out of my peripheral, I see him fall in step beside me. I swear I feel the smile on his lips. "I've never had a quickie before and I've got a little less than forty-five minutes before I have to be at Tate's. Think you can get me off in that time?

"Phew!" Crew tips his head back as if what I said is ridiculous. "I can do it more than once in that amount of time."

"Show me the ways, you sexual Jedi."

I don't even have time to worry if he'll get that nerdy reference because he chuckles and replies, "Please can I be Obi-Wan and not Yoda? The young Ewan McGregor version not like that old guy."

"Alec Guinness."

"God your brain is hot, Fireball."

I can't help but smile.

Chapter 15

Crew

As soon as my orgasm has ended, the weirdest thought pops into my head. I haven't had sex with the same person this many times since I was married. And the weirdest part is that, even though I've barely pulled out and taken the condom off, I'm already thinking about when we can do this again.

I kiss her forehead and go into the bathroom to clean up. When I come out she's already dressed and I let out a sad, "Boo!"

She gives me a soft smile. "I told you this was a quickie."

"Your first," I remind her proudly. "How'd you rate it?"

"Ten out of ten," she announces laughing, which is a sound I have come to adore the same way a puppy likes belly rubs. "I will probably remember it when I'm ninety-nine."

"Probably?" I grab my sweats off the floor and pull them on. "That's not much better than perhaps. I think we might have to go again."

I grab her gently by the shoulders and pull her back toward the bed, but she breaks free of my loose grip and picks up her bag off the floor. "I've got a date with my favorite second cousin

151

and even your ten-out-of-ten orgasms aren't going to keep me from it."

"Fine. Fine." I mock grumble.

I walk Olivia downstairs to the door and it gets adorably awkward again. She looks everywhere but my face. "So... thanks. See you around."

She reaches for my front door but I grab the handle first and hold the door open for her. Then I follow her out, and she gives me a look. "You said earlier you don't like walking alone in the dark."

I point up at the twilight sky. She smiles thankfully. I wrap an arm around her shoulders. "So this is clearly not a one-night stand anymore. I think we can both safely say that."

Her head snaps up and I'm finally able to see those deep dark pools. I lean down and give her a soft kiss. She flushes deeper. "I have to go babysit Dylan."

"Okay well... if you ever want to get together again and give this a name, let me know."

"You don't do relationships, Crew. I don't do one-night stands. I mean even when I try it turns into... this." She motions with her hands like there's a mess in front of us.

She shakes her head, her silky brown hair mussing around her face. I reach up and brush it back where a few strands cling to the corner of her mouth. "We can think of something to label it. I think we'd do our best brainstorming naked though," I go on as we reach her car and she clicks the remote to unlock the door. "That's how our best work has been done so far anyway and why mess with success?"

"My God, you are something else."

I laugh. "I'll take that as a compliment."

"Goodbye Crew." She winks. She fucking winks and I am on fire again.

I watch her drive away until her taillights disappear on

Abbott Kinney. As soon as I'm within a couple feet of my front door I hear my cellphone screaming from the hall table where I plunked it with my keys as I was leading Olivia to the bedroom.

I see Nash's name on the screen and walk away, leaving it to ring until it goes to voicemail, which I don't intend to check. I head into the kitchen and stare at the contents of my fridge, trying to figure out which of the pre-made meals I ordered from my meal service I should eat tonight. Everything is so healthy and after really good sex I usually want something sinful and satisfying, like a cheeseburger.

But we're days from the first real game of the season and there is no way I'm eating a cheeseburger so someone, like my brother, can comment that I don't take the game as seriously as my dad did. My phone rings again and I walk back out into the entry and see my dad's name on the screen so I pick it up. "Hey."

"Nash is right. You're avoiding him."

Shit. I should have known he would bitch to Dad. I grit my teeth but try to sound light-hearted—and innocent. "I see him just about every day. How can I be avoiding him?"

"He says you bolt from practice and games without a word and that you don't answer when he calls," Dad says, and I can tell by his tone he's unimpressed. Not just with me doing this, but with the fact that he has to get involved. Dad has a younger sister, but they never had a disagreement let alone a rivalry of any kind. He doesn't get the way Nash and I sometimes—and lately more than not—grate on each other's nerves. He has zero patience for it.

"He likes doing press. He's good at it so I let him," I reply and walk through my house to the living room. I drop down on the sofa and close my eyes, pinching the bridge of my nose. "And he always calls when I'm busy, or in the shower or whatever. That's on him, not me. Also, we haven't had a real game yet so let's not be dramatic."

Dad sighs. "Okay well, I fully expect this to simmer down before that puck drop in four days."

Of course, he knows the exact countdown to our first game of the season. He's going to be there and, like with everything else to do with our careers, he's going to be proud. Dad has never pushed us into hockey, but since we both chose it, he's been nothing but a pillar of support. I can't fault him anything, to be honest. He's a great dad.

"Is that the only reason you're calling?"

"That isn't even the reason I'm calling, but I figured I would bring it up," he retorts. "Your mom will be the next person calling if you don't heed my advice here and cut your brother some slack or whatever. And trust me, you do *not* want her on your case."

"I do not," I agree. My mom has always worn the pants in our little family.

Stephanie Deveau-Westwood is a smart, savvy, accomplished business woman and she's also a great human being but she doesn't mess around when it comes to squabbles between her sons. She and my uncle Seb are as close as siblings can be. She often tells us Uncle Seb is the only reason she lived long enough to meet our dad and have us because when she was younger she had addiction issues and it was Uncle Sebastian who got her the help she needed.

"Stop threatening me," I tell him. "I'll call Nash tonight and sing him bedtime lullabies or something, okay? Just tell me why you called so I can have dinner. I'm starved."

"Okay," Dad pauses. "They're doing a little thing in San Diego when the Quake play the Saints at the beginning of November. It's a ceremony thing and they want you and Nash there a day early so you can do some press with me so can you guys get permission from your coach?"

Dad could call up Jude Braddock and ask him right now. He played with the guy... well, against the guy. They're acquaintances who have huge respect for each other. But he vowed to never interfere in our hockey lives because his dad tried to basically orchestrate everything about Dad's life when he was playing. He treated him like a commodity not a son for a very long time. Dad never interferes or steps in, unless I accidentally light a car on fire in my driveway after catching my wife in our bed with someone else. Then he ignores his instincts and takes charge, thankfully.

"Of course. I will ask the coach tomorrow first thing, but wait... is this finally it?" I ask and sit up on the couch. "Are they finally retiring your jersey?"

"Yeah."

"Oh my God Dad! Congrats! This is awesome. Well overdue," I exclaim and I'm on my feet again.

Having your jersey retired is one of the biggest honors a hockey player can have and it's insane that the Saints haven't done it before now. I think they're salty because Nash and I signed contract extensions with the Quake after our rookie contracts expired. The Saints management had reached out to Dad, and our agent, explaining how badly they wanted to sign one of us, they didn't care which. But Nash and I wanted to stay together *and* with the Quake —aka their biggest rivals. Anyway, that seems to have passed. It's about time they acknowledge the finest player who ever lived, and the reason they have a Stanley Cup banner hanging from their rafters.

"Thanks. It will really mean a lot if you two can be there," he says quietly.

"Of course we can. And they're doing the ceremony during our game? That's great!" I'm truly excited for my dad. I know he's wanted this, but he's never let on. Still, I would want this so I assume he would too.

"Okay cool," Dad says. "How is the wrist? Nash says it's bothering you."

"Nah. I mean it tweaked for a second there but I'm confident now it was a false alarm." There I go lying again. "Don't stress."

"Okay. Your brother's lingering injury seems to have cleared up too, which is a relief. And how is everything else?" Before I can answer I hear a muffled sound. "Steph, I'm doing it my way."

"Is Mom there?"

"Yeah."

"Oh okay." I grin. "So by everything else you mean, how's my mental health, and have I finally let someone else in, or is Anne-Marie still winning?"

"Shit, Steph he has your number and he isn't afraid to dial it." My dad starts laughing and then makes whimpering noises as I'm sure my mom is hitting him with one of the hundred throw pillows on their bed or couch. I hope it's the couch. I don't want to think of them calling me in bed together. Weird.

"Crew, I'm sorry I ever said that out loud!" Mom's voice calls out.

"Tell her it's fine. She's not wrong. I am not dating anymore because of Anne-Marie," I admit. "But it's not a bad thing like she thinks. I'm happy. I'm good."

I think of where I was twenty minutes ago, with Olivia. "I'm really good, actually, so everyone relax."

"Okay. Good. We're happy you're happy," Dad replies. "Now go call your brother."

"Fine."

"Love you, kid," Dad says.

"Love you, baby boy!" Mom hollers in the background.

"Love you both."

I hang up and scroll through my contacts until I get to Nash. I hit the button to connect the call and wait. The asshole lets it ring four times and then finally, just before the voicemail kicks in, he answers. "Oh hi. You're alive."

"You spent all morning running drills with me on the ice, Nash."

"Yeah but like where are you outside of work?"

This is one of the very many subtle differences between Nash and me. He calls hockey work. I never have. Everyone sees the blatant differences, like how I'm tattooed and he's not. My eyes are a lighter shade of hazel. I like to keep my hair a little longer and shaggy, and it's naturally a shade darker than his. He's reserved, I'm anything but. However, it's the little things, like this, that always really hit hard for me.

We are so different and I always fought the differences, forcing a friendship, not just a genetic obligation to get along. I stopped doing that and he's finally noticing. He just doesn't know why I did it. I'm sure that question will come up soon.

"And just now," he continues and his voice is one deep decibel away from whining. "I call, no answer. Dad calls thirty seconds later and you pick up."

"How did you know that?"

"He texted me."

Fucking hell. Why is Dad making this a bigger issue? I grit my teeth. "I was saying goodbye to someone when you called. I had company. Dad called right before I could call you back. Nash, please stop being a nagging girlfriend. If I wanted one of those, I would have one."

"So it wasn't a girl who you had over?"

"So we're changing gears from nagging girlfriend to jealous wife?" I snark.

"Fuck off, Crew. I'm a concerned brother," he barks back

defensively. I can picture him pacing the oak floors in his immaculate, soulless house. "Not concerned. Wrong word. I know you're still fine."

Indicating I wasn't previously. I get super irked by that as I head back into the kitchen and contemplate hanging up on him. But the thing is, he's right. I wasn't fine. When Anne-Marie left me and did what she did, I had some kind of mental break. I admit it. Nash knows the gory details, thanks to our parents. Anne-Marie and I decided to open our marriage. She was convinced we were too young to stay together if we didn't. I agreed because I was scared she was right and I didn't want to fail. I wanted us to work. He knows all of this but we haven't talked about the fact that he knows all of this. I have wondered more than once since I found out he knew I was bi, if he also knows I tearfully confessed, to Mom and Dad I stayed in this open marriage for five and a half months, and that everything was okay because there were rules. No secret hook-ups, everything must be approved by the other person ahead of time, and never in our home, always rent a hotel room. But the rules weren't being followed and I found out the hard way when I came home from a road trip and found Anne-Marie in our bed with a guy I didn't know. The dude ran before I could punch him, which I fully intended to do. And then Anne-Marie asked for a divorce, right there, half-naked, with the other guy's stink still on my sheets. I lost it, dragged the mattress outside, and lit it on fire. She got in her car and left screaming. But my car was still in the driveway, way too close to the burning mattress and it went up in flames. The only decent thing Anne-Marie did that night, and maybe in our entire marriage, was call the cops as she drove away. If she hadn't the whole house would have likely gone up and me with it, because I was too broken to stop it.

I told Nash a little about the breakup, that she cheated and we were divorcing, but I didn't tell him about the mental break.

And I didn't want him to know. He wouldn't have broken like that. He wouldn't have needed Dad to sweet-talk the police into writing the whole thing off as an accident and then whisk him away for a weekend to get a grip. Dad took me to this place up in the California mountains. A lodge by June Lake. We stayed in a cabin and in the cabin next door, Dad flew in and paid for one of the top psychologists in America, and that's where I would spend my days. In therapy. It was there I told Dad, with the encouragement of the psychologist, that I was bisexual.

I didn't tell him how I figured that out. That the arrangement Anne-Marie and I had also included three ways and sometimes that meant another man in the mix, not always just another woman. That Anne-Marie had been the one to suggest it, and that she said she was cool with it, but then she used it as a reason for divorce. "I don't think you even like women, deep down. I think you're lying to yourself and to me. You hook up with guys way too easily." And that later, during the divorce proceedings, she threatened to reveal it to the media if I didn't give her more than the prenup she had signed said she would get. I agreed to give her more money, not because I was gay, or ashamed of being bi, but because I would give all my money away to be rid of her. Also, I was not going to let her control my coming out. I would tell people the way I wanted when I wanted to.

I kept all that from Nash for a million reasons, for his sake and mine. But he knows now, thanks to Dad, and his reaction has been worse than I could have ever imagined. Our relationship can't recover from this.

And so here we are with me being a dick to him and him getting annoyed and acting like he has no clue why. Nash is the absolute king of poker faces. If he looks confused, it's because he wants you to think he's confused. He doesn't have an expression hit his face that he isn't aware of. He's the most self-aware person on the planet, not to mention thoughtful, articulate, and calm. So the way he looked like he'd swallowed durian fruit when we fumbled around the subject of my sexuality at the rink made his feelings about it loud and clear.

"So what? What can I help you with Nash?"

I stare at the contents of my fridge. It's all less appealing than it was before. I grab a chicken kale salad and drop it on the counter. "I wanted to tell you about Dad. And ask if you were... do you want to carpool? We're going to have to get up there before the team and so I figured we could go together."

He knows I hate riding with him because it's like traveling with a ninety-six-year-old man. He hates riding with me because he constantly thinks I'm speeding and that I don't wait at stop signs long enough. I do. So if he wants to travel together, he must be really desperate for us to spend time together. "Yeah. Okay. But I drive."

"Fine."

"Cool." I sigh. "Gotta go. Dinner is calling."

"I also wanted the name of that lawyer Dad got you hooked up with when you needed one." And that has me stop in my tracks, halfway to the water cooler to fill my Stanley.

"The lawyer Dad hooked me up with? For my divorce?"

"Yeah. I mean he does other stuff too right?" Nash asks and his voice is off. His words are clipped and his tone is kind of uneven when everything about Nash is usually even.

"Divorces and custody agreements," I inform my twin. "You got a child I need to know about? A wife?"

"Ha. Ha," he says but his tone isn't dry. It's kind of... anxious.

"Seriously, what's up?" I say, softening a little. I know how hard it was to be going through something and thinking I had to do it alone. I don't wish that on anyone. "Why do you need a lawyer and what can I do to help?"

"Answer the phone when I call," he snaps. "And I don't need a lawyer. It's for a friend."

I almost snort at that because Nash doesn't have any friends that I don't also call friend. He does nothing but eat, sleep, and hockey, and I know no one on the team needs a divorce lawyer. Divorcing in hockey is rare and so when it happens, news gets around fast, but the only thing that would be less believable than Nash having a friend I don't know, is Nash needing a lawyer himself, so I guess he must know someone I don't. "Charlie Sullivan. And it's a *she*, not he."

"Charlie is a she?"

"Charlotte Sullivan but she goes by Charlie," I explain. "She's young. Like fresh out of law school, but she's good. But, like I said, she is divorce and family law."

"It's fine," Nash blows me off. "Maybe she knows someone who can help with this girl's situation."

"You have a female friend?"

Yeah, I sound shocked and he's rightfully offended.

"I could. I'm not a fucking monk," Nash snaps as I fill my Stanley and walk back over to the counter to unpack my chicken kale salad hoping it magically turned into a cheeseburger. "And I think friend is an overstatement. She's this woman who lives in my building. A real pain in the ass to everyone who meets her but she's like, in a bind, and I thought I would be neighborly and offer help."

None of this sounds normal, or legit, but I know if I push him right now he'll just get more pissy, so I relent and make a mental note to answer more of his calls and quiz him about it on our trip to San Diego if he hasn't confided before that. "You're a good neighbor, Nash. Mr. Rogers would be proud. Now can I go eat my salad? You'll be happy to know I decided to give your private chef a whirl."

"Yeah?" He sounds instantly thrilled. "He's good, eh? Have

you tried his pumpkin ravioli? My god, the pesto sauce is insane."

"I'll have that tomorrow before practice and report back."

"If you don't like it, we can't be twins anymore."

He's been making that joke since we were, like, seven and it never fails to make me smile. "Later."

I hang up and head back into my living room with my meal, turning on ESPN to help distract me from my thoughts of Olivia. As much as I want to flip through the highlight reel of what we did today, I shouldn't because it's only going to make me want to do it again. And she hasn't agreed to that. Maybe it's best she doesn't. This can't go anywhere anyway.

Olivia is a sweet girl who wants a serious relationship. She also has something that catapulted her into my bed but she hasn't said what that is. I don't want to find out. I don't want to be involved with someone. So instead of thinking of Olivia, I think of all the drama and trauma my marriage caused me. By the time I finish my dinner, I'm very happy with letting this thing with Olivia go. It was fun but now it's done, which is best for both of us.

Chapter 16

Liv

I watch the kids file out of the classroom. A few of them are humming, one of them is playing air guitar, and all of them are smiling. They like me! They like my class! I glance over to the corner where the actual teacher has been observing and she smiles and nods approvingly.

Carlos also shoots me a confident, happy smile. "We did good, Garrison."

I grin. "We did, didn't we?"

I lift my hand and high-five him. The teacher heads toward her desk and we collect our own belongings, say goodbye, and walk out together. "She's gotta give us five stars. The kids are totally engaged in our classes."

"It's not an Amazon review, Carlos," I laugh. "But yeah, I think she'll give us a glowing assessment. Now we have to talk about the quiz. Can you email me your half of the questions and I'll build the file for the kids. I want it to be interactive, with sound clips too, so I emailed the principal to see if I can have access to the school server to store the file so they can access it right from the classroom computers."

"You are the best partner in the world, Garrison." He grins again and wraps a friendly arm around my shoulder.

I fight the urge to flinch and win. It's not Carlos. He's great. In fact for a while there, despite what I said to Tenley and my cousins, I had entertained the idea of maybe pursuing him after our work relationship was done. I'd run a scenario in my head about our end-of-term party and how I would make some smooth comment that we should stay in touch and then if he reacted well, I would invite him to a movie or something. But... I haven't run that scenario in my head since.... since I slept with Crew Westwood.

We round the corner of the outdoor hallway and I step out of his side hug casually and look up and smile. The building these kids get to go to school in is right out of a movie set, in my opinion. There are huge outdoor marble hallways with painted ceilings and their cafeteria seating is in the middle of a court-yard with colorful canopies to keep the sun off them while they munch on lunches that look like something Jamie Oliver made.

"You are enamored with California, aren't you?"

"Well, yeah, in general," I reply as we start down the steps. "You have to understand Silver Bay, Maine, is lovely and quaint, like something out of a Hallmark movie, when it's not sub-zero freezing and coated in ice. But it's that about six to seven months of the year."

"So no outdoor eating at lunchtime in your high school," Carlos replies, and I shake my head. "It's not all that, though. I mean I had outdoor eating in Arizona, but my friend got bit by a rattlesnake because of it."

"What? Shit. Did he live?"

"Yeah. But it was nuts," Carlos replies. "See, if you don't live in the rich school districts and your cafeteria is outside, you have to live with pests because there's no budget for pest control. And there're drive-by shootings."

"You've been in drive-by shootings?"

"Yeah. Once. Zero stars." He winks at me. "But I'm going back there to teach once I'm done next year because they need people to not give up on the area."

See. I should be making heart eyes at him right now. He's handsome and noble and kind and driven. Instead, I'm thinking about Crew and wondering if he will be at Tate's for the barbecue tonight. It's been four very long, boring days since our third encounter and I haven't seen him. I haven't heard from him, but to be fair, I haven't reached out either. Still, it feels like he's avoiding me, which is stupid. It's just... he knows where to find me and he doesn't. But I don't want him to, right? Right.

My phone dings as we get to the staff parking lot. I pluck it from my purse and read a text from Tenley.

TENLEY: Sorry! Can't pick you up. There was a thing I couldn't get out of & then Parentals showed up.

"God damnit Ten."

"What has the number Ten done to you to deserve such blasphemy?" Carlos kids.

See. He's charming too. What is wrong with me? Why did I flip the off switch on him and how do I turn it back on?

"Ten is Tenley. My cousin I live with."

"The one who picks you up sometimes?"

I nod. "Only not today apparently. She just bailed."

LIV: WTF am I supposed to do?

TENLEY: Uber? I'll pay! In fact. I'll order. Gimme the addy.

Uber. The idea spikes my anxiety instantly. I do not want to get into a car with a stranger right now, especially because every Uber driver I've ever had has been male. I know I'm overreacting to this attack, letting it affect my daily life, but... I can't help it.

"I can drive you wherever you need to go."

I look up into Carlos' friendly brown eyes. My gaze shifts to the minivan he drives, which he inherited from his grandma. "Where do you live again? I don't want to put you out. I'm not going home. I'm headed to Venice to my cousins."

"I live in Manhattan Beach so I'm heading that way anyway," he replies. "If you were heading back to West Hollywood it would be out of the way, but I would insist on driving you anyway."

I am an idiot for not being attracted to him anymore. I total brain-dead idiot. "Thanks, Carlos. I owe you."

The drive is painless. Comfortable even. We laugh a lot and even get a chance to talk through the quiz we're planning so we're both on the same page and have gotten a ton of work done by the time he pulls onto Tate and Mallory's street. "Whoa. Someone is having a party."

Carlos eyes all the cars lining the side of the road and the catering truck in Tate's driveway. "My cousin. He is hosting his teammates before the start of the season."

"He plays hockey, right?"

"Yeah."

"Sorry. I know nothing about hockey. I'm a football fan," Carlos explains. "The American and British kind."

There's a tap on the glass of the passenger window beside my head and I not only jump but squeak. Carlos puts a hand on my knee, meant as a friendly comfort, I'm sure, but judging by the look in Crew's eyes he's taking it as something much more.

Carlos rolls down the window from the controls on his door. "Hey."

Crew doesn't even glance at Carlos. His eyes are glued to me. "I didn't mean to interrupt. I saw you and thought you were with Tenley or one of your other hundred relatives."

"I... no this is Carlos. I work with him. And go to school with him." I turn to Carlos and try to smile but it feels wrong.

Tight. "Carlos this is Crew Westwood. He plays with my cousin Tate."

"Hockey. Plays hockey," Crew adds, and I laugh too loudly.

Carlos moves his hand from my knee to reach across me toward the open window to shake Crew's hand. Crew shakes like it's not a big deal but his expression is tense and dark. Like he's... jealous? No. No way. Couldn't be.

"Nice to meet you," Carlos says. "I was just delivering Liv to her party."

"Thank you. I'll email you when I have the quiz ready for proofing," I say and scramble like a feral raccoon to get my seatbelt off, grab my shoulder bag, and open the car door. I do it all so fast that I actually smack Crew in the forehead with the door because he was still leaning into the window. He falls backward onto the grass between the road and the sidewalk, swearing.

I leap from the car and stare down at him while he rubs his forehead. "Are you okay? I'm so sorry!"

"Yeah. Fine," he grumbles.

Carlos must have been worried about him too because he's turned off the engine and got out of the car. He's standing right beside me. "Dude. That looked brutal. Are you sure you're okay?"

"Yeah. I've been concussed before and this ain't it," Crew replies and ignores Carlos' outstretched hand. He gives me a quick glare as he hauls himself to his feet.

"Sorry," I say again and then turn to Carlos. "Thanks again. I'll see you in class tomorrow."

"Yeah."

"Why rush off, Carlos?" Crew asks and my head ricochets back in his direction. "Wanna grab a bite before you go?"

"I mean..."

Okay, clearly Crew *is* concussed. What the hell is he doing?

"You can meet the rest of the local NHL team. It's an invite a lot of people would kill for." Crew smiles. "Not enough though, in this town. LA isn't exactly a big hockey town, but maybe we can woo you and you'll spread the word."

"I..." Carlos looks at me.

I smile. "Sure. Yeah. Join!"

I mean, what the hell else am I supposed to say? And obviously, Crew isn't jealous. He doesn't care if this leads to something unprofessional with Carlos or else why would he be encouraging us to hang out? Clearly, Crew hasn't been thinking about me the way I've been thinking of him.

I might not still be attracted to Carlos but maybe with some effort, I can change that. Because being attracted to Crew is a dead end now. Clearly.

So I blink and channel my mom. Her courage. Her passion. Her wild side. I hook my arm through Carlos' and give him what I hope is a flirty smile. "Come have some barbecue with me."

"I'd love to."

I lead Carlos toward the backyard. I don't bother to turn and see if Crew is following but I'm sure he is. And I hope he's happy about this.

Chapter 17

Crew

I'm miserable and I have no one to blame but myself. Why did I encourage that school friend of Olivia's to come to the barbecue? He hasn't left her side all night. But, I mean, why would he? I wouldn't leave her side either. And it probably helps that she's the only person here he knows. But still, fuck him. And fuck me for inviting him.

"Hey growly," a voice says, and I turn and see Tate standing beside him. "You got heartburn from the ribs or something?"

"No," I growl the word out so yeah, he has a point. I take a deep breath and a sip of the beer. "It's a good party, Tate. Thanks for hosting this year."

"Our pleasure," Tate says and his eyes are on Mallory, the love of his life, who has a tray of appetizers in one hand and Dylan on her hip. She's chatting to Tenley and the wife of one of our defensemen. It's nice to see him happy but I'd be lying if I wasn't a tad bit jealous. Mallory is all in. She loved Tate even before Tate loved her. I never had that with Anne-Marie, and now thanks to how jaded I've become, I'll never have that with anyone.

My eyes move through the crowded backyard filled with my teammates and their significant others to Olivia who is perched on the arm of a chair by the doors to the house. Her friend Carlos is standing beside her.

"So seriously, what is up with you?"

"Nothing. Nothing important anyway," I mutter.

Dylan lets out a frustrated squeal. Mallory struggles to balance him as he squirms in her arms. Tenley grabs the tray of appetizers and Olivia bolts up to grab Dylan. I can't hear what she is saying to Mallory but she's got a happy, reassuring smile on her face. She takes Dylan by the hand and lets him lead her into the house. Carlos follows along and I swear he checks out her ass.

"Who's the dude?" I ask with a tilt of my head in their direction. I know who Carlos is, but I want to see if what Olivia told me matches what Tate says.

"Liv's classmate, I guess." Tate shrugs and his eyes darken. "Tenley swears he's cool, and she usually has great judgment. Don't tell her I admitted that."

I smile. Tenley and Tate have a relationship very similar to Nash and I, probably because they're very close in age. As close as you can be without being twins. "So just friends?"

He turns his stare to me. I really shouldn't have asked for clarification. I mean, I'm supposed to barely know Olivia. "I mean, just wondering because Tenley is always teasing Olivia that she's innocent and stuff."

"We try not to tease her anymore," Tate replies. "She's got a lot on her plate right now. I think... I'm worried about her if I'm honest."

"Why?"

He hesitates, sipping his own beer and stopping one of the catering crew to pluck an appetizer off the tray.

"She's my favorite cousin," he admits, offering me one of the veggies sticking out of the hollowed-out mini red pepper filled with a caramelized onion avocado dip that's to die for. I know because I've eaten several of these already. I grab a carrot stick. "She's always stuck to her own way, you know? Never bent to peer pressure, or worse, Garrison family pressure. She's just... she's special. And something happened that has made her question herself. I usually stay out of my female relatives' personal lives, and I don't intend to meddle now... but I don't want her with some loser who just wants to use her, you know? It's more important than before because she's kinda vulnerable right now."

"That's very good-hearted of you," I say when I finish chewing and swallowing the carrot and delicious dip. "But women kind of hate that shit where you control their lives. Or try to. She looks capable of making her own decisions."

"Yeah, and she was but right now..." Tate shakes his head and the look that washes over his face is intense. He looks like someone died. It makes me instantly uneasy. "Let's just say that Carlos dude better have the best of intentions because I'll make sure he regrets it if he doesn't."

"Garrison!" Hendrix our backup goalie calls out, waving Tate over to where he's gathered with a bunch of other players, including our main goalie who is on crutches. Coach is waiting on the results of his latest MRI before he decides if he'll have to put him on injury reserve and find another goalie.

Tate walks away to join the group. Nash takes his place beside me. I instantly grit my teeth. He doesn't notice. "Hey. I'm probably going to Irish goodbye in a minute."

"It's not an Irish goodbye if you tell people you're leaving," I remind him and he gives me a small, sheepish smile that doesn't reach his eyes.

"Yeah well, you don't count. Anyway, just wanted to make sure you're okay," he says. "You have looked like you're about to bite someone's head off since you got here."

"Sorry. Yeah. I don't know why." I shrug. "Resting bitch face is contagious I guess. I must have caught it from Tenley."

I motion with my beer bottle toward Tenley who is eyeing us. Suddenly she looks like there's too much lemon in her Corona. Nash stiffens so quickly beside me that I feel it. "You've been hanging with Tenley?"

"No." I shake my head and turn to find a scowl on his face. "But why does the idea bother you? She hates you and last time I checked you didn't think much of her."

"I don't. She's bossy and overbearing and annoying," Nash replies and crosses his arms. As usual, there's no drink in his hand. Nash only drinks, like, twice a year. Three times if we win the Stanley Cup. He doesn't like to lose control. "And trust me, I tried to see past that. In Vegas we…"

I lift an eyebrow and hold my breath. Is he about to tell me he hooked up with Tenley? He can't. He wouldn't. That would violate the team code, one because she's Tate's sister but also because of Nash's own strict personal rules about not dating. Of course just because he hooked up with her doesn't mean they're dating. But then that would violate another of his personal rules —no one-night stands.

"What? No. Do not look at me like that. I did not sleep with her or anything." His voice is a heated whisper and his eyes dart all over the place, making sure no one overhears. "We hung out. I tried to like her. She's just… an emotional bully. I don't like her. And if you were dating another person I don't like it would be hard. I'm sick of stuff between us being hard."

"Well, don't worry. I was simply making a joke about Ten," I reply. "And you don't have to worry about me dating anyone. I don't do that anymore."

"Right. Mr. Random Hookup guy." Nash nods. "Keeping your options open."

I don't like the way he says that. It slices into all my insecurities related to him like a hot knife through butter. I bristle. "Well, I think I'll Irish goodbye it myself. I'm in a pissy mood, as my face reflects, so I'll see you tomorrow."

I put my mostly empty beer down on the nearest table and walk away from Nash, and most of the party, finding my way inside. There's a powder room off the front hall but I'm betting someone is in it so I make my way upstairs. I walked here, which means I have to walk home so I better drain the bladder first.

I take the stairs two at a time, headed for the main bathroom nestled between the two spare bedrooms, across from what used to be Anne-Marie's office. When I get upstairs I come face-to-face with Olivia who looks sweaty and disheveled as she slips out of one of the guest rooms.

Our eyes lock and she freezes. "Oh. Hey."

Some switch I didn't know I had flips inside me. I'm suddenly raging with jealousy. "Are you... with Carlos? Am I catching you...?"

Her face turns bright red, probably as red as the fiery rage that is burning in my chest. I know this makes me an insane asshole but the idea that she snuck up here to fuck—or even fool around with—that guy, while I was downstairs... is making me crazy.

She doesn't say anything so I grab the handle of the door she just closed and open it. I expect to see a half-naked Carlos in there and my fist balls at my side. Am I going to hit him? No. But I could and Tate would probably thank me. After all, he's worried about Olivia and wants her protected.

But inside the bedroom is nothing but toys. Tons and tons of toys including a giant wooden truck. Wait... it's not a real truck.

It's a bed shaped like a truck and a tiny little blond human is asleep in it. Dylan.

There's no one else in the room. I turn back to Olivia, feeling so stupid I'm speechless. She reaches for the door, closing her hand over mine on the handle and pulling it shut. "Carlos left. I came up here to tire Dylan out so he would go to sleep. You really think I would sneak up here in a house filled with people, my family, and *you*, and fool around with some random guy?"

"He's not a random guy," I argue back. "He's in your class and you seem to like him. And he definitely likes you."

"We're friends and we work together at our teaching internship," Olivia says.

"But he likes you," I argue. "It's written all over his face."

"So then I must be up here fucking him?" Olivia counters and her boldness is a shock. A shock that wakes up my dick because it's hot to see her get riled up enough to have a potty mouth with me. "Because I fucked you more than once so I must be ready to fuck whoever else wanders my way now, right?"

Oh fuck. She thinks I'm calling her a whore. I shake my head gently take her wrist and tug her away from Dylan's door. I don't know much about toddlers but I do know he's started learning words and I don't think anything we're saying should be added to his vocabulary.

"No. Of course not. But I wouldn't judge you if you did want to sleep with someone else." I inhale sharply and exhale slowly. "I'm sorry. I just... I saw you with him and I didn't like it."

"Why?"

"Because you were just with me."

"Days ago," she corrects me. Her eyes glimmer with a nervous glint but she is forcing herself to be cocky anyway as she tilts her head and puts her hands on her hips. "I'm new at this, remember? So is there an amount of days I have to wait after a one-night stand?'

"It was more than once," I correct in a calm, factual monotone. It gets the reaction I was hoping for—Olivia's lip quivers as she fights a smile. "And no. There's no required wait time. However, if it's great, I mean, like mind-blowing fantastic, there's no need to rush out and add to the body count. It simply wouldn't be fair to the poor sucker who has to follow an eleven out of ten. Or fair to you."

She bats her dark, impossibly thick eyelashes. "Did you just seriously call yourself an eleven out of ten? To my face?"

"I didn't." I shake my head. "I'm just explaining facts to you, hypothetically. But if you think of me when you hear 'eleven-out-of-ten', then that's very flattering. Thanks, Fireball."

That's it. She breaks. I can feel the light of the smile that takes over her face. It hits me in the chest and blooms like the night jasmine that peppers pockets of the city.

"Stop with the sex Jedi mind tricks, Inky," she mutters and turns for the stairs.

I grab her wrist. She lets me. She stops moving but doesn't turn to face me. It's not much but it's an invitation to continue whatever it is we're doing. I step up behind her and use my free hand to slowly, deliberately lift her hair off her shoulders, exposing her long, delicate neck. My lips tingle with the need to touch her there. "If you're still curious, don't go looking to experiment with that guy."

"Why not?" she counters, her voice firm but low. "How many women have you slept with since you lost your virginity?"

"Women? About..." There's a brief moment of hesitation. Do I tell her the truth? Then I remember the promise I made to myself not to be ashamed of who I am. "Twenty-six. I guess you make twenty-seven women."

"Holy shit," she hisses and then clamps a hand over her mouth. "I'm sorry. I don't mean it like that."

"No slut-shaming, Fireball. Remember I lost my virginity at sixteen, not twenty-two and three-quarters."

She turns around finally and we're so close that I feel every part of her graze every part of my front and it's so hot I'm surprised we aren't shooting off sparks. Her cheeks are pink again and she drops her hand. "I really didn't mean it that way. I mean you're a hot rich hockey player. And you were in a relationship for years that turned into a marriage. But it's not even close to the numbers I bet some of the other guys have pulled. And I bet my own cousins, some of them, are nearing triple digits. I mean... Theo. I worry about Theo. But anyway, I just, I mean, sixteen? That's the part that blows my mind. At sixteen I think I was barely kissing boys. I was just so... anxious about it that it was never really enjoyable. And you were already getting naked and everything."

"With my ex," I explain and run my fingers through her hair again. Even though it's just a little past her shoulder blades, it's thick and lush and feels incredible. "We'd already been dating exclusively since we were fourteen so I mean, we knew everything about each other. It was a safe space, not some random thing. Looking back I think it was pretty damn romantic and poetic. But it should have ended in high school."

Lifting her hair and letting it slide through my fingers fills the air with the scent of her shampoo, which is heavy with lavender and something citrusy, like orange. "That's the woman you were married to?"

I nod.

"I'm sorry it didn't work out."

I stare at her as that statement hits me like an anvil because no one has ever said that to me about my marriage ending. Not a single person. She must take my stunned expression as a sign

I'm upset because she backtracks. "I mean, obviously I'm not sorry you aren't married now because I'm not sorry we... did it. And I would be if you were married. I don't want a married guy so I'm glad you aren't but I'm still sorry because you seem like a really good guy and I don't think you went into marriage expecting it to end. I mean no one does, right? So I'm sorry you had a dream die, I guess. Is that weird? Well, anyway. I am. I'm sorry you went through that."

"Can you stop talking so I can make out with you, please?"

"Uh... but we shouldn't."

"Right. We shouldn't." I nod. "But we're gonna."

"Okay. If you insist."

I'm chuckling as I lean in and capture her smiling lips, but we both get serious as soon as our tongues meet. The kiss sucks all the humor out of us and turns it into passion and the next thing I know I've got her pressed up against the wall, her arms pinned above her head, and my rock-hard dick rutted up against her inner thigh because she's wrapped her leg around my hip and over my ass.

She feels so damn good all warm and soft and breathy as she whispers my name against the column of my neck and grips my shoulders with her delicate fingers. "We have to stop."

"We do. I know," I relent verbally but physically I'm still rubbing my dick all over her and she's still bucking her hips a little. "Just tell me you like it."

"I like it. I think of this all the time," she confesses softly, her fingers scraping down my back just hard enough for me to feel it through my shirt. "Running into you, kissing you, doing more than kissing with you..."

"Do you touch yourself when you think of it? Of me?"

I roll my hips and shift to the left so I'm no longer bumping against her inner thigh, now I'm lined up with her sweet center and praising whoever invented the thin gauzy fabric her skirt is made of, because it doesn't make for much of a barrier. I can feel her warmth through it, even though it's bunched up between us.

"Olivia...?"

"I do..." It's such a faint whisper I have to strain to hear her. "I have... touched myself while thinking of you."

Oh God, that confession makes me feral. I swear I might come in my pants right this second. I lean in and claim her mouth with mine. I want to not just explore every inch of her, but claim it, if only for these stolen seconds. My dick bumps her again and a fuse lights. I will explode if I'm not careful. So I do what I do best, make it worse.

My mouth leaves hers and as she pants her way to recovery. I kiss her neck, and her jaw, and when I reach her ear I command, "Show me."

"Wh... what?"

"Show me how you touch yourself."

"Now? Here?" Her eyes are quickly losing the glassy quality as they shift toward the staircase and the dull murmurs of the guests downstairs.

"Now. Here." I kiss her just below the earlobe, where a small fleck of a diamond stud is. "Show me how you touch yourself when you think of the way I fucked you."

Everything about her stills. She's not even breathing, I don't think. I move my head so our eyes can meet and at the same time, I reach up and take her arm, which was resting on my shoulder, and move it down. I pause only long enough to kiss her palm and then I rest it in the crook between us. "Show me."

She blinks once, twice, three... so many times it's just a flutter. Like I'm sure her heart is doing. But Olivia likes being told what to do. She likes being guided and she complies like the perfect student that she is. I watch with lust swirling in my veins as she slips a hand under the waistband of her skirt. I yank on it. It's an elastic waistband so it gives easily without breaking, so I can peer down at her hand as it slips into the pale green cotton underwear she's wearing.

"Ahhh..." A perfect little sound escapes her perfect lips and she sighs.

I take a second to snap my eyes to the stairs, which are blissfully devoid of anyone, and then I focus back on the delicate little hand and those long narrow fingers that are doing a demure dance inside her panties. I wish I was Superman and had x-ray vision because I need to see what's happening in there. "Oh..." she sighs and her back arches a little.

"Are you touching your clit?" I ask and she nods.

"Are you wet?" She nods again. "What are you thinking of?"

"Your tongue," she whispers. "The way you looked when you tasted me for the first time."

That's it. I am going to explode if I don't come. But I don't want to ruin what's happening in front of me so I clench my jaw and use the hand not holding the waistband of her skirt wide open to rub the front of my jeans. I shudder at the contact. She shudders too but it's deeper. Her whole body jerks and a wave of heat climbs up her chest to her neck and cheeks and her back is arched off the wall. She's coming all over her hand. It's beautiful.

When her body starts to slack, I reach between us and slowly pull her hand up. Her index finger and middle finger are glistening and I stare at them like they're the ceiling of the Sistine Chapel. Glorious, incredible, a work of art. She doesn't see my look of awe because her eyes are still shut, and I get it's embarrassment more than euphoria keeping them shut. This is all so new to her. So I show her how okay I am with what just happened. How much I fucking love it. I open my mouth and wrap my lips around her fingers.

Her eyes are wide open now and she's watching with rapt attention as I suck her juices off her fingers. Now it's my turn to groan as the salty perfection that is Olivia Garrison coats my tongue.

Footsteps.

Oh fuck!

I leap back and she launches herself off the wall and past me, clipping my shoulder with her own as she bolts into the bathroom. Olivia manages to quickly close the door without so much as the slightest thump just as Tate appears at the top of the stairs.

I'm not facing him. I'm leaning against the wall, my back to the stairs, thinking of all the gross pictures I've seen of pucks to players' faces, hoping the bloody visions will make the steel rod in my pants wither and die.

"Crew?"

"Hey!" I look over my shoulder. "Just waiting for the bathroom."

"I thought you left," he says and walks around so we're in front of each other. I turn and lift my leg so my foot is against the wall, knee bent, hopefully camouflaging my shrinking, but not shrunk, cock.

"I was gonna, honestly, but there was a line for the bathroom so I came up here to try this one and..." I motion toward the door.

Tate nods. "I came up here looking for Liv. Have you seen her?"

"No. I mean try Dylan's room or... maybe she's the one in the bathroom," I suggest casually. I sound casual, right? And my heart that's beating at twice its normal rate is doing it quietly, right? He can't hear it, can he? "Does she take an obscenely long time in bathrooms? I don't have sisters or female cousins so I don't have any idea."

Tate laughs at my joke but moves to the closed door beside

me and cracks it open. A proud smile slides over his face. "He's dead asleep. And alone. So where is Liv?"

I point to the bathroom door. Tate pauses, his face contorting in anxiety for a second as he lifts his hand. "Please may she be alone in there."

He knocks twice. "Liv?"

The door opens slowly and she appears. She looks one hundred percent normal. Calm, cool, and collected, not like a woman who just orgasmed on her hand and let me lick it clean. I'm stunned by her recovery. Impressed. "Hey. Can't a girl tinkle in peace?"

"Sorry. I was just getting worried," Tate explains and he tilts his head to try and see over her shoulder, into the bathroom, which makes her frown. "You and Carlos just disappeared with Dyllie a while ago and... I just wasn't sure if everything was okay."

"Carlos went home," Olivia explains, pushing the door all the way open and stepping out of the bathroom. "I played with Dylan until he fell asleep and then spent a little time just chilling by myself. You know parties aren't my thing. And then I had to pee."

"Speaking of..." I slip past both of them and gently close the door.

I rest my whole body on it and relax. Phew. That was close.

They continue to talk outside the bathroom door as I pace inside, still trying to get my dick to fully deflate. I can't make out everything they say but the more they talk the harder Olivia's tone gets. Also, the higher Tate's tone gets—like he's worried or guilty or something.

So of course I lean into the closed door.

"I am fine. Look at me? Do I look not fine? Please stop," Olivia is saying, her tone hard. "Because the only thing making me not fine is all the fussing and worry you and your sister are doing. It happened to *me*, okay? Let *me* handle it the way *I* see fit. I don't have to make this okay for you. I never would have even told you if I knew this was how you'd react. I'm handling it my way."

Then there's the stomp of feet down the stairs.

I have no idea what the hell that was about but I have a very strong feeling that I need to know. That I *should* know. That Olivia doesn't *want* me to know.

Chapter 18

Crew

The Quake arena is buzzing. The fans got here early and in droves. We're a sell-out crowd tonight and, in Los Angeles, that's a big deal. I should be more energized than I am, but I just walked out of a meeting with Coach, and he's delaying the official announcement of the new captain... or captains, as he says it will be.

"Look, I just don't want to take away from the moment," Coach Braddock told me as I sat across from him in his office in my pre-game suit. "Let's let this be Burroughs last hurrah, and we'll move you two up from alternate captains to actual co-captains the next home game."

"Sure." It sounds logical on paper. Burroughs, our Captain, retired at the end of the season, but he's coming back for the first home game today because we're raising the Stanley Cup banner.

Every time a team wins the Cup they put a banner in the rafters of the arena. This is only the second banner for the Quake and it's a major moment. Media is covering it from all over North America. So, in theory, what Coach Braddock is saying makes sense. Still, it triggers a tingling that says something is off.

"That is, of course, if you still wanna be co-captain with Nash."

And there's the reason my Spidey-sense was tingling. I stare straight at Coach and examine his expression. It's not dark with annoyance or cloudy with guilt. He hasn't decided he doesn't want to give it to me. He's honestly got doubts I want it. I adjust my shoulders back defensively anyway, like I've done ever since we were seven and the first person, a parent of another player on our baby hockey team, turned to my dad and asked 'So which one is better?'

"You think Nash wants it more than me?"

"I never said that." Coach keeps his tone light even as he leans forward props his elbows on the desk and tents his fingers. He wears a thick, plain titanium wedding ring and no other jewelry. "I asked if you wanted it. Because you've seemed kind of... checked out. Not of the game. On the ice, in practices and preseason games, you've been one hundred percent. I see that clear as day. But the captaincy is more than on-ice performance, and you haven't really stepped up. You gave more as Alternate Captain last year than you are giving this year as figurative Captain."

"I didn't realize that I was still auditioning for the position," I say and yeah, it sounds kinda bitchy. Coach's raised eyebrows are his way of telling me he thinks so too. "I was overly worried about the wrist and I'm in the process of trying to find a new house. And it was preseason. If ever there was a time to be distracted, it's before it counts, right? Now that the season is here, I'm fully focused and ready to lead, Coach. I *want* to lead."

He looks unconvinced but he nods. "If you don't want it, that's fine. It doesn't mean you're any less accomplished than your brother. Know that. You'll always have an A even if you don't want a C."

"I want the C," I say it because it's like a reflex more than an actual desire. This is part of the plan. My dad has big endorsements lined up for the hockey twins, who are co-captains, not just the hockey brothers who play together. Our whole image has been built on the fact that we do everything together. I can't... I mean I don't want to bail on this joint position, which would be one of the first co-captaincies in league history.

"I want it," I repeat and we both stand up.

"Your dad here tonight?" Coach asks as he comes around his desk to walk to his office door with me.

"Yeah."

I reach for the door handle as a wry smile blooms on Coach's rugged face. "Guess I should go say hello. He's a hell of a guy, your dad, but it still chaps my ass I wasn't able to beat his overall goal record."

I smile. "No one is going to beat that for a very long time."

"So that's not on your bucket list?"

"I'm not in this league to best my dad," I reply. "I genuinely just want to play the game my way. And just enjoy the ride."

Coach shakes his head, but he's smiling. "That's an amazing attitude but not one that the world wants you to have. When it comes to this sport, the media and the fans are always trying to pit sons against fathers. Ask mine. It's why my son Dec stopped playing."

"I think Nash felt the pressure more than me," I tell Coach as we turn the corner of the arena hallway towards the VIP. "But never enough to quit."

"I have a feeling you two wouldn't quit for anything."

"Wouldn't quit what?"

I look over my shoulder and Nash is in the hallway a few

feet behind us. He must have come out of the restroom. I smile. "Hockey. No matter how much pressure there is."

"Yeah. Never," Nash says solemnly like he's taking the Boy Scout oath or something.

"You boys better get ready," Coach says before he walks into the lounge and over to my dad who is in the corner of the room, arm around my mom's back.

I give them both a quick wave and head to the dressing room. They got to town last night and Nash and I had dinner with them so it's not our first time seeing them. Still Nash hesitates before following me the few steps across the hall to the dressing room entrance. "Should we go in and let the staff snap a pic or two?"

"You mean Christine?" I question, and he nods. Nash rarely refers to the back office staff by their names. He's always using departments. "PR lady" or "the marketing guy" or "Staff" and it makes me nuts. "She got shots when we walked in and Dad was there to greet us. She says she's more interested in covering the San Diego game and ceremony next month. Wants to put a Quake spin on it so the Saints don't take all the glory."

"Dad played for the Saints," Nash notes the obvious. "It's their glory."

"Yeah, but she says there's a Quake angle, with the way we're making our own legacy away from Dad's team and history," I explain. "Speaking of history, I assume Coach talked to you about his plans for delaying the C announcement?"

Nash nods tersely. "Yeah. And I bet you told him it's okay, didn't you?"

"Well, basically, yeah." I shrug as we dodge half-naked teammates to make it to our own dressing room stalls that are right beside each other this year. "You didn't? I mean it's his call, Nash. He's the coach."

"I said I was disappointed because it would have been great

to do it today and also finally clear up all the media speculation." He sighs as he shrugs out of his pale gray suit jacket. "But I guess the speculation doesn't bother you since you hardly talk to the press. I'm the one fielding all the Captaincy questions."

"I've been asked a few times," I reply defensively. "I just don't let it bother me."

"Must be nice not to care enough to be bothered."

"Stop being a dick, Nash," I snap. "I care. Just because I don't hinge my entire life and personality on it doesn't mean I don't care. Now will you shut the fuck up so I can get ready in peace and enjoy the moment we're about to have? It's going to be epic to watch that banner go up with or without a C on my jersey."

He mutters something I don't hear and turns his back to me as he unbuttons his dress shirt. Good. He's stewing in private. I act like he isn't here as I get out of my suit and into my game gear. I joke with Collingwood tease Hendrix and take over the playlist pumping out the pre-game tunes through the speakers. Everyone is in high spirits except for Nash.

We're playing the Seattle Winterhawks in the opener. They've got Grady Garrison as their goalie. He's another of Tate's billion cousins. I try not to think about facing him on the ice. I definitely avoid thinking about the fact that he is also related to Olivia. It's weird to think of her and him being relatives since I've seen them both naked.

The intro is complete chaos. The crowd is on fire and so loud that I swear my eardrums will ring all the way into next week. Everyone settles down a little as the montage of our last season plays on the Jumbotron. The entire current roster is lined up at center ice staring up at the screen. I feel every moment deep in my chest and I swell with pride. God, it was a magical season. And for the first time, I'm not exhausted thinking about doing it again. I'm energized.

Our former Captain, Burroughs, walks onto the ice when

the video ends and the crowd roars. After going down the line and hugging every guy he hugs me and stands next to me since I'm the last in line. He leans in. "Do it again, Westy One."

Burroughs has been with the team since Nash and I were drafted and he nicknamed us Westy One and Westy Two. I smile but it's tinged with sadness as I realize we'll likely never hear those nicknames again. End of an era.

The banner goes up and I know I can't be the only one fighting emotion. I look up as I skate to the bench. The friends and family section is to the left of our tunnel and there, in the middle of it, is my mom and dad. Mom waves like an excited teenager and wipes her eyes. Dad nods with a proud grin on his face and gives us both a goofy, typical dad thumbs up. My gaze drops and I see a row of familiar faces. The Garrisons. Jordan and his wife and Tenley. Mae Garrison is beside Tenley. Also, Devin Garrison, Tate's uncle is there and Liv's mom. I recognize her mom because I saw her when I was younger at hockey stuff that my dad and the Garrisons attended. Nash and I always begged to tag along. I guess Liv never wanted to go to those things, like league-wide charity events or All-Star games because I would have met her sooner. And two gray-haired people who must be the grandparents. And... between the grandparents, handing them both tissues as they clap and shed tears, is Olivia.

I wasn't expecting to see her here tonight, because she notoriously avoids hockey stuff, but it's a very pleasant surprise. We lock eyes and I flash her a grin. She looks away, but not before I catch a hint of a smile on her lips too.

Unfortunately, the rest of the night isn't filled with pleasant surprises, just unpleasant ones. Like some shitty penalties against us, two very sloppy goals by the Winterhawks, and no response from us, sloppy or otherwise. The game ends with a loss. Two-nothing. We didn't even score. I only got two shots on net and while one hit the crossbar the other was easily gloved by their Grady.

Coach Braddock is more than a little grumbly when he joins us in the locker room after the game. "Not the start we wanted. It's the end that matters and to ensure we immediately turn this around and are in playoff position at the end of the season, I want everyone in the breakdown room tomorrow at eight."

There's not even a murmur of protest even though I know inside, the guys are groaning as hard as their muscles. I am. The breakdown room is where we go over footage of previous games. I have a feeling we will be painfully dissecting every minute of this disaster to ensure it doesn't happen again. Coach heads for the door but not before turning to me and pointing. "I want you taking press today. Nash too. And Garrison and Collingwood. Not Hendrix though. You hit the showers."

Duke nods without lifting his head. He should have had both those goals that sailed over his left shoulder. The fact that Coach doesn't want him to own up to that with the press is weird. He's usually all about accountability.

I towel the sweat off my face and throw a cap on my damp hair. As the media files in I also pull off my pads and my Under Armor. It's ridiculous but I get less of the hard-hitting questions when I'm half naked with my ink on display. And I'll use any trick in the book right now, to make this go easier.

The media is like a school of sharks that smell blood in the ocean. They act like this one loss has set the tone for the rest of the season. Like we're done before we even began. They love to tear down the winners. I hate this part of the job, but I manage to keep my answers positive, calm, and unbothered. Nash does the same but that's Nash no matter what. Robot.

After a dip in an ice tank and a scalding shower, I'm shocked to find that the VIP Lounge is still hopping. Usually after a loss the fans and special guests clear out rather quickly. But there are still at least fifty people in there as I saunter in. And the first person I notice is Olivia. She's sitting at a high-top table with Tenley and Mae.

Olivia's hair is wavy like she used a curling iron and half up in the front. She's wearing jeans and Tate's jersey again. And the fact that I wish it was mine annoys me. When someone wears your jersey it's a sign of attachment I shouldn't want with a bed buddy. I've never wanted it with one before.

"Hey! Come here often?"

The deep voice is directly behind me and when I turn I see nothing but chest. Well, a broad manly chest covered in a soft gray checkered dress shirt, opened at the top to reveal skin dotted with freckles. Grady Garrison is a ridiculous six-foot-five. The tallest in the league. When my eyes reach his face I find it smiling. Warmly. But also very casually. Grady is firmly in the closet and intends to stay there. He told me this the one time we hooked up at the All-Star game last year.

"Yeah. I come here all the time, but not usually too lose to a giant redhead," I reply and flash him a friendly smile because I've always liked Grady in a friendly way. The hookup was nice but there are no lingering feelings about it. I can't say the same for his cousin. "You think just because your last name is Garrison you can infiltrate our private sanctuary?"

My tone is confrontational, in jest, which is why it doesn't make Grady bristle. He runs a hand through his dark copper hair and then scratches his wild ginger beard and says, without missing a beat, "Yeah the name helps. But you should know by now I'm all about infiltrating private places. It's what I do best."

Oh okay. He's going straight there. Do not pass go, do not collect a hundred dollars. Just straight to innuendo-ville. I did not mean to get on this train tonight. My eyes flick over to Olivia who has noticed I'm here. She's sipping what looks like a Coke and eyeing me.

"If I recall, I was the one doing the infiltrating," I reply quietly.

"Well if you want to go over the details, I'm at the Beverly Wilshire tonight," Grady replies. "Team flew out but I'm staying an extra night to see family and I have a photoshoot for Bauer tomorrow."

"I should be all in," I say and pause. Because I'm not. Grady was a great time. He has the added bonus of being in the closet and wanting to stay there so there's zero worry with him. But after being with Olivia... "But I kind of have this thing with someone at the moment and they're here and..."

"Say no more. You already have plans." Grady doesn't look the least bit bothered or wounded by the information. "We're cool."

"Good. Thanks."

"It helps that I just kicked your ass."

"You barely lifted a finger," I argue. "We didn't give you the chance to count in that win."

"Ouch." His giant hand goes to the center of his chest like he's been wounded. "That hurts more than knowing your new bed buddy is here."

"No. They aren't. I mean I did hook up with someone here but have no plans to do it again," I explain and now his eyes are narrowing. "It's just awkward because... well, I just... it's awkward."

"Hey! You giving Grady a hard time?" Olivia asks because suddenly she's right in front of us, reaching past me to hug her cousin. "Great game. Congrats on the shutout? I'm allowed to say that word now, right? Because the game is over?"

"Thanks, Livvy, and yes. Saying shutout is only bad luck if the game isn't finished. You're basically cursing the goalie to let one in." He squeezes her tightly with a warmth that lights up his eyes. Now I'm jealous he gets to hug her. When Olivia turns to me she smiles and gives me a quick jerky wave but nothing else. Which is fair. "Where's the fam jam?"

"Back corner, except for Dad and Uncle J. They're talking with the press." She looks at me again, reaches out, and gently but firmly pokes me square in the middle of my chest. "With your dad."

"What is it? Oldies night?" Grady quips.

"Shooting a quick promo for Bengay," Olivia adds with a dazzling snarky smile.

"As long as it's not for Viagra, it's cool," I add and they both gasp and follow it up with groans. "They're getting celebrity endorsements now. A retired basketball player and a football running back from the nineties have both done Viagra ads."

"Oh gross. Oh my God. I'm going to have nightmares!" Olivia proclaims.

"Liv are you getting scared by the big bad hockey player?" a teasing voice asks, and I see Olivia's mom walking up behind her daughter and hugging her lightly from behind. Liv does what daughters do after the age of thirteen and rolls her eyes while struggling to break free. So her mom turns her attention to me. "Don't tell me you didn't get your dad's disarming charm? I mean, you clearly got his hockey skills, but is that it?"

"Hello, Mrs. Garrison."

"Caplan-Garrison," Liv and her mother correct me at the same time.

"Sorry. Mrs. Caplan-Garrison." I extend a hand and she shakes it more firmly than most men. "Nice to see you again."

I have met Callie Caplan-Garrison a few times but I still feel like we should be formal. Especially now. She smiles as brightly and prettily as her daughter. "Just call me Callie. It's easiest. Sorry about the loss. Tough one, but don't let it steal any momentum. You guys are Cup champions for a reason."

"Thanks. You should be a motivational coach," I smile at her. "And sorry for scaring your daughter."

"Shut it," Olivia warns with a nervous laugh.

"What exactly did you say?" Callie wants to know.

"He was talking about Viagra," Grady replies for me and I fight the urge to cringe. I do not need to be talking boner pills with my bed buddy's mom. Or my best friend's aunt. And she's both.

"That will do it." Callie sighs and kisses her daughter's cheek. "My precious flower."

"I can talk penis pills Mom," Olivia blurts out a little too loudly and a couple of nearby guests glance over. She flushes but keeps going. "He was talking about them *and* Dad though, and even you have to admit that is not something a daughter needs to hear."

"Devin takes Viagra?" Tenley asks innocently, and way too loudly, as she stumbles into the conversation.

"No Ten, he does not. The man needs no help. He's still as... capable as he was the day I married him," Callie explains to everyone.

"Oh God, how did we get here?" Grady scrubs his face, which is turning as pink as Olivia's already is.

"How *did* we get here?" Tenley repeats and her body quakes in over-exaggerated shudders. "And how do we get somewhere else?"

"I made a joke about endorsement deals for the retired players and it's somehow spiraled." I take a step away. "I should go find my mom and brother before I say something else that lands us all on TMZ Sports."

"Don't kid. That shitty site almost ruined me," Mallory adds as she walks over with Mae. "Crew have you met Mae? Callie and Devin's youngest."

"Mayhem Garrison," I say holding out my hand to shake hers. "The next big thing to happen to hockey."

"Shut up," Mae covers her face with her hands for a moment and then sighs looks up at me sheepishly, and shakes my hand. "You read the article?"

"It was in *Sports Illustrated* Mae, not the Boston College school newspaper," I say. "Of course, I read it. Also, Tate mailed everyone on the team copies this summer when it came out."

Mae Garrison was given a two-page article about being a female goalie on the men's hockey team at Boston College where, last year, she crushed the record for most shut-outs in a season. Rumor is they wanted to photograph her in a bathing suit and sandwich the article into the Swimsuit Issue but she refused, which makes her even more badass in my opinion.

My eye leaves Mae, and I see my dad walking in with Jordan and Devin. He's making his way to my mom who is by the candy bar, no doubt popping Sour Patch Kids into her mouth since they're her favorite. "I should get going. Good seeing all of you again."

My eyes linger on Olivia and she smiles just a little bit. Just enough to give me a chub in my dress pants. I turn but Tenley grabs my arm. "Wait! I wanted to say Shelby says hi."

"What?" I turn back to face her and Tenley does a little excited jump grabbing my attention. Her big blue eyes are wide and she claps. "Right! How did I almost forget? Shelby, my cousin that you were interested in, she's single. She never got the chance to make that clear the night you introduced yourself to her. Anyway, she's coming back to town in a couple of weeks for a visit."

Every single set of Garrison eyeballs is burning into me right now. But the two pairs I feel like hot pokers on my skin are Olivia's and Grady's. He clears his throat but his voice comes out in a low rumble. "I'm sorry do we mean Shelby, *my sister?*"

I wouldn't exactly call his tone menacing, but I wouldn't not call it menacing either. I can't look him in the eye. I can't look Olivia in the eye either so I stare at Tenley. "I didn't... I never said I was interested. I was meeting her, yeah, I mean I haven't met all the Garrisons. Every time I think I have, you guys multiply or something. I don't know. Anyway, I... I'm glad she's coming back to town. I hope you guys have fun. She seems like a great girl."

"She's the best," Mallory says.

"A sweetheart," Tenley chirps and nudges Olivia. "Livvy tell him something awesome about Shelby."

"Shelby is great." Liv's voice is small and unconvincing. "I need a glass of water."

She leaves.

"She's my *sister*," Grady repeats.

"Oh don't go being all protective older brother." Tenley waves her hand in front of Grady's face like she's trying to swat a fly. "Shelby can handle herself just fine and you and Crew are friends. I will never understand dudes who don't want the people they love with the people they love. I mean, hello that's a no-brainer."

"Ten has a point," Mallory adds. "I mean, I would love my brother Emmett to settle down with one of my friends. I'm sure Crew would love for Nash to date someone he is friends with."

"Crew wouldn't dare inflict Nash and his wet noodle personality on a friend," Tenley mutters lowly but I catch it.

"It's because they don't want to think about their friends naked with their siblings," Callie tells Tenley. "Trust me I used to want to puke when I would think of Big Bird naked on top of my sweet, kind, gentle older sister."

"And now we're back to talking about sex and our parents," Grady groans, then turns and walks away.

"Mom! No one needs to picture other people having sex.

Just don't do that, for anyone, especially Uncle Jordan. Gross," Mae barks out. I guess Callie calls Uncle Jordan Big Bird.

"What about me is gross?" Jordan asks, walking over.

"I hear Viagra is looking for ambassadors, Big Bird, you in?" Callie blurts out and as everyone erupts in groans and complaints, I disappear into the crowd and swim through it until I find my own, much tamer, family.

Dad is happy to see me and hugs me and tells me to shake off the loss. Mom kisses my forehead and rubs the back of my head and tells me how proud she was to see the banner go up. Nash is Nash, silent and moody. He takes losses like they're his responsibility alone.

We make our way out of the building, curling our way through the concrete halls to the elevator that goes up to player parking. My mom is chattering away about life in Nova Scotia and her business. My mom started her own shoe company when Nash and I were babies and it's been a complete success, as my dad will tell anyone and everyone. He's beyond proud of her. So are Nash and I.

As soon as we step into the parking area Nash comes to a halt and lets out what seems to be a sigh of relief.

"What?"

He looks at me like I'm insane for not reading his thoughts. Sometimes I think he believes the hype the media spews that we're telepathic and that's why we always know when and where the other is going to pass the puck. "The wind!"

Nash jabs a finger into the air. I look around the garage, the side facing the street is wide open, as we're several levels up near the roof of the arena. There is a wind swirling through the openings, picking up garbage and leaves. As the wind hits my face it's warm. "Santa Ana winds."

"Yes! Right?" Nash is too excited for a California weather phenomenon that hits every fall. He's got his phone out and is googling it because he has to be one hundred percent certain. "Yes. Yes! It's the Santa Anas! That explains the loss."

The Santa Anas are warm winds that can occur sporadically from October through March in California. They're rumored to mess with people the way they say a full moon does.

"Those winds are worse than mercury in retrograde," Dad adds.

I roll my eyes and Mom laughs. "You two and your superstitions."

"What caused the loss was the fact that you and I couldn't find the back of the net to save our lives. Tate was skating like an amateur. Our top goalie is out and Hendrix was playing like he was made of Swiss cheese."

"It's the Anas."

Nash has spoken, and I roll my eyes again. We make our way to our cars. Mom and Dad are parked across from Nash who is two cars over from me. "Enough about the winds, your dad and I have to talk to you."

My parents stand side by side in front of their car and my mom loops her arm through Dad's. I get a weird feeling in my gut.

"Okay..." Nash and I say in unison with the same trepidatious tone.

"We were approached to do this thing," Dad says and he seems as uneasy as I feel. Never a good sign. "It's not something we would normally consider but... I mean it's similar to something I've done before but on the team, you know. Never thought... but it's more about your mom and I left the decision to her."

"Don't make decisions in the Santa Anas. They mess with your brain chemistry," Nash interrupts.

"I made the decision before the winds, Nash," Mom says and frowns as the winds in question gust and her blonde hair, which is cut in a simple, straight bob flies up and strands smack her in the cheek. She brushes them back into place before continuing. "We're doing a documentary series."

"More accurately, we've agreed to be filmed for a pilot a documentary series. If it gets picked up, we'll be in the series," Dad adds. He's always the one who talks details.

"For what? Why? How? When?"

"Nash, chill," I mutter and turn to my mom and wait as patiently as I can for an explanation.

To be honest, I'm just as shocked as my brother. This is out of character for them. As Dad mentioned, there was a documentary about hockey that featured the Saints when he was on them. It was right after he got married, when Mom was pregnant with us, and for years afterward Dad bitched about the process and how much he hated it.

He also had some seriously bad experiences with the press when he was dating Mom, and it almost broke them up, so I wouldn't think she'd jump at the chance to be on display in anything like this. Guess I was wrong.

"It's covering hockey life from the family's perspective," she explains and she actually sounds excited about it. "You know I have a pretty unique perspective because I grew up in a hockey family and I married a hockey player."

"So this is a WAGs thing?" Nash looks like he just got a giant whiff of cat piss or something equally rancid.

"No. Not exclusively. They'll also be featuring hockey moms and dads at a junior level. And retired players, like your dad," Mom explains. "And some really difficult cases like the families coping with long-term traumatic brain injuries and stuff."

"So... it's not another Housewives type of garbage?" Nash confirms.

"Absolutely not," Mom says firmly. "I agreed to do it

because it wasn't that, and I can showcase my company and how players' wives have their own careers and ambitions. And I trust the producers because it's being championed by Tenley Garrison."

Well, that's a shocker. I wonder why Tate has never mentioned this. Neither has Olivia. Or Grady.

"Jordan Garrison is signing on too," Dad interjects. "And Landon Casco and his family."

"He didn't mention it," I mutter. Landon is on Injury Reserve and not currently playing since he was diagnosed with leukemia at the end of last season. But he's still in contact with the team regularly, despite opting for treatment in San Francisco near his family. I text him a lot privately too because he's a good friend.

"I won't do it," Nash blurts out suddenly. "Dad, we've talked about this before. It's not good for our brand. You said it. Stick to only sports publications and stations for interviews and never talk personal stuff. We don't even have social media for that reason."

"We're not asking you two to take an active part," Mom assures us. "But they will be filming your dad's jersey retirement ceremony."

"Fuck."

"Nash!" I snap because for the golden robot boy to swear it's a big deal, and this really isn't. I mean sure, I don't like it either, but it's Mom and Dad's decision and it's not like Nash is featured. He'll be in this one segment. "It'll be one extra camera at an event filled with them. Stop being a bitch."

"Really, Mr. Torchalicious?" Nash snarks and glares at me. "You think more cameras on you is a good idea. Imagine if they'd been filming this when your wife left you and you lit your house on fire."

"Are you really fucking going there?" I bark. "Shut up!"

"Both of you stop. Now." Dad's voice is deep and hard. He's not messing around. His dark eyes dart around the parking garage, which is empty except for the security guard down at the other end. "Never mind the winds, you two are never going to lead a team together if you snap like this other everything."

"We weren't going to say anything but I see no choice now," Mom adds and her blue eyes are filled with worry. "Something's changed between you two and I don't like it. It hurts my heart to see you two like this."

"I haven't changed anything," Nash says. "Not how I talk to him or what I say or what I do. He's different and I don't know why."

I grit my teeth so hard my jaw aches. I will not get into this here. And not now, with Mom and Dad. And I just kind of had a grenade lobbed at this thing with Olivia/Shelby/Grady and I need to figure out how to clean up the mess. So I just want to extract myself from this as soon as possible so I can think.

"I'm cool with being on camera a little for this thing you're doing Mom," I say and lean in and kiss her cheek. I hug my dad briefly and nod at Nash, trying not to scowl as I do it. "Sorry. I really need to get home. Let's talk more tomorrow."

"See?" I hear Nash say like a whining child as I slide into the driver's seat. I punch the *Start Engine* button to drown out anything else he might say about me.

Nash doesn't know why I'm pissed off at him? For real? He's the biggest over-thinker I know and he couldn't piece this mystery together? I think deep down Nash knows why I'm angry and he feels too guilty to admit it. I mean what would that conversation even be?

Me: Hey so I know you know I'm bi and you haven't said a word about it.

Nash: Yeah well it was either tell you I think you're disgusting or keep quiet.

Me: Thought so. Thanks for being honest. Been nice knowing you. I'm asking for a trade now, from this team and from this family. Bye.

I do not have the time or emotional energy for that right now. I have to figure out what to do about both Olivia and Grady thinking I want Shelby. That's not a misunderstanding I can let simmer because, even though they're both supposed to be nothing but bed buddies, I don't want them hurt. And then there's the fact that they're both related and don't know about each other.

Sigh. How did my uncomplicated life get so complicated?

Chapter 19

Liv

"You're different."

"Stop."

"No. You are!"

I don't want to look my mother in the eye but I know I have to because if I don't it's a sign of weakness. She'll take that as proof she's right and then she'll dig and dig until she uncovers the truth. And I have too many secrets to even begin to worry about which one she'll unearth.

"I'm happy Mom. I'm content. Isn't that all you're supposed to care about as a parent?" I ask and lock eyes with her. Even I have to admit sometimes it's like looking in a mirror. Same feeling when I look at Mayhem, only it's a fun house mirror that makes me taller and leaner and giddy about hundred-mile-an-hour black rubber discs flying at my face.

Now Mayhem is pretending not to listen to us as I putter around the kitchen making breakfast. Mom watches from a bar stool at the peninsula and Mayhem sits in the swinging chair Tenley insisted on putting in the corner of the dining room reading a book.

"I do care about that. I also care about the why," Mom replies and suddenly puts down her coffee and lifts her hair off her neck, swearing like a trucker under her breath. "Hot flash. They're trying to kill me."

"I hear they're like someone turning your blood to gasoline and lighting a match in your heart," Mayhem says, her eyes never lifting from the page she's reading.

"Yes. Only worse." Mom sighs.

"Are you in perimenopause?" Tenley asks.

"Full-on menopause," Mom replies. "And it's hell. I actually had a hot flash during sex the other day. Threw your father right off of me and ran to the window for air. Thought I would literally burst into flames."

"Like I wish I could after hearing that story," Mayhem says and squeezes her eyes shut.

"TMI Mother! Seriously." I groan and flip the eggs in the pan with a flourishing swoop of the pan.

Tenley whistles, impressed. Mom has seen my cooking skills a million times before so she says nothing and sticks to the topic. "Relax, baby. I'm lucky I still have a sex drive. A lot of women lose that with menopause."

"You better find yours soon, Liv, before it's gone."

Great. Now Mayhem is jumping on the make-fun-of-Olivia train. That's a new twist and I don't like it. "Says the girl who gets her only romance from paperbacks."

"I work with hot sweaty men every single day," Mayhem counters. "Eye candy is enough at the moment. Plus it's hard to find a date when you're the only chick on the men's team. College boys have such fragile egos the last thing they want to do is woo the woman who can bench press them, or who pals around with the biggest, toughest guys on campus."

"You keep doing you, Mayhem," Mom says proudly as she

continues to fan herself. "I was the scariest girl in Silver Bay and landed the best man in town so don't dim your light for anyone."

I carefully plop a perfectly cooked feta fried egg on top of each of the toasted sourdough slices slathered in Tenley's famous smashed avocado and tomato with Everything Bagel seasoning and homemade hot sauce. Then I drop the plates on the peninsula in front of my mom and the empty seats. I stand on the other side to eat mine, since we only have three bar stools. Mayhem abandons her book on the swinging chair and joins us.

We chat about life. Mom updates us on the latest with the extended family and I'm shocked and pleased to learn my brother Conner is shopping for engagement rings for his girl-friend Mac. Mom is teary-eyed as she explains. "He's between two different rings, but he won't ask my advice. He does however have lengthy calls with your dad as he strategizes how to ask her. He doesn't want it to be a big deal but he doesn't want it to be a small deal either. And he's working on the courage to ask Alex for permission."

"Ugh. That's so archaic," Tenley groans. "I'm not the prop-erty of Jordan Garrison. My husband isn't asking permission."

"It's a symbolic thing," Mom argues. "And as someone who didn't have a dad to ask, I thought it was absolutely adorable when your dad asked for my permission to marry Jessie. Well, he didn't so much ask as tell me it was going to happen and please do not kill him."

We all laugh because that is so on-brand for the aggressive but oddly loving relationship Mom has with Uncle Jordan. Tenley is still frowning though.

"Ten, Uncle J will literally murder a dude who doesn't show that level of respect but intends to marry you. You know it."

"What if I elope?"

Mom gasps like Tenley just confessed to murder and drops

her fork with a dramatic clang. She points at Tenley first but then her finger moves to each of us. "Not one of you should ever entertain the idea of an elopement. Garrison weddings are magical, joyous events and we will not be denied one. We're too close a group to exclude each other from important life events."

"I don't think it's that big a deal," Tenley mutters and shoves food into her mouth, chewing aggressively. She swallows her bite. "What if it's just a starter marriage? It won't even count so you guys don't have to be there."

"Who in this family would go into a marriage knowing it won't last?" Mom asks. "It's such a huge financial and legal thing not to mention it's sacred. I was so scared of the emotional significance I didn't ever want to do it."

"It doesn't always have to be emotional."

"Yes Tenley it does," Mom counters. "You won't understand that until you do it, but that's fine. You will figure it out one day. Do it right the first time and there are no regrets. And even if the marriage ends up ending, like Devin's marriage to Conner's mom, we're all still glad there was a big family wedding because Conner can look back on those pictures and see the love."

I think about that as I sip my coffee and slice into my avocado toast again to devour the last few bites. Am I about to become an Ashleigh? Can I handle it if Crew starts dating Shelby? I was up half the night mulling over the feelings that swirled inside me after that tidbit was dropped like a lead balloon. Up until that moment, I thought I was very cool with everything that had happened with Crew. And I was even convincing myself that if we hooked up one or two more times, it would be okay. Good, even. And that I could do that—*him*—a few more times and stay chill about it. Crew made it clear he doesn't date, so that was off the table but it wasn't just off the table for me, which made it comforting. It made it okay. But now I hear he's interested in dating someone who isn't me and it hurts. The fact that the person he is interested in was a relative makes it way worse, of course. And I am both horrified and angry at him. I mean, it would be like me dating Nash. How insanely inappropriate and uncomfortable would that be?

"Livvy why did your whole face just go dark?" Mom is way too in tune with me. I used to love it when I was little and she could read me like a book. Now, not so much. "See? Something is going on. Talk to me, goose."

"I do not understand why you would call me goose."

"You need to watch *Top Gun.*"

"Miles Teller is so freaking hot in that," Tenley interjects and makes a chef's kiss gesture with her lips and hand. "That's my type. Tall, dark, handsome. Fighter pilot, not a stupid hockey player. Emotional. Not a robot. Hey, we should go to San Diego and hang out at a bar by the airbase. Catch ourselves some real-life Miles Tellers. Who's in?"

"Miles Teller is *not* in *Top Gun,*" Mom corrects and rolls her eyes as she pops some toast into her mouth. "He was in the sequel. Watch the original. And getting back on topic, I need some alone time with my baby girl *numero uno.* You two make yourself scarce when breakfast is done."

"I have to go to campus anyway and discuss my final grade with my teacher," Tenley says as she licks her now empty fork and hops off the stool, carrying her plate to the sink.

"Can you drop me off at the Orangetheory up the street?" Mayhem asks, carrying her own dish to the sink.

"Sure thing."

They file out of the kitchen and a few minutes later, as I'm loading dishes in the dishwasher, they leave the house. Mom is staring at something on her phone. "Your uncle Big Bird and your Aunt Jessie agreed to be in Tenley's documentary about the Pro Hockey World."

"Wow? Why?" I ask stunned. "And please don't say you and

Dad are doing it. I do not think you have a safe for TV mouth, Mom. I love you but some of the stuff that you blurt would get you in trouble with the FCC."

She laughs and puts her phone down on the bar, reaching for her coffee. "I agree and so does Ten, which is why she didn't ask me. Don't worry, no cameras for us. But I wanted you to know. The Westwoods are also doing it. And I think a Braddock or Casco or someone else is too."

"Oh, cool." Crew is going to be on TV, maybe while dating my cousin. This just keeps getting better and better.

"There's that darkness again," Mom notes and I turn away from her, bringing the frying pan to the sink. "Leave that and come sit. We need to talk. I don't think you're okay."

I can't tell her about the attack. Not yet. I'm not ready. But my mom is relentless and has the strongest motherly instincts of anyone I've ever met so she will not let this go until I give her something. I take a deep breath and turn from the sink, leaving the pan to soak.

Mom has moved the coffee machine and is refreshing both our cups. She glides to the fridge and her long pale yellow sundress swooshes after her. I zone in on the tattoo on her inner wrist. It's an outline of three heart balloons, their strings overlapping here and there. Inside each heart is a year, the birth years of Conner, myself, and Mae.

It's not her only tattoo. She has another one at the base of her neck, the Japanese symbol for family which she got long before we were born. That's the one thing we have in common, more than our appearance. The fact that both my mom and I have always believed family is sacred. And we both have always known we wanted one of our own. Crew is divorced and never wants to remarry. He doesn't trust women at all anymore. That means he's not fit to fulfill my wants and needs. Shelby has never expressed any need for marriage, children, or a family of her own. Maybe she is the better fit for Crew.

"Hey, overthinker," Mom calls out softly, pulling me from my mental spiral. "Let's chat it out over coffee."

She holds out my cup to me and I walk over and take it and follow her into the living room. As she sits at one end of the couch, I sit at the other and we both tuck our legs up at the same moment like twins. Twins... Crew...

"I'm not a virgin anymore by the way so you don't get to keep teasing me," I announce and it feels incredibly good to get that out. "But I am not ready for the entire fam to know so, like, don't tell anyone, please. I know that's asking the world from you but please."

Mom blinks, almost like I just tossed cold water on her face, but she recovers quickly and nods. "I don't think I can stop teasing and keep it a secret at the same time. If I'm not razzing you, the way I do everyone about everything, someone in our family will get suspicious. Probably, Tenley, you know how she makes it her job to unearth secrets."

"She's been busy lately with trying to make the doc happen," I tell Mom. "She's hardly ever home and when she is, she's locked in her room. Very unTenley-like, but exactly what I need right now."

"So... I guess I don't get to ask for details." Mom sips her coffee as I make a face at her. She smiles wryly. "I'm not saying *gory* details. I don't need to know his dick size or anything. I don't want to know anything that will make it impossible to keep a straight face when I meet him. I just... was it okay? Did you enjoy it? And be honest, I swear I will never tease you about this, no matter what you say."

"It was great," I say and a smile blooms over my pink cheeks before I can stop it. I'm trying to keep this vague and casual but clearly failing.

Mom grins back and sighs, putting a hand on her chest. "Oh thank God! I know my first time was subpar at best and I thought if that happened to you, after waiting as long as you have, you'd write off sex forever. Not that there is anything wrong with that. If you were pan or whatever I wouldn't care but I just want you to be happy with yourself."

"Mom, a pansexual is someone who is attracted to people regardless of sex," I correct gently. "Someone who isn't sexually attracted to anyone is Asexual."

"Okay, that. If you were that, I'd be fine, I just want you to be whatever makes you happy." Mom reaches out and grabs my hand giving it a squeeze. "But I'm glad you had good sex. With a man?"

"Yes." I laugh. "And before you say it, I know you'd be fine if it was with a woman."

"I would." Mom nods. "So this man... when do I get to meet him?"

"I will not be disclosing any more information at this time," I announce. "Or ever. Just know that it was exactly what I wanted and I have zero regrets."

Well, except for the fact that I'm not dating him.

Yeah, that's right. I realized last night, when it was revealed that Crew was interested in Shelby, that I wanted him to date me, even if I hadn't heard about this apparent infatuation with my cousin, I think the reason I have been keeping my distance from Crew a little when he's made it clear I could call him up and jump into his bed again, is that I don't want to be his bed buddy. It isn't enough for me.

"So how long have you been dating him?" Mom asks, ignoring what I just said.

"He is not my boyfriend. I'm not dating him," I reply and sip my coffee again, hoping it looks as casual as I am trying to be.

"It's not an ongoing thing. That was what I wanted. No more questions."

"Oh. Okay." Mom pinches her eyebrows. "No judgment but... did you really wait all this time to give it up to a one-night stand?"

"You're right, I didn't think I wanted that," I agree and try not to sound too annoyed because I'm the one who opened up this conversation. I'm not sure why I did. I guess, after the sting of last night, I just need to talk to someone about it, even vaguely, before it becomes a memory. "But I changed my mind and I'm glad I did."

Mom doesn't look like she's buying it. She keeps shooting me leery looks. "As long as you're happy and safe. I just... I would like to know what changed your mind."

"It just started to feel like pressure. Like it was this fragile thing that was destined to shatter but that might just break when I didn't want it to, you know?" I say and wrap both hands around my mug because one hand doesn't seem like enough suddenly. The mug is getting heavy and my hands are shaky.

"I sort of understand, maybe." Mom puts down her mug and sweeps her long chocolate hair back behind her shoulders. The silver strands, which seem to have doubled in the last year but still aren't enough to call her salt-and-pepper, glint in the sun coming in through the window behind the couch. "I was hell-bent on losing mine from the age of fifteen. I was flirting with every guy in Silver Bay. Looking back I have to admit that I took rebelling to a new level because I was so angry at my grandmother for abandoning your aunts and me. Anyway, what made me finally do the deed was that a guy I fooled around with... he tried to do it without my consent. Luckily your Uncle Big Bird and your Uncle Luc had taught Rose, Jessie, and I had to throw a proper right hook and it was enough to stop him and get the hell out of there. But that spurred me on to find someone I wanted to do it with and do it with sooner rather than later. Take charge of my own destiny type of thing, I guess."

I nod slowly. Why do I suddenly feel like I might burst into tears? Why is it hard to swallow? Why can't I take a deep breath?

Mom leans forward, slowly, deliberately. Her voice is even and calm, two things it rarely is. It's unnerving rather than soothing. "Honey, did something happen to make you want to take charge of your own destiny?"

The doorbell rings. I jump ten feet, spilling coffee on the throw rug. Mom scrambles off the couch. "I'll clean that."

I swear and put my mug down on the coffee table, shaking my hand because it's been scalded by the coffee as I rush to the door. I'm not expecting anyone so I'm hesitant to open the door. I rock up on my tip toes to peek through the peephole and see Crew.

"What the heck!" I whisper as my mom rushes back into the living room with a dishtowel and cleaner she must have found under the sink.

"Who is it?" Mom asks. "Is it a serial killer? Do I have to find something to clobber someone with?"

"No." I shake my head. "I don't think it's for me. I'm just going to ignore it."

I start to walk away from the door but Crew knocks again and then speaks. "Olivia?"

Both of Mom's eyebrows shoot to the ceiling. And she stops scrubbing the stain. I shake my head and hold a finger up to my lips. Her mouth opens but she shuts it without a word. Then her eyes move. To the window. Our building is one of those classic two-story jobs with outdoor hallways that look onto the pool and courtyard. We have a big window next to the door that looks over the courtyard, and the open hallway runs right by it.

"The curtains are open." I make the realization out loud. Mom nods. "He sees me."

"He does," Mom confirms and waves happily at Crew.

She stands up and walks over and opens the front door. Now there's nothing but the metal storm door between me and Crew, and my mom. How could this be more awkward? "Hey Mrs.... Callie. Hi Olivia."

"Hey. What's up, dude?" I ask like he's a bro and we're homies from the same frat house.

My mom's eyebrows shoot up again. She reaches past me and opens the storm door, motioning for Crew to come in. "Please excuse Olivia's manners. They must be on the floor with her coffee."

Crew looks baffled but only slightly, which is a feat. I glare at my mom who smiles innocently at me.

"Olivia, I... I was hoping I could get a minute with you. Alone," he starts and then he clears his throat. "And spoiler alert, I might need more than a minute."

"I have company."

"I'm your mother, not the queen of England," Mom butts in like only a mom can do. "I'm going to go tidy the kitchen. Why don't you two go for a walk."

"It's Los Angeles, Mother," I remind her with the tone of a moody teenager. "People don't walk."

"We could go for a drive," Crew suggests, shoving his hands in his pockets and gluing his eyes to the hardwood. Guess I'm not the only one acting like a moody teenager.

"Yes. Go do that. I'll tidy." Mom grins like she's Cupid and her arrow hit someone right in the ass. I glare at her again and she shrugs then waves the coffee-stained cloth she's holding. "Have fun. Make good choices!"

"Oh my God," I hiss and roll my eyes. Crew hands me a coat off the row of hooks next to the door. It's actually Tenley's faux leather bomber, but it's cute and coincidentally goes well with the jumpsuit I have on so I just shrug into it instead of arguing.

I send one last glare at my mother from over my shoulder as Crew exits the apartment, holding the storm door open for me. She winks at me, gives me a thumbs-up, and actually mouths two words very clearly—'Great choice!'

She knows. She knows I slept with Crew Westwood. Kill me now.

Chapter 20

Liv

I don't know what we're doing. I mean, he's interested in Shelby. Why is he here? It must be because he doesn't want me to tell anyone about what we did. Maybe he's worried it will ruin his chances with Shelby.

We get to the sidewalk in front of the building and I stop walking. He is a few feet ahead of me and doesn't realize I'm not behind him for another couple of feet. He turns back to find me.

"I don't think we need to do this," I tell him, trying to be strong and ballsy like the woman tidying my kitchen.

He starts walking back toward me. He's a vision, honestly. Crew is wearing a pair of jeans and a navy T-shirt that tugs and pulls in all the right places, and he's got a camel-colored corduroy jacket in his hand. "What don't we have to do? Talk?"

"Yeah. I mean I know why you're here." I shrug and force my eyes to stay on his face, even though the afternoon sun is catching the golden strands of his hair and between that and the darker stubble on his jaw, it's making his eyes look brighter and lighter than I have ever seen them. His face is just flat-out devastatingly handsome.

"Okay, I'll play. Why do you think I'm here?"

His voice is light but the look on his face says he is not, in fact, amused. He folds his arms over that lovely chest of his. "You know what I heard last night," I say square my shoulders and clench my fists so I don't fidget or shake. "You are interested in dating my cousin, Shelby. You're here to talk about whether or not I'm going to tell her about what we did. Because I, unfortunately, have the power to mess up your shot."

"Really?"

I can't read him right now. He looks equal parts smug and annoyed and I don't know exactly what to do with that. I wish I dated more complex men... or had more complex relationships. I'm once again a fish out of water.

"As I recall you're the one who doesn't want anyone to know that we hooked up," Crew reminds me as the wind picks up and slaps me in the face with a warm gust.

"You have a teammate rule you didn't want to get caught breaking too, remember?" I wait for a response. All I get is a half-nod. "Can you just tell me one thing? Why would you break the rule for Shelby and not me?"

"I did break the rule for you."

"You didn't know you broke it."

"And then I did know. And then I broke it again."

Palm fronds above us rustle their discontent as the wind picks up again. I brush my hair back as it hits my cheek. "I'm bad at this."

"At what? Going for a drive. Yeah, you kinda suck at it because you're rooted to the ground like the cement dried around your feet," Crew says. "Can you walk to my bike already?"

"Bike?"

"Yeah. I'm on my motorcycle today. It was easier to cut through Sunday traffic." Of course, the hot, tatted hockey star who looks like he could have been Charlie Hunnam's stunt double in *Sons of Anarchy* has a motorcycle. Of course.

He starts walking backward, his eyes still on me, his hand stretched out toward me. "Come on, Fireball. Your mom told you to go for a ride with me and you are not the type of girl to disobey a parent."

"I can be," I counter but I'm already walking, following him.

He grins. "Oh I've seen the glimmer of the bad girl in you and I approve."

Now I'm the color of the fire hydrant across the street. Crew comes to a halt one building down in front of an intimidatingly large matte black Honda Shadow. He unclips two helmets and hands me one. "Do you know how to buckle this up correctly?"

I take the helmet and drop it on my head. "Nope. Not a clue. You're my first biker dude."

He chuckles and starts doing up the strap under my chin. His fingers keep brushing my skin and I force myself to ignore how much I like it. He's not mine. Never was and isn't going to be. Stop with your nonsense, heart.

"I like being your first in things, Olivia," he says in a raspy whisper and he gives the strap a final tug and steps back to put on his own helmet.

It feels weird standing here with the giant heavy thing encasing my head. It's way heavier than a bicycle helmet, which is the only other kind I've worn. He straddles the motorcycle, grabbing handles, pulling it upright, and kicking the stand back with the heel of his boot. "Okay, hop on."

I look at the sliver of seat left behind that sculpted bubble butt of his. I cock my head in hesitation. "There isn't enough room."

"There is," he promises. "You're going to have to get real close, wedge yourself right up against me. You're good at that, Fireball."

Helmets are hot. I'm hot. I fight the urge to fan myself. Instead, I slam down the tinted visor grab his shoulders, and, as gracefully as possible, haul myself up and onto the back of the motorcycle. He's right, I have to squish right up against him. My crotch is pressed up to the back of that hard firm ass of his like I'm trying to become one with it. Every inch of his back is touching every inch of my front. My hands are gripping his sides lightly, but he reaches back and tugs them forward until my hands meet between his pecs.

"Hold tight," he says and the bike roars to life, and before I can blink we're gliding down my street.

I'm slightly scared but in that good, rollercoaster way. I feel safe with Crew. We get to Sunset and he turns left onto the busy street. The warm wind has the ends of my hair flying everywhere as buildings and billboards blur. A few blocks later he stops at a light and as he puts his feet down to steady the bike while we wait for the green he turns his head. "You okay back there?"

"Yeah, but I thought you wanted to talk?"

"I do. We should probably pull over somewhere, but I like having you wrapped around me like a koala bear," he says and I smack his chest with the flat of my hand and suppress a giggle.

"I am not a koala," I reply. "Turn right at Crescent Heights. I know a place we can talk."

"You got it, Fireball."

The light changes and Crew takes off. He follows my directions and as Crescent Heights turns into Laurel Canyon I take my hand off him long enough to point to the low, squat orange and teal building pressed into the foot of the hills. He signals and gently glides the bike around the side of the iconic little bodega to the parking lot.

As soon as he cuts the engine, I peel myself off the bike and Crew. I fumble with the tie but finally manage to get it undone and yank off the helmet. He's watching me with amused eyes. I try to smooth my hair and hand him the helmet.

He locks both helmets on the bike and looks around. "What is this place?"

"Are you serious?" Does he really not know? "The Laurel Canyon store."

"Okay. Cool. We're shopping." He shrugs. "Like a grocery store? Is my Fireball out of sugar?"

He used *me*. That feels unfair. Actually, it feels good and that's why it's unfair. I bite my lip and start toward the store. "Follow me. It's a literal tragedy that you don't know what this place is. Consider this a gift. I'm about to introduce you to a piece of music history and the best millionaire's shortbread you've ever tasted."

"What now?"

As we enter the store, I explain to him everything I know about this little piece of Los Angeles history. How the store was a haven for the Southern California Rockers in the seventies. How David Crosby used to spend days wandering the porch, and Jim Morrison lived behind the place. How the Eagles would roll down from the hills and pick up beers or smokes to head back up the hill and jam some more at whatever house they were squatting in while they struggled to get gigs. How Joni Mitchell would shop and flirt here.

"Wow. I think you were born in the wrong decade," Crew says with a soft smile as we wander the cramped aisles of the tiny store, browsing all the wonderful and sometimes ridiculous items that are crammed onto the shelves. There's Cheerios next to Jesus candles. Brightly colored containers of Cuban coffee next to pastel mugs that say 'Give Peace a Chance'. "I can tell by the way your whole face is lit up like a Christmas tree that this place really speaks to you."

"I'm an Art Education major, remember?" I touch a pile of

Teddy Bears wearing sunglasses. They're soft and velvety. "Music is art. In fact, I'm currently teaching a music and music history class at a middle school as part of my internship."

"Do you love it?"

"I do." I smile. Crew smiles back. It's not sexy or sarcastic or sly. It's just a smile. Simple, pure, and gorgeous.

"I can tell you love it because you look like I feel when I'm talking about hockey."

God, this is a good moment. I am in love with this moment. This connection... this... but wait. We're not here to connect. We're here to disconnect. He likes Shelby. I inhale sharply and step around him—no easy task in the cramped space. "Let's grab some chai and that shortbread I was mentioning."

I march up to the counter in the deli department, where they also have all the fancy coffee equipment of a Starbucks and a healthy baked goods section. The girl behind the counter gives me a warm smile because she's seen my face before. I used to come in here a few evenings a week to study. "Hi Rosie, can I get a chai tea, two millionaire's shortbread squares, and... what do you want to drink?"

I glance over at Crew. He shrugs. "Surprise me."

I turn back to Rosie. "Two chais please."

Rosie punches it in grabs two of the pre-wrapped shortbread squares and hands them to me as I dig out my money. "Haven't seen you in a while. Thought maybe you moved away."

"Nope. Still here."

"No late-night study sessions anymore?" Rosie asks. "I liked having you here until close. Kept me company. Now it's just me and Bobby McGee and he doesn't curl up on me like he does to you. Just keeps trying to scratch me, the rat bastard."

"One day I'll be back," I promise. "Give Bobby my love."

She finishes making the teas and slides them across the counter. Crew reaches over me and picks them up and then follows me to the little porch on the front. There are rickety old sets of tables and chairs out there. I pick a bright green set in the corner.

"Wait!" I command as he sits his giant self down in the teeny chair across from me. I take a sip of the chai and then start unwrapping the shortbread. "If we are going to have this painfully awkward conversation, I am going to at least have some of this deliciousness in my belly to distract me."

"What painfully awkward conversation are we having?" Crew wants to know as he blows on his tea. It's totally unmanly and absolutely adorable at the same time.

"The one where you ask me if it's a problem if you date my cousin," I say, and already I want to die of humiliation. I bite into the shortbread. It's not helping the way I want it to but it is delicious. "And I say it is a problem for me and then you remind me how a one-night stand works and that I don't have a right to any feelings because one-night stands don't matter. And as you said before, I was the one who wanted to keep this private. I don't get to change the rules now. And I need—"

"You need to stop talking."

My mouth is frozen, half open, but silent as requested. Crew sips his tea. "This is weird. It's like someone heated up wheat grass. I don't think it's my thing."

He puts it down on the table. I reach across and pick it up. "More for me."

That amused look is back in his eyes, which glints with copper tones in the sunlight shining down on us. "Are you done now? Can I speak?"

I nod and then immediately shake my head. "Nope. I'm not done. You can date Shelby if you want to date Shelby. She'll never leave Silver Bay. She's very happy and has a great job. But maybe that distance makes dating easier for a self-proclaimed commitment-phobe like you."

"When did I proclaim myself commitmentphobic?"

"You said you don't want anything after your ex," I remind him and he averts his eyes. Yup. I nailed it. "I remember everything. Anyway, I can forget this ever happened and you go be with... whoever. Even if it's Shelby. My cousin. A direct blood relative in a family that's closer than peas in a pod. But yeah. Whatever."

I stare off at Laurel Canyon Boulevard where there's a constant stream of cars zipping to and from the San Fernando Valley. I'm trying to look cool and unaffected. I sip my tea. I bite off a piece of my shortbread. But he stays silent so long that I have to steal a glance at him.

Crew is staring at me with the most deliciously intense gaze. Like he's trying to peel off my clothes using telepathic superpowers. And it's so hot that I find myself wishing he had those powers. I bite my lip. He leans forward, big forearm covering almost the whole top of the table, and with his free hand he presses his thumb to my chin and tugs my lip free from my teeth. "You can't forget our time together."

"No. I can't. But I can pretend I forgot."

"What if I don't want you to."

"If you tell Shelby we... did it... she won't date you," I warn him.

"That would be a tragedy if I wanted to date Shelby," he replies and leans back in his seat, finally unwrapping his shortbread. I'm already halfway through mine. "I don't. I have never had a single ounce of interest in Shelby Garrison."

"Why not?" I demand. "Shelby is gorgeous and she's smart. She's got a great career and big heart and an incredible sense of humor. She's also sporty. Loves hiking in the summer and skating in the winter. She and Harlow were state figure skating champions you know. Who doesn't want a champion?"

He chuckles. It's such a deep, satisfying sound. "So you're not just okay with me dating Shelby, you want me to."

"What? No!"

"Then stop shaming me for not being interested. FYI I went into the lounge to find you that night, but Tenley saw me and I couldn't tell her that so I stupidly asked to meet your cousin and she took it the wrong way." He bites into the shortbread and after chewing a second he moans and I feel it like he just licked my clit. Sweet Lord, this man. I have never been this physically reactive to someone. How does he do this to me? "This is incredible? What's it called again?"

"Millionaire's shortbread," I say and smile at his praise. "Rosie makes it herself. Not hockey diet-friendly though. It's got a whole pound of butter in it, which is probably why Bobby McGee hates Rosie. He loves butter and always wants to steal a bar from behind the counter and she has to shoo him off because of the chocolate layer. He can't have chocolate."

"Who the hell is this Bobby McGee?"

I scan the area and find him in one of his favorite haunts, under a potted palm in the far corner of the porch. I point. Crew's eyes land on the long-haired tabby cat. "A stray that showed up at the store as a kitten. They lock him in at night so he doesn't get eaten by coyotes or smoked by a car."

He nods. "The name is because of the history of the store?"

"Yes. But more specifically Rosie thinks his meowing sounds like Janis Joplin singing." I lean forward and whisper the next part because I know it sounds crazy but I don't not believe it. "Rosie swears the cat is Janis reincarnated."

Crew's eyes widen and he slides them back to the cat. Then back to me. He is trying so hard not to laugh. "Who are we to say no?"

"Exactly." I break first, giggling, and he lets his laughter fly.

We giggle so long and hard that I have to wipe tears from

my eyes. He finishes the last of his shortbread in one big bite and after he swallows he says, "How can something that feels so easy be so complicated?"

I blink, the cup of chai against my lips. "Huh?"

He motions to me and then to himself. "We're easy. Together. This.... isn't work. It's easy. I've never had an easy relationship."

I don't want to say anything to that because I don't want to ruin the feeling that's washing over me. It's warm, sweet, happy. I smile and sip the last of my tea.

"But it's also fucking complicated as fuck," he announces and balls up the shortbread wrapper. "If we go public with this then I have to explain to Tate and the team, I broke the teammate policy. And I mean... there are other factors."

He pauses and doesn't tell me what those other factors are. Instead, he tosses the wrapper through the air and it swishes into a garbage can across the patio. Pleased with himself he grins and then stands and gives me his hand. "Let's get out of here."

I take his hand and stand. He yanks me to his chest so unexpectedly I squeak but then his lips are brushing mine and I sigh, tip my head, and kiss him. He softly cups my cheek and kisses me back, long and hard and like no one is watching. But someone is watching—Bobby McGee. I catch his judgy glare as we break apart.

Hand-in-hand we walk back to the bike. "So Inky, are you saying you want to go public with this one-night stand?"

"I'm saying... if you're game, I'd like to keep doing this, for an undesignated amount of nights," he replies. He turns and pulls me into his chest again. "And maybe some days too."

This is not happening... I never get everything I want exactly when I want it. I'm not that girl. I'm okay with it. I mean, my life works out, no complaints.... I mean no big ones. But this... Crew is willing to test the dating waters, after everything he's been through, with me. I'm getting what I have chastised myself for dreaming of. Hoping for.

He snaps his fingers in front of me, a careless smile on his lips. "Are you in shock? Was I that much of a long shot?"

"The longest shot, the biggest risk, the one-in-a-million shot in the dark." I can't stop smiling. My cheeks hurt. My heart is pounding. I feel like dancing.

"We should go back in there and buy a lottery ticket." He winks, cheeky bastard.

He pulls me to him and kisses me again. It's long and slow and warmer than the wind swirling around us. I did it. I stopped being scared and timid and I got everything I've wanted.

Life is so good.

Chapter 21

Crew

What now? That's the memo my brain is currently sending my heart. But my heart is too busy flopping around like a fish on a dock to come up with an answer. I like this woman. It's not something I planned or even wanted but damn, I like her. A lot.

There's still a lot she doesn't know about me though, so the fact that she's beaming right now isn't something I take solace in. I have had this talk with my therapist, about what would happen if I found someone else I wanted to seriously pursue. I blew him off when he asked the question because it seemed impossible. I would not let myself fall. He backed off when it was clear my only answer to his questions about how I would address my sexuality was 'Don't have to worry. Not going to happen.' But he did say in order to start a relationship authentically I should be upfront about it as soon as possible.

The question is, now that I'm in this situation I never thought I would be in, how do I do that?

We pull to a stop in front of her apartment and she lingers, clinging to my back for a few minutes as I turn off the bike and pull off my helmet. I love the feeling of her against me like this.

When she finally lets go, she lifts herself off the bike and yanks off her helmet. Her hair is all over the place so I put down the kickstand, get off the bike, and stand in front of her, smoothing her dark silky hair back into place. "So... now what?"

I wish I knew, Fireball, I think and give her a little shrug. "I think I need to have a chat with Tate. Then I'll swing by the team store and grab you a jersey with my name on the back."

She grins. "I understand the Tate thing being a priority, but the jersey?"

"Huge priority," I promise her. "Because I do not want to see Tater or Tot or any version of that on you again. Also, feel free to wear the jersey, and nothing else, on date nights. Home date nights of course. When I get a home. I'm working on that."

"You are something else."

"I am. But... I think you can handle it." I wink at her because I know she loves it. I can tell by the way her skin tinges pink. "So you good with me telling Tate?"

She nods. "You can tell whoever you want. Just... what exactly are you telling them?"

"That you and I are seeing each other," I say. "The details of how and where and when it started are ours alone. You good with that, Fireball."

She nods. "And you're good with me telling people too? Because FYI, I think my mom has already figured it out and will likely say something stupid in our family group chat."

"Okay, then I better get to Tate sooner rather than later."

She bites that perfectly plump bottom lip again. "I also... I mean will this be exclusive because I just... I can't handle sharing."

"I can't either," I reply. "And for the record, I haven't been with anyone since our hookup in Vegas."

"Me either, but I'm betting you guessed that."

"I did."

"I'm a little self-conscious at how different our experience levels are," she admits and her head is tipped down so I'm looking at the top of her head and not her face. "I feel like... I worry it will bore you."

"I don't even think about it, Olivia," I promise her as I scoop her chin in my hand and force her to look at me. "I'm not going to lie, I've had a good amount of sex with a decent amount of people. But when I'm with you, I think of only you. I get excited at the idea of discovering things with you. What you like, how you like it. I want to be your plaything, Olivia. Nothing is off-limits with us, and I want you to know that. Whatever you want to try, let's try it. Except sharing. I don't want to share you with anyone. For any reason."

"Oh... okay." She looks a little bit relieved but only a little. "I just... what if I'm vanilla?"

"It's a valid flavor, Fireball." I smile and kiss her lips softly. "I like vanilla. Whatever you are, sweetheart, I'm here for it. You turn me on with clothes on and off, mentally and physically, and I can't tell you the last time that happened."

"Your ex-wife?"

Huh. That's a loaded question. "Maybe. Sort of. Not really."

I'm scrambling in my head to figure out a way to explain that to Olivia. I am not a guy who is good with words. At least, not when they matter. Nash is the far more articulate one. Anne-Marie always used to tell me I have the communication skills of a toddler.

"You started dating her when you were...?"

"Fourteen."

"So, the connection was mental and physical but it was also juvenile, right?" Olivia says, glancing up at me timidly through her lashes. "When couples get together at such a young age, it can be hard to grow emotionally. Not always but sometimes you get stuck in the less developed communication patterns you started in."

I must look as stunned as I am because she smiles sheepishly. "Yeah I mean, I was connected to my ex emotionally and physically, obviously, but that didn't grow like it should have, like you said. But how did you know that?"

"I took a few psychology courses," she replies. "And when everyone else was exploring human connection and acting on hormones I was just thinking about them. Analyzing them. Reading about it. Also, I've had boyfriends and some pretty solid relationships. But they always ended when I wouldn't... I mean, there's a place we would get to and I wouldn't go farther so they always ended."

"And then you just decided to pick a random guy in Vegas and go all-in?" I ask because it still doesn't make sense to me. I keep telling myself it doesn't have to. And it doesn't. A woman has a right to make her own decisions, about sexuality or anything else, without anyone else's approval or understanding. But I'm so damn curious.

"Well the universe kind of gave me a wake-up call that I should get on with it," Olivia confesses, but before I can quiz her about that statement because it seems slightly ominous, she keeps going. "And you weren't exactly, totally random. I recognized you, remember? I knew you were a stand-up guy. I was safe and it would be a solid effort on your part, even as a one-night stand. So... here we are."

"What was the wake—"

"Oh shit."

Olivia and I both snap our heads toward the voice and as soon as I see Grady's face I take a step back, away from Olivia. I regret it immediately because it makes me look guilty. And I'm not. I've done nothing wrong. Grady's eyes flare and our gaze locks, but he turns away and focuses on his cousin. "Hey, Liv. Did I interrupt something? Sorry!"

"No. We were just saying goodbye," Liv says as she walks over to him and gives him a hug. Over her shoulder, his eyes stay on me and they're hard. "You know Crew, right?"

"Yeah. Through work," Grady mutters.

She glances at me and I nod and toss a "Hey. Hi." to Grady who ignores me. He starts up the steps to Olivia's apartment.

"I'm here to see Uncle Devin."

"Is Dad here?" Olivia asks. "He wasn't when I left."

"Left to go on a date with Crew?" Grady asks her.

"It wasn't a date," I interject for some stupid reason. Holy shit this is next-level awkward and I'm making it worse. "It was me trying to smooth over a misunderstanding. I... I should go. I guess, but actually, Grady I wanted to talk to you for a second about a hockey thing."

"Talk to me tomorrow," Grady says without looking at me. He reaches for the door to the building. "I'm supposed to do an interview with Devin for TSN. He told me to meet him here."

"I thought you were leaving tomorrow."

"Not anymore." Grady yanks open the door but finally stops to look at me. "I was traded."

"To who?"

He cocks his head and looks at me like I've lost every single one of my marbles. I guess I have because it hits me at the same moment Olivia squeals the text abbreviation, "O-M-G! You're a Quake?"

"Yeah. Their goalie is out for at least six months so they needed someone cheap and easy," Grady announces as she leaps into his arms again for a celebratory hug. "I mean, someone other than Crew."

Ouch.

He smiles like he's making a joke but it doesn't reach his

eyes. Olivia smacks his chest and rolls her eyes, not getting how personal that dig was. "Why do hockey players always talk shit to each other?"

"It's called chirping," I explain. "Integral part of the sport."

She turns back to me. "Talk to you later?"

"Talk to you soon," I confirm and manage to muster up a smile for her. Then my eyes skitter over to Grady. "Talk to you tomorrow."

He doesn't answer. He just disappears inside Olivia's apartment complex with her. I feel nauseated as I get on the bike. He could say anything to her. He could ruin things with Olivia before they even really start and I can't help but wonder how the hell I got here. Caring about someone screwing up a relationship I never even wanted.

Chapter 22

Crew

The one thing that made it possible to sleep last night was that I knew Grady wouldn't tell Olivia about our night together, because it would mean outing himself and Grady swears he never wants anyone to know his sexual preferences. I texted him twice last night but he never got back to me. In the last text, I told him I would swing by his hotel before practice so here I am, walking through the lobby of the Beverly Wilshire.

I don't have his room number and I don't feel like dealing with the front desk so I text him again and tell him I'm downstairs and then park my ass in one of the fancy chairs facing the bank of elevators and wait. It doesn't take more than fifteen minutes until the elevator on the left opens and Grady Garrison saunters out.

I stand up and cross the travertine marble floor. He shoves his hands in the pockets of his jeans. "Hey. I'm grabbing some breakfast before I head to practice. You wanna join?"

I nod. "Sure. I ate but I can grab a coffee."

Grady nods and I follow him back across the lobby to the entrance to their restaurant called Boulevard. The hostess smiles brightly and seats us at a table next to the windows facing Rodeo Drive. The waiter takes our order, a black coffee for me and an egg white cheddar and ham omelet for Grady with a chai latte.

"What is with your family and chai?" I ask. "Olivia had me try it and it tastes like the inside of a bag full of grass clippings."

Grady laughs soundlessly at that. "Anything is better than black coffee dude."

I shake my head. "Agree to disagree."

"On hot beverages, sure. Are you here to ask me to do that on the subject of you dating my family members?" Grady asks, his red eyebrows pinched.

"I know it seems weird," I admit and my fingers play with the edge of the fancy woven napkin, but my eyes stay on him. I want him to know I'm sincere about this. "And this will probably make me sound like an asshole, but I didn't even realize you two were related at first."

"Me and Liv? Or me and my one and only sister Shelby?" His eyes are narrowing by the second. I am doing a shit job at this. For the first time in my life, I wish I was Nash. He is so much better at communicating.

"I am not interested in your sister. Never was. She's lovely though. Seems great," I say cautiously. "But I was already involved with Olivia when I met Shelby and honestly, I haven't thought of anyone since I met Olivia," I confess and flash him a quick smile. "She caught me by surprise. And of course, when I realized she was your cousin I panicked, but I knew I couldn't tell her."

"No. You can't. Please." Panic is darkening his eyes now. "I have no intentions of ever telling anyone, in my family or otherwise, and I don't want you to out me."

"I would never, Grady. I promise." God, I can't imagine doing something so cruel.

He looks out the window. "Is it going to make things harder for you and Liv?"

"No. I mean I don't think it's mandatory that you list the name and social security number of every person you've never been with to your new girlfriend, is it?" I ask, trying to be light and slightly jovial because the situation could use a little levity. "I'm not exactly an expert on this because I've had exactly one serious girlfriend, who I married and almost ruined my life over."

Grady shoots me a sympathetic glance. "So in a way, you are almost as new at relationships as Liv is at sex."

"Umm... yeah, that's one way to look at it and the only thing weirder than you knowing I'm with your cousin is you talking about her sex life," I confess, and he smiles.

"I'm just saying I know my cousin," Grady says and pauses as the waiter drops off our order. Grady thanks him and reaches for the pepper on the table as he continues. "I adore her and to be honest, I'm happy she's found someone who makes her beam. She was literally beaming all night after she left you. She's happy. You look happy too."

I nod and stir a packet of stevia into my coffee. "I like her, Grady. Truly."

He nods.

"Is that weird? Did you think... you and I..." I let the sentence trail for two reasons—we're in public and also it's an egotistical assumption, that he still wants me, and I hate sounding egotistical.

He shakes his head. "It was good. I would have done it again. But like... no offense, it doesn't hurt me that it won't happen again, or even that you're romantically interested in my cousin. I wasn't looking for that from you."

"Okay good." I smile at him. He smiles back.

"So I guess this is the part where I threaten to end you if you hurt her in any way," Grady says, taking a bite of his omelet and chewing it. When he swallows, he points his fork at me for a second. "There. Done. Consider yourself threatened."

"I've been warned. I will take it seriously," I promise.

I sip my coffee, and he chews another bite of omelet. "Does she know about your proclivity for... shooting right and left?"

A hockey analogy. That's a new one.

I shake my head. "Not yet, but I will tell her."

"Okay."

Our conversation moves to the team, and how he feels about being traded, which is good but he also feels pressure because of our previous Cup win and trying to repeat it being the Quake's main focus for the year. I offer to give him a ride to practice since he doesn't have his car here yet and he accepts. As we drive down Wilshire, I finally find the guts to ask him a question that has been eating away at me.

"Grady, do you think she'll care?"

"That you're bi?" he asks freely because we're alone in my car. I glance at him and nod. "Nope. My whole family is very progressive and pro-LGBTQIA. She might have questions but they'll be curiosity-based, not judgement-based. Livvy is a bit of a Bambi when it comes to sex but she is definitely not a bigot."

I don't ask him why he won't tell them who is he if they're all so progressive but the question is at the front of my mind. When we get to the arena everything that could have been awkward about this is a distant memory. Grady is relaxed, joking, friendly. "Thanks, man."

"Honestly no worries. I'm happy for her and you," he says, and I feel he genuinely means it. Then he points down the hall where Tate is waiting at the elevator that takes us from player parking to the bowels of the facility. "I'm actually more happy for Livvy because she doesn't have to deal with him, with knives on his feet, after he finds out. I heard about the Quake code."

Right. Tate. The code.

We're so close now Tate hears us and turns. He smiles, and I drink it in because it may be the last one I see directed at me in a while. "Hey! My cousin and my bestie. I like how this year is shaping up."

He lifts his fist to tap mine, the Grady's. "How's Hendrix taking this?" Grady questions as we all get into the elevator and Tate punches the right button.

"He's bummed, but he gets it," Tate says. "He's happy he's still in the league, and there are worse teams to be traded to than Seattle. What did he say to you, Westy?"

"I..." I swallow. Fuck. "I haven't talked to him yet."

"He left last night for Seattle," Tate says, and he is full-on judging me for not reaching out. A team captain would always reach out to say goodbye to a traded player. I'm sure Nash did. I fucked up.

"I can still reach out," I argue. "I had a lot going on in the last twenty-four hours, but I'll talk to him soon. Right after practice."

Tate nods, but he still has that look in his eye that reminds me I fucked up.

"So..." Grady says as the elevator settles and the doors start to glide open. "Crew is dating Liv."

He steps out of the elevator and misses me glaring, wide-eyed at his back. Tate laughs and steps out after his cousin. "Who is Liv?"

"Our cousin."

Tate's smile trembles and then his eyes find mine and then move back to Grady who waves. "Off to meet the goalie coach."

Tate turns to me. "You don't date."

"I didn't for a while." I shrug my shoulders. "But I changed my mind."

"Liv? My cousin?"

"Yeah. That Liv." I swallow. "And I just want you to know that I didn't knowingly break the code. The first time I met her I didn't know she was your relative. And honestly, we said siblings when we made up that code."

He folds his arms over his chest and I can see his jaw flex. He's processing but he is also pissed. I get it. "When did you meet her?"

"In Vegas."

And as our eyes lock we both think of the very same memory from that trip. Me, in a woman's hoodie. On his floor. His light eyes darken and he shakes his head slowly. "No. No. You did not."

"I didn't know who she was," I remind him.

"Fucking hell, Crew!" He balls his hands into fists at his side and swears again under his breath.

"We're dating. Like full-on, dude. It isn't a one-night stand. I mean I think we both thought it would be that, but it isn't," I confess and he looks angrier at that. "I like her. I respect her. I'm not going to hurt her."

"Did she tell you?" I blink and wait for him to elaborate. When he just stares at me imploringly I have to shrug. He swears again. "Well, I can't fucking be the one to tell you."

"Tell me what?" I don't like the cold knot tightening in my chest.

"I'm more protective of Liv than I am of Tenley or anyone else in the family, but there is a reason for that," Tate explains, stepping closer to me and pointing. "You need to be careful here. For your own sake because I know you've been burned before."

"Scorched," I correct. "Like the earth in the Bible."

"If you two aren't honest with each other then it will happen again, and she's not telling you something," Tate says quietly. "And I'm actually more worried about you than her at this moment in time."

"Wh... What?" This was not how I thought this conversation would go at all.

"Boys! Let's move. Coach wants us suited up and on the ice in fifteen!" Nash's voice fills the hallway and without another word, Tate stalks off toward the dressing room.

I'm left with nothing but an ominous feeling in my gut.

Chapter 23

Liv

I glance at Dylan who is occupied with his giant plastic dump truck, sitting on the AstroTurf-covered patio and making dump truck sounds with his little mouth. I take the moment to glance at my phone again. The family group chat has been blowing up since I made my little announcement. All I wrote was *Morning Gang. New boyfriend alert: I'm dating Crew Westwood. K Thx Bye!*

There's been a tsunami of texts ever since. So many I had to completely turn my phone off during classes this morning. I pull up the group chat now and scan over the texts.

Callie: I am so happy for you baby! Crew is good people. But if that changes let me know and I will knock him over the head with something.

Uncle J: She's not kidding. Trust me.

Uncle Luc: She isn't kidding. Anyway, happy if you're happy kiddo.

Auntie Rose: Avery and Steph are such lovely people, I'm sure Crew is a fine man. Yay for love.

Harlow: Relax Mom they just started dating. Do NOT throw around the L word.

Theo: Now I know who to target on the ice when we play the Quake next week. Gotta show West-wood we've got your back.

Grady: I already did that when he told me.

Shelby: Happy for u Livvy! Is his twin single?

Uncle Cole: You really wanna date a guy on the other side of the country?

Shelby: I didn't say anything about dating.

Uncle Cole: I am going to delete this entire conversation from my brain now.

Tate: We will chat when I get home Liv.

Oh... that one is foreboding.

And oddly, not a word from Tenley. I haven't been home to talk to her in person about this so I hope she's there when I'm done watching Dylan. I glance down at my little monster who is rolling the dump truck toward the rattan coffee table and making noises I'm sure he thinks are engine noises.

My phone buzzes again but this time it's not the group chat. It's my boyfriend. A smile blooms as I open his text.

Crew: Wanna come over when you're done at Tate's? Would love to see you.

Liv: Sure. Ten has our car but if you don't mind driving me back to WeHo later I'm in.

Crew: I can do that. Tomorrow morning.

I smile so big it's ridiculous.

Liv: I'll be by around eight.

Crew responds with a thumbs up and I put my phone in my pocket and get down on the ground with Dylan who has moved from the truck to the ukulele I bought him. "Ba-da-ba-ba!" He wails happily like he thinks he's Kid Laroi or something.

"You might skip hockey and be the first Garrison pop star," I tell him and he grins at me.

* * *

Hours later, I'm settling Dylan in his room for the night when the door to his room creeks open behind me and I jump, my heart lurching into my throat.

"It's me!" I turn and see Tate standing there, arms up like he's in a robbery. "Sorry, I thought you heard the front door."

I press a hand to my chest, my heart thundering. "I didn't. I..."

I can't finish that sentence. There is not enough air in my lungs or this room. I move away from Dylan's bed as he yells "Da!" and lift his arms toward Tate who scoops him up and kisses his cheek.

I walk out of the room, make my way downstairs, and into the back yard where I stare at the stars and listen to the canal water tapping Tate and Mallory's paddle boat, and force long, slow breaths into my lungs. A few minutes later, Tate walks out to join me.

"Sorry," I say. "Did you get Dyllie down okay?"

"Yep. He's out," Tate replies and watches me intently. "You okay?"

"Yeah. I was startled."

"That's an intense reaction for startled," Tate notes and I feel judgment from him, which I don't like one bit.

"Remember when we were kids and there was a bat in the barn gym," I say as I recall the building on his parents' property that they converted into a gym for off-season workouts. "You were the one who discovered it and it swooped down at your face and you freaked out for weeks afterward when anything flew by you, from a moth to a sparrow?"

"I was nine."

"Yeah and I was physically assaulted," I remind him. "That's gonna take a minute to get over. I am not abnormal."

243

"I never said you were abnormal," Tate replies, his shoulders tense as he gets defensive. "I think jumping at noises or unexpected things is very normal after what you went through. I don't know if sleeping with a freshly divorced, anti-relationship hockey player on a random trip to Vegas would be considered normal though."

It's like Tate just dropped an anvil on my head. I take a sharp breath and my exhale is shaky. "He told you about Vegas?"

"He didn't have to," Tate explains. "I ran into him that morning when I went back for my wallet. He was on our floor in a woman's hoodie. I didn't know at the time it was your hoodie and he was leaving our suite, but I'm not an idiot and it was easy to piece together once he said he met you in Vegas."

"He's been divorced for a year so I wouldn't call that fresh," I argue. "And we are dating now, his idea FYI so I wouldn't call him anti-relationship anymore."

"Does he know? What happened to you?"

"No. And I don't see why he has to," I mutter. Tate frowns and it makes me sigh. "Look, I will admit that maybe the whole reason I ended up with Crew the first time was because I was responding to trauma. However now it's something else. At the moment I see it as a bright spot, the only good thing that came out of this random attack I had to endure. That I'm still enduring until the asshole's trial happens."

Tate scratches the hair at the back of his neck and hangs his head a little. "Look, he's my best friend so I have to look out for him too. I need to know this isn't just a distraction for you because he's been really fucked over by a woman before and if you do it too..."

"Tate, do you realize who you're talking to?" I demand, exasperated. "I was going for a one-night stand, trying to be like you, or Tenley, or my mom. But I fell for Crew, okay? I'm not going to hurt him."

"I don't think you will," Tate agrees but then adds, "On purpose. I just think someone with unresolved trauma might not be thinking clearly. And you even trying to have a one night stand when all you've ever talked about is the perfect romantic relationship, is a sign that—"

"I'm done having this conversation." I flip up my hand, palm out to get him to shut up, and then storm past him, back into the house where I grab my book bag and purse before heading to the door.

"Wait! I have to drive you, remember?"

"I'll walk."

"You can't walk to West Hollywood from here, Livvy."

"I'm walking to my boyfriend's." I slam the door behind me.

Anger has me halfway to Crew's house before I realize it's dark out. I'm on a side street with no streetlights and I never texted him to say I was on my way. When the reality of my situation starts to take hold, the anger gives way to fear. I want to pull out my phone to text Crew, but I don't want to appear distracted. I keep my eyes up, scan the street, and make my way over a block to the main drag of Abbott Kinney.

There will be lights there and also people. Maybe some sketchy people but also patrons on patios and people to hear me scream if I have to. I started watching YouTube self-defense videos and so I dig my keys out of my pocket and wedge each one between my knuckles, even the stupid little mailbox key. A man is approaching, he's got his hood up and his head down so I move as close to the edge of the sidewalk as possible. I would rather jump into the street if he tries to grab me than be shoved into one of the dark doorways of the closed shops.

He doesn't even glance at me as he bustles by so that's good, but my nerves are fraying more and more with every person I pass and every sound I don't expect, like a dog barking at the end of an alley and a car horn a block over. By the time I see the corner of Crew's gated complex, I start to sprint. The security guard gives me a strange look from inside his box as I get to the gate and lean on it for support.

"I'm... I have the code. I just need a minute to..."

"Olivia!" Crew appears on the other side of the gate and he hits a button on a remote and the gate gently hums as it opens.

He's standing there in just a pair of shorts and a white t-shirt but he's never looked more gorgeous to me. I have never wanted to see a familiar face so badly. I slip through the barely open gate and hug him. He wraps his arms around me and I finally take a deep breath, sucking air into my lungs like I've been holding my breath. Maybe I have. And why are my eyes watering?

He kisses the top of my head. "Tate called and said you took off on him. He was freaking out about you walking to my place."

"I'm fine. I did it," I say, wishing I sounded confident. Wishing I felt confident that the little trip felt like a milestone, but it didn't. I don't ever want to do that again.

"Honey, can you tell me what's going on?" His voice is so soft and gentle.

I look up at him just as a hot wet tear slips down my cheek and he cups my face and wipes it away with the pad of his thumb. "Hey. Hey. You're okay. You're always okay with me."

"I know," I croak out and let him turn us and, with an arm wrapped tightly around my shoulders, he walks us back to his place.

Once we get there, he closes the door behind us and guides me around all the half-packed boxes to his sofa. I drop down onto it easily because my legs are sick of holding me up apparently. He smooths my hair, tucking it behind my ears and then he kisses me again, this time on the forehead. "Olivia, you can tell me anything."

"Okay." I sniff and take a few deep breaths. "But I don't want to. Not right this instant."

He looks taken aback by that and I feel bad but I can't stand the idea of him looking at me the way Tenley and Tate do, like I'm even more of a timid little baby than they thought I was. Plus Crew is a smart man, he'll look at the timeline from the attack and think that me sleeping with him was simply me using him to get rid of my virginity and he would be right. But that's not what it is now and what if he doesn't believe me when I say that part. What if he thinks I used him? He already admitted he doesn't trust women and this isn't going to help that.

Crew gets off the couch and I watch him head into the kitchen. He comes back holding a drink in a blue labeled bottle. Wait, the bottle isn't blue. The drink is. "I tried your wet grass latte, now it's your turn to try my drink," Crew says. "It's an iced caffeine-free lavender latte. I drink them at night when I can't turn my brain off."

I stare at it as I open the cap and it makes a popping sound. I take a tiny sip. I've never drank lavender before but it's delicious. "Not bad. And chai lattes aren't wet grass."

He gives me a small grin. "Are you up for drinking that on the road?"

"Yeah. Where are we going?"

He doesn't respond. He just holds out his hand, so I take it, and the next thing I know we're in his car, driving toward West Hollywood. So I do what any inexperienced woman new to relationships and recently traumatized would do—I jump to conclusions. "Are you taking me home already? I thought... you said morning. I know I'm a bit of a disaster tonight but I fought with Tate. Are you really ditching me?"

"No. I'm not ditching you," Crew replies calmly as he drives down Santa Monica Boulevard toward my house. "But I have to be a bit worried you have something big you won't share with me. I know sexual relationships are new to you, but romantic ones aren't, right?"

"Yeah, I've had boyfriends before."

"So did you lie to them too?"

"There's a difference between lying and working things out on my own," I argue. "I know that this isn't something you ever thought you'd do again—date—and so why in the world would I emotionally vomit all my baggage on you and potentially make you regret your decision?"

"This sounds like, and looks like, a pretty big deal Olivia," Crew says calmly as he turns left on Crescent Heights, towards Laurel Canyon, instead of continuing on to my street a few blocks away. "You showed up tonight pale as a ghost and barely breathing. Like you were in the throes of a panic attack. That's something you should share with the guy who sees you naked regularly."

"I have much to learn, apparently," I say a little bitterly because I am sick of feeling like everyone knows more than me. My own fault, but still.

"I think I've proven myself to be a pretty good teacher, though." I glance over at him and he gives me a cheeky grin as he takes a left on Lookout Mountain and now my curiosity levels are through the roof.

"Where are we going?"

"I told you, I'm looking for a new house," Crew explains as I take another sip of the blue drink. "I was driving the realtor crazy because I've seen every house in Venice and the surrounding area and I don't have the urge to even make an offer on any of them. She has been asking me to branch out and try new areas. So after our day at the Laurel Canyon Store, I started to poke around listings here."

He slows right before arguably the most iconic house in the Canyon, at least still standing, and turns onto Stanley Hills Drive. I swivel my head to look back and try and catch a glimpse of the famous house. "Joni Mitchell lives right over there."

He hooks a right into the first driveway and gravity pushes me back in the plush leather seat as we climb. "Well, this place caught my eye and I came to see it with the agent. I really like it so I asked if I could come see it at night and get the vibe after dark. The agent gave me the keys since it's empty."

"Real Estate agents do that?"

"Maybe not with just anyone but with a relatively famous local athlete with a five million, all-cash budget, yeah. It happens." Crew rolls the car to a stop and I peer out the windshield at the beige stucco beauty in front of us.

"Is this a Spanish or..." I climb out of the car and catch sight of the turret with the oblong windows peppered like dominos across it. "Something else?"

"The agent referred to it as a Spanish Victorian. She said it was built in the mid-sixties and that the architect was experimental, like everyone who lived here back then."

Crew reaches for my hand again and I gladly give it to him. For the next twenty minutes, I am in silent awe as he unlocks the front door of the house and guides me through, explaining what he's been told about the features of each room. The house is amazing. Inside are wood beams colorful tile floors and pale stucco walls. There's an amazing, huge patio off the back that Crew says he'll install a cold plunge and a hot tub on as well as a grill for barbecues. He walks back in and stands in the middle of the den. I lead him over to the wall of windows and point. You can just see the tips of the forest green-colored house. "Joni Mitchell's house. The woman is an icon. This place is a dream and it's right in the middle of history."

"Well, now I really have to buy it." Crew moves to stand

behind me and wraps his big arms around my shoulders. I lean against his chest and whether it's the drink I consumed, or him, I feel grounded and calm for the first time since I left Tate's house. "Joni is Canadian you know. We can make this the Canadian block of the Canyon."

I laugh. "Rumor is she's never really here anymore. Spends most of her time back in Canada."

"And you?" he asks quietly. "You running back to Maine when school is done?"

"Nope. California has better schools for the kind of teaching I want to do right now," I reply. "And I'm happy here. When hockey is over you running back to Canada?"

"Hell no. I mean, thankfully that's about a decade away," Crew says, squeezing me a little tighter. "I love Canada but I don't really know if I'll move back. We'll see what happens next when this career ends. I'm open to anything."

His words hit me because he really has been open, and fearless, in following this thing between us wherever it went. And now here he is, trusting me with his feelings, letting me into his life when he swore he wouldn't let anyone else in, and I'm shutting him out.

I tip my head back against his wide chest and the words tumble out of my mouth much easier than I'd ever thought possible. I tell him about the attack. About how I'm still confused as to why it happened and what his goal had been. I explain how bruised up I was, how scared it made me, and how lucky I was that my punch connected and that couple jumped in when they did.

It feels good spilling my guts. It's like I'm shedding weight I didn't know I was carrying with every word. By the time I stop talking I feel lighter. Crew kisses my temple and whispers, "I wish I could kill the guy."

"Get in line. Tate's first." I sigh. "I'm just lucky he's going to be prosecuted so he doesn't attack someone else. I am freaking out about having to face him but I have to testify because he's trying to deny the charges. Did you know half of these types of cases get off because the courts are so clogged and either a witness doesn't show up or they get time served because the prisons are too crowded?"

"What are you going to do if his sentence is time served?" Crews wants to know and I shrug my shoulders because I don't have an answer.

He moves and turns me in his arms. We're face-to-face now. "Thank you for finally confiding in me."

I tip my head so our lips can connect in a brief but sweet kiss. "I told Tate something tonight that I didn't realize was true until I said it. The one good thing that came out of this ordeal was you and me. I wouldn't have gone to Vegas, hell-bent on losing my virginity, if that monster hadn't tried to jump me. And I'm very glad I did."

"I am too, but I still wish that had never happened to you." He kisses me, longer and deeper than the time before. "You still up for a sleepover?"

I nod but I'm fighting a yawn. "I might actually just sleep though. That drink relaxed me a little too much. I'm exhausted."

He wraps an arm around my shoulder and guides me to the front door. "That's not just the drink, it's your adrenaline dropping," he explains as he pauses to snap the lockbox on the door back into place as we make our way down the stone path to the drive. "It's okay, we'll go straight to bed, for sleep only tonight. And then in the morning, I can be your first-morning sex."

"Another first?" I say, acting both shocked and annoyed. "When will it ever end?"

"I'm hoping never, Fireball." He chuckles as he lets go of me to open my car door.

I like the sound of that more than I care to admit. But I can think of one first I don't want to experience with Crew, a first big breakup. But I feel so solid in this thing with him now that I doubt that will happen. I've told him my big secret and he's still here, still holding my hand, still making me feel like a queen. *His* queen.

All is right with the world.

Chapter 24

Crew

"Where is your brother?" I haven't heard my mom sound this agitated in probably over a decade.

I watch her pace the small holding room where the camera crew asked us to wait before they interview us. They're interviewing my dad right now. Then they'll interview my mom and then me and Nash together for clips they can splice through a montage they're doing tomorrow night before the game when they retire my dad's jersey.

"Did he say anything on the drive here? Was he going somewhere? Meeting someone?" Mom wrings her hands.

"I told you, didn't I?" I ask but I honestly don't remember. I may have only told Dad and assumed he told my mom that Nash bailed on me. She blinks. "Nash didn't ride with me. This morning he texted me to say he was going to make his own way here."

"What? Why?" She lifts her hands to rake through her blonde hair, a move she does when she's stressed but then remembers her hair is professionally blown out and goes back to wringing them instead. "So we don't even know if he's here. In the building? In San Diego?"

"I'm sure he is," I reply as I sit on one of the padded chairs they have throughout the room, which looks like a friends-and-family lounge. "Nash doesn't fuck up when it comes to hockey. Or anything."

Other than being a good brother.

Mom sighs and shoots me a skeptical look. I swear she heard that last part that I only said in my head. I decide to change the subject. "I'm dating someone."

She at least stops pacing at that announcement. "For real?"

"Yeah. Oh, and I found a place to live. A new place. A house in Laurel Canyon," I explain. "I'm signing the paperwork as soon as we get back."

"Please do not say this new person is living in this new place too," Mom warns. "I love you Crew but I don't want you rushing into anything like last time."

"No worries there, this one is slow and steady," I promise. "So slow in fact that I'm not introducing you guys yet."

"Can I at least get a first name?"

"Olivia."

"Californian? Hockey fan?"

"Mainer. And no. I mean she's aware of hockey but I wouldn't call her—"

Mom gasps and grins. "Olivia Garrison?"

"How did you get that so quick?" I ask as she walks over, motioning me to stand up.

"Because I thought I saw you two making eyes a couple weeks ago at the first Quake game," she tells me and pulls me into a hug. "I'm happy for you, Crew. She's a nice girl from a good family and with a solid head on her shoulders and a gentle spirit."

"She's all of that," I agree and give her a quick squeeze back as the door opens and my twin steps into the room.

"What are you hugging about?" Nash grumbles.

He's wearing the deepest darkest scowl I've ever seen on his face, and that says something. He's got on a button-down shirt and some pants that are wrinkled. And the shirt is buttoned wrong too. His eyes are ever so slightly bloodshot. I motion for him to move his sunglasses from his head to his eyes. He blinks but does it as Mom lets go of me and turns around.

"Your brother's girlfriend. Crew just told me he's dating Liv Garrison," Mom tells him, smiling. "So glad you got here. I was beginning to panic. You're never late."

"And Crew is never dating again," Nash says, a hard smile flashing on his lips that says he's kidding, but not really. "Guess everything is a lie!"

His tone is high and bright. Too high. Too bright. My brother is not only in a mood, he's also drunk. Or close to it. My mother tilts her head and takes in her other son. Her mouth starts to open but thankfully so does the door, bumping Nash straight in the ass. He curses. "Nash!"

A head pops in through the opening. A dude with dark wavy hair and clear blue eyes says, "Hi. Oh good both twins are here. Stephanie, we're going to interview you now. Can you follow me? Guys, I'll be back for you in a few. Thanks for your patience."

Mom shoots Nash a concerned look but follows the producer guy, who told me earlier his name was Fisher, out of the room. As soon as the door closes behind them Nash rips off his sunglasses. "So Mom and Dad know about Liv. When were you planning on telling me?"

"I figured you'd heard because Tate and Grady and other teammates know." I shrug. "Nash, have you been drinking?"

He ignores me and shoves a hand into his hair, which isn't as neatly styled as it usually is. "So Mom gets an actual conversation but I get to rely on the hockey gossip chain?"

"I would have talked to you about it on the ride down but

you didn't want to come with me anymore," I reply and step closer to him. But not too close. He's got an energy I don't recognize and I don't like it. "Have you been drinking?"

"I had some bloody marys at lunch," he snaps.

"Some?" I echo, horrified because this is so not like him and so not appropriate. "How many and why?"

He rolls his eyes in the overdramatic way only someone inebriated can do. "I don't know, like four. And why? Because they didn't know how to make a Caesar. Had to settle."

"You knew we were going to be interviewed today."

"Yeah. And it's a puff piece." He waves his hand in the air, dismissing my concern. "They want light, cute, entertaining sound clips from The Greatest's only offspring. You are constantly telling me I'm never light or entertaining so I thought this would loosen me up so I could be the charming, funny twin for once."

"Fucking hell, Mom's film crew is here too, Nash. The one for the documentary." I dig in the pocket of my coat which I tossed over one of the armchairs when we got here. I think I have a pack of gum in one of the pockets. I pull out three sticks of Big Red, which is the worst gum ever and has probably been in there for years but whatever. I hand one to him.

He shoves my hand away way more aggressive than necessary. "Keep it so you can make out with your new girlfriend later."

"Olivia isn't here and seriously, stop being a shit. I am trying to save this situation for Mom and Dad. And so they don't think of you as a fuck up, okay?" I shove the stick of gum at him again. "Trust me. You don't want that feeling."

"Fuck you, you don't give a rat's ass what feelings I have or don't have." He slaps the gum out of my hand.

Rage ripples and swells in my gut. Fury. I stare at the gum

where it landed by one of the baseboards. I force my eyes back to him. He is glaring right back at me.

"Why didn't you tell me? About Liv. Why not just fucking talk to me?"

"You want to know the truth, Nash?" I seethe. "Because I didn't want to see the look of relief on your fucking face when you found out I'm dating a woman and not a man."

The room is dead silent. You can't hear either of us breathing. There's nothing but the gentle rhythmic hum of the ceiling fan as it swirls above us. Nash looks like I just sucker-punched him. His eyes are wide with disbelief. His mouth twisted in confusion. His skin growing redder by the second. "What the fuck did you just say?"

"You are embarrassed by me. By what I did with Anne-Marie, by who I am. I'm bisexual and that disgusts you," I tell him. "You've made it clear."

"Fuck you. I'm done. I don't want anything to do with you. Anywhere. Ever again. Fuck you!"

He pushes past me so fast and close that our shoulders clip. I swear as pain shoots up and down my arm and I reach out and grab him because he's heading for the door. "This is for Dad. You better not let him down."

"Don't touch me."

"Nash."

"Fuck off. You are such a stupid selfish prick," Nash hisses and shoves me.

That fury in my belly swells like a tsunami and washes over me until I can't see straight. I shove him back and he hits the wall with a thump so hard his sunglasses tumble backward and the door rattles. And then he's in the air. I can barely register what's happening before he's hurtling through the air, inches in front of my face, fist cocked.

I've taken many punches before, mostly on the ice. Some I

saw coming. Some I didn't. But I've never taken one from Nash. The pain in my cheek is so intense that my eyes instantly blur and I fight to stay conscious.

"Holy shit!" I hear a voice, panicked and not Nash's, but I can't see who it is because I'm on the floor in the corner. I must have stumbled backward and tumbled over a chair. Nash is on top of me, so I guess I took him with me for the fall.

I swing. I make contact with something... his shoulder maybe? Nash grunts. "Fuck you!" And I resume my swinging again. This time I make contact with something softer. I feel a squish. And his groan gets much deeper and louder.

Then he's gone and there is nothing but air in front of me. Until there's nothing but Dad. Even through my watering eyes, I can see the ashen color of his face, the way his brown eyes have doubled in size and are bright with panic and confusion. "Oh my God. What the hell is going on?"

The door opens over his shoulder. He doesn't even turn around. "Get out."

Fisher disappears, closing the door behind him. Nash is in a heap in one of the chairs, blood sliding down his chin from where I split his lip. Dad grabs my shirt and shakes me. "What the fuck is wrong with you?"

He lets go, grabs the front of Nash's shirt, and hauls him up. "I swear to God I have never been so disappointed by anything or anyone in my entire life. This day was important to me. And your mother. That producer from the documentary just saw you two brawling with each other like mortal enemies. Why would you do that to us?"

I suddenly don't know how we came to blows. It feels so stupid. We hurt him and Mom and for what? I look over at Nash and he's crying. There's a steady stream of tears pouring out of his eyes. Now I'm fucking scared.

"More importantly," Dad goes on, "what the hell would make you two do that to each other?"

There's a hesitant knock on the door. Dad does an about-face and marches over, cracking it just enough for his words to carry to whoever is on the other side. "I need a bucket of ice, some paper towels, and fifteen uninterrupted minutes. Do you understand? Thank you."

He closes the door, then walks over to Nash and pulls him into a hug. My vision is blurring again but this time it's my own tears. They're not out of pain but out of fear. I have never seen Nash break down like this. He sobs into Dad's shoulder. Dad looks as scared as I feel. I wipe my tears and turn away. When someone knocks on the door again I pull myself together and take the ice and paper towels from the Fisher dude.

I kick the door shut with my foot and walk to the only table in the room, making space for the stuff next to the coffee and pastries sitting there. Dad pulls back from Nash who I think is pulling it together. He examines his lip. "You won't need stitches."

He walks up to me, grabs me by the chin gently, and tilts my head to the lights. "You are going to have one hell of a bruise, but no broken eye socket or cheekbone."

His fingers press my tender flesh just to make sure and I wince. Nash has his head hanging, eyes on the carpet as Dad says, "I'm going out there and I'm going to distract your mother and the crews. You two are going back to your hotel and you are going to talk this out. And I am going to see the difference in you both by tomorrow morning or you won't be involved in the ceremony. At all. I will ask that Braddock bench you both."

"What? Dad!" I stare at him in shock. "What about the sound bites for the ceremony reel?"

"They've got enough older footage of you talking about me

and my career. I will make sure it's fine," he says and then he hugs me. "I love you both but this, whatever is going on between you two, is heartbreaking, and fixing it is all that matters. So go fix it."

He lets me go and I watch him leave the room. I turn to Nash who is still staring at the carpet. "I took a rideshare here."

"I drove. Come on." I move to the door, and I half expect him not to follow but he does.

Luckily the hotel is less than five minutes from the arena so we are back in my room within ten minutes. I shut the door behind Nash and he walks over and stands by the window, holding ice in a dripping wet paper towel to his lip. I stare at his back. I don't know where to start. He didn't say anything in the car on the way over except, "Want some ice?"

I toss my car keys on the small table by the window and just say what I'm feeling. "I don't know where to start."

"I'm not a homophobe or whatever," Nash says flatly and finally turns around to look at me. His lip is swollen so his words are kind of slurred. "I don't mind that you're bisexual, Crew. I don't care if you're gay or trans or anything. I can't believe you think I'm that guy. You're supposed to know me better than anyone."

"You were always so cringey when the subject came up. You bristled, you got weird or shifty," I explain.

"Because I was embarrassed," he admits and tosses the ice and wet paper towel onto the table next to my keys. It hits with an audible splat. "Embarrassed that I found out accidentally. You didn't confide in me. Dad assumed you would. That's why he mentioned it, but you didn't. So every time it came up I felt anger and shame and embarrassment that you thought you had to hide that from me. That you didn't want to tell me. Why? Because you don't give a shit about me."

"Are you crazy? I love you. I want to be you when I grow up, Nash." My voice is raw, and it cracks a little and I'm fighting tears again. "I didn't purposely not tell you. Do you remember that night? That night I caught Anne-Marie with someone. In my bed? Our bed?"

He nods. I continue, trying hard not to let the images of my mental meltdown that night come back too vividly. I want them to stay in the past. "I don't. Not all the details. I remember feeling shame and anger and like a fucking failure. I gave her everything she wanted, a big house, an open marriage, everything she asked for instead of a divorce. I didn't want you, and Dad and Mom, to say I told you so. I didn't want the world to think I had made a mistake even if I had, but I definitely didn't want you to see me fuck up that badly."

"Crew, she was the fuck-up not you. I would always have your back and never say I told you so." Nash looks young and tired. Like he used to look after a particularly grueling weekend tournament when we were kids. Only now what's put him through the wringer isn't a hockey team, it's me.

"What you might not know... what Dad knew but I was too ashamed to tell you is that..." I swallow, my cheek throbbing with white-hot pain. "Anne-Marie used my sexuality as a reason to end it. The reason she cheated. She's the one who wanted to try threesomes. She's the one who wanted to try a guy. I did it and I discovered a part of me I didn't know about, and I thought she supported it. I thought we were growing together. I didn't want to leave her but then she turned it all around and said, to Dad and the lawyer, that we needed to up the money despite the prenup because she would argue in court that I had lied about my sexuality. I was gay so that would void the prenup."

"Are you fucking kidding me?" Nash looks horrified. His eyes darken with outrage. "Is that why you paid her so much? Why didn't you tell me? I thought you still had feelings for her. I was so pissed it was like, why is he throwing money at her and letting her get away with everything and risking his career by burning shit and almost lighting the whole house on fire?"

"I had a bit of a breakdown from all her bullshit. I can't explain it other than it was everything boiling over." I sigh. "You handle feelings better than me."

"By not letting myself have any," Nash quips, and our eyes meet.

"You bawled today and you punched me. That looked like feelings to me." He almost smiles. "I'm sorry I drove you to that."

"I drove myself," Nash replies and walks to the small club chair in the other corner of the room. He drops down into it like a sack of potatoes. I lower myself the same way onto the edge of the bed. "And if I'm so much better than you at handling things then why didn't I have a conversation with you about everything instead of just being so hurt that I made you think I was a freaking homophobe?"

"Well... bright side of this is it turns out we're way more similar than we thought," I say because I can't not make light of even the heaviest of moments. "We both are fantastic at misinterpreting and assuming the worst."

He lets out a burst of air and almost smiles but winces instead because his lip is rightfully fucked. "Is that why you've been bailing on everything to do with the captaincy? Because who wants to share the C with a homophobic jerk?"

I nod a little because now I feel super bad about it. "I wanted to share the C with my brother. My best friend since birth and I didn't feel like we had that bond anymore."

He nods and looks away. I wish I could be in his head for just a second. I think it's about all I could handle. Nash is so intense, he vibrates at a whole other frequency. I love him but I also worry about him. "I fucked up. Something big. I've been trying to tell you for a while. Since Vegas."

"Okay. So tell me now."

Nash leans forward, then back, then forward again. "I always wanted to be you when I grew up. Carefree and cocky and so fucking sure that no matter how stupid the move, you could talk or walk or work your way out of the consequences."

"Warning: I can't. No one can."

"Yeah, well I didn't get that memo and took a stupid dare and..." His hazel eyes lock with mine. "I got married."

"You... did you say *married?*" He nods and my brain fumbles the word around in my head like a slippery football. My brother. The king of 'I'm married to my career' got hitched. "To... to a woman?"

He stares. "No. To a hellion. The devil's daughter. A goddamn nightmare dressed as a daydream... I married Tenley Garrison."

I swear on top of my black eye and bruised cheek I'm going to have carpet burn on my chin because my jaw just unhinged itself and is currently on the ground. Nash stands up. "I know. I'm a fucking idiot. She was just so fucking annoying all night teasing me and I can never come up with the smart remarks as fast as you so I just kept drinking and trying to loosen up and then next thing I know we're in some Vegas chapel in the middle of the night and she dares me to do something stupid so, like, we got married."

"Holy shit. I honestly... I don't know what to say."

"It's fine. It's being annulled. As soon as that train wreck finds the damn marriage certificate." Nash groans. "I can't even remember the freaking chapel. I've called like a hundred of them. I've got that lawyer you recommended looking into the Nevada marriage registry but it hasn't been filed yet I guess because she hasn't found it. So maybe we didn't actually get married. I really only remember barfing in a ditch by the Vegas sign."

"Who are you and what have you done with my brother?"

Nash wants to smile but his lip makes it impossible. But I can see it in his eyes. I reach out and hug him. He hugs me back so tightly I can probably add rib injury to the list of issues I have. But the one I don't have anymore is a broken relationship with my twin and that counts more than any bodily injury. "I love you."

"I love you too," he says back. "And I would love you just as much if you were dating Grady Garrison instead of Liv."

I let that one slide. He has no idea what he said is so close to the truth.

"Let's order room service and talk about what I can do to help fix this Tenley situation," I suggest as I let him go.

"I'll take anything I can eat through a straw and a bucket of ice."

I smile. And then I stop because ouch.

I order two buckets of ice.

Chapter 25

Liv

"Texting lover boy, again?" Tenley groans and hip checks me as she walks by carrying a fern that wasn't in our apartment yesterday.

"Yeah. He's taking his pre-game nap soon and I wanted to say sweet dreams," I confess but I leave out the part where I just went into the bathroom and also sent him a cleavage-filled selfie in case he can't sleep and needs something to entertain himself with.

Tenley smiles. "I did not see this plot twist with you and the cool Westwood coming."

"Neither did I but I'm so happy Ten." I grin at her. "I feel like I can tell him anything. And that he tells me anything. Maybe because we started so... candidly. I don't know but it's real. And it's good."

"Did he ever tell you why he and Nash-hole looked like they'd lost a *Fight Club* match with The Rock at their dad's jersey ceremony?" Tenley wants to know.

"Okay so maybe he doesn't tell me everything." I laugh as I tuck my phone in my back pocket and move to the wall she hung the backdrop on. It's a little crooked so I tweak it. "He said he'll explain everything when he gets back."

"When is that?"

"Friday afternoon. They play Seattle tonight and Vancouver Thursday." I stand back and look at the gray backdrop Tenley borrowed from the UCLA film department. It looks good.

"Look at you with the schedule memorized." I am amusing Tenley way too much. "I love this journey for you."

"Shut up or I'll walk and you'll have to find another unpaid production assistant," I warn but she knows my threats are empty. I need to help her with the additional footage for her documentary proposal because tomorrow I have to go to court and give my side of the incident and face the guy who did this. I have no classes today no internship and no Dylan so if I don't help Tenley, I'd do nothing but stress out.

"My therapist said I should tell Mom and Dad before the trial," I announce, and Tenley stops moving. Her head spins to face me. "So I emailed them."

"Liv!"

"I'm better with things written down," I argue. "And that way Mom couldn't interrupt and freak the hell out. It was the best option. I also begged them not to jump on a plane and promised I would call as soon as it's all over tomorrow."

"Your mother will not respect that wish."

"I know. But I also googled the flights and there isn't really an easy way for her to get here in time," I reply, and Tenley looks shocked.

"I'm almost proud of that sneaky move. And I am very proud you're finally seeing someone about this."

"Crew gave me the name of a very good psychologist," I admit. "We do Zoom meetings. It's helpful. I am also going to go to that group at school this week. Not because I'm a victim but because I'm a survivor."

She smiles brightly at me and her face is filled with relief. There's a knock at the door. "Okay, that's the film crew. The girlfriend should be next."

Tenley rushes to the door and I walk over and get the bar stool we're going to have this hockey girlfriend sit on. Tenley's meeting with the Amazon guy went well, but he had two things he was requesting Tenley tweak before he brings the series trailer to his boss. He wanted more young, current wives or girlfriends and a broader representation of more teams.

When Tenley mentioned this in front of Mallory, she suggested that Tenley interview her brother Emmett's new girlfriend. Emmett Echolls had recently been traded to the Quebec Nationals. But he'd started seeing a girl from California at the beginning of the summer and they'd agreed to try long-distance. Mallory wasn't all that close to her siblings, so she didn't know much about the woman, but she got her contact information for Tenley and the woman agreed to an interview. Tenley could splice that into the trailer and hopefully, it would appease the Amazon guy.

The interview was last minute so she decided to use our apartment for it. So now a camera guy, a sound girl, and a make-up artist are cramming themselves and their equipment into our space. I stand back and let them do their thing and admire Tenley who is flawlessly running the show. She's so confident and calm. I hope I look like that when I'm teaching class.

My phone buzzes and it's a text from Crew.

Crew: Miss you.

Before I can write back I get a picture from him. The outline of his very hard cock through a very thin sheet on his hotel bed.

Crew: He misses you too.

Oh my God, I leave the room to go splash water on my very red, very hot face. Then text him back.

Liv: I miss you both.

I fan my face again and head back out. Our guest has arrived—and she is stunning. Long dark wavy hair, big thick lashed brown eyes, olive skin. She's wearing an outfit I could never dream of pulling off, a silky slip dress with a business-like blazer on top. The sound girl is struggling to find a place to clip the mic.

"So I'll ask you some really simple, day in the life, what's it like questions," Tenley is explaining. "And you just give me candid, honest answers. Keep your eyes on me, or my assistant, not the camera."

Tenley motions toward me and the pretty woman's eyes find mine. "Hi!"

"Hi!" She sounded bright and cheerful. I sound squeaky and hyper. Great.

She turns her attention back to Tenley. "This is going to be so much fun. Honey, I am just the glitter you need to make this thing shine."

"That's what we're banking on," Tenley says, and I don't know how she keeps a professional demeanor. I would want to either laugh or roll my eyes at that comment. "The long-distance aspect of you and Emmett's relationships is definitely different."

"So if your docu-thingy gets bought by someone will I be a featured cast member? Like a regular?" she asks.

The makeup artist stands back, done. Yeah, she somehow managed to make the pretty woman prettier. The sound girl gets the mic to clip to her lapel finally and she gets out of the way. Tenley starts giving her directions on where to sit, and how to angle herself. "So the casting thing? You didn't answer."

"Well, you'd likely be asked to be in a few episodes, yeah.

But we don't call it cast members as it isn't scripted," Tenley corrects. "Okay. We ready Anne-Marie?"

Wait... what? She has the same name as Crew's ex. I study her, really study her, from across the room. I have, like any bed buddy who hoped to be more, googled Crew and saw pictures of his ex online with him from when they were married and she would attend games. She had darker hair and maybe a bit of a rounder face and... thinner lips but... well no. It couldn't be.

I subtly slip my phone out of my pocket and pull up my Google search but I don't get to punch her name in because Tenley calls my name and asks me to bring her clipboard. I rush over carrying the notes she left on the dining room table and she settles into one of the other bar stools and the next thing we know we're filming.

Everything seems fine. Anne-Marie talks at length about Emmett and dating a hockey player and having a long-distance relationship and all is smooth sailing and I remind myself that there were four other Olivias in my fourth-grade class. There are two in my program at UCLA. There could easily be more than one Anne-Marie involved with a hockey player. And I've almost convinced myself when Tenley asks her why add the stress of long-distance to a relationship that's already difficult due to the travel and schedule of a pro hockey player.

"Because honestly, it's not my first rodeo. I was married to a hockey player previously, so I know that the distance, being apart from them, isn't the hard part."

Tenley's head snaps up from her notes. Her blonde brows are furrowed. "I'm sorry, you were married to a different hockey player?"

"Yeah. Emmett knows so I didn't think it was a secret. Did you not know?" Anne-Marie smiles and leans forward a little bit, lowering her voice. "I thought maybe that was the reason you guys wanted me. Because I've got double the perspective. I had the worst marriage possible to a player and now I'm in a healthy, albeit long-distance, relationship with a man who knows loyalty and how to be faithful to their partner."

"Who were you married to?" The cameras are rolling. I'm not supposed to be the one talking. And I am certainly not supposed to be the one asking unscripted questions. But Tenley doesn't yell cut or chastise me. She's staring intently at Anne-Marie waiting for the answer I'm scared I already know.

She flips her brown hair over her shoulder, creating a rustle in the mic but I don't need the mic. I hear her loud and clear when she says, "Crew Westwood."

"Cut!" Tenley bellows and jumps off her stool. She hands me the clipboard she's holding and our eyes meet. She looks absolutely blindsided so I know she was as clueless as I am. She waves the sound woman over. "You can unmic her. This isn't going to work out. Thank you for coming Anne-Marie. I didn't mean to waste your time but this isn't going to work out for us."

"Why? What happened?" The sound woman plucks the mic from her jacket, and Anne-Marie stands up. "I'm not saying anything untrue. We were married. He had sex with other people. It's over. All true."

"I do not have permission to discuss anything related to your former marriage," Tenley says like she's suddenly a world-class lawyer. "Mr. Westwood has not signed on and I can't allow his name disparaged without his ability to defend it. Sorry."

The tone of that sorry says she is not sorry at all. Anne-Marie hears it too, but she doesn't appreciate it the way I do. Her voice gets tight, her hands slip to her hips, and she gets a defiant glint in her eye. "But his dad is doing this, right? I heard from Emmett that Avery Westwood was in this. My ex-father-in-law. He knows. He knows all about it. The cheating... the three ways he wanted to have with me. And the men."

"What?" The word hurls itself out of my mouth.

She nods, thinking she's hooked us. I'm not a fish taking her bait. I'm a girlfriend getting her feelings bulldozed. What the hell is even happening here? Anne-Marie leans in. "So I can't say this on camera, but we're not rolling so, yeah. We had an open marriage and it all went south when our three ways became M-F-M. Crew is gay."

"He is not," I say with all the firm belief I have in my heart.

Anne-Marie stares at me. "How would you know?"

"Thank you for your time. Sorry, you aren't a fit. Have a great day," Tenley announces as she swings open the front door to our apartment.

Anne-Marie stares at her completely confused and visibly annoyed. But then she snatches her bag from the table next to the fern and walks out without another word. Tenley shuts the door behind her with a firm thud and then turns to her crew. "Sorry, all. I promise I'll pay you for the full three hours I booked but you're all free to go. And please, I beg you all to remember you signed confidentiality agreements. Absolutely nothing heard at these interviews can be shared with anyone."

The group is quiet as they gather their things as quickly as possible and disappear out the door. It's only once we're alone that Tenley looks me in the eye. "I don't believe her," Tenley tells me and leans against our closed front door, pushing the heels of her hands into her eyes. "I know that intimate relationships are a new area for you, Livvy but trust me when I say that it's rare one person is entirely at fault for a failed relationship. She came here with an agenda. She wanted to slander her ex. She's bitter and petty and we both know Crew isn't gay."

"No, he isn't," I agree and then bite my lip. "I know he's not. I do. But I need to know if anything she said was true. Does that make me a bad person? A jealous girlfriend?"

Tenley smiles and shakes her head. "No, it makes you a caring one. One that is worried she's setting herself up for a fall.

It's okay to be cautious and anxious. Talk to him. I'm sure you'll work this all out."

I nod and try to flash her a confident smile but I'm sure my lip is quivering. I am the opposite of confident. After we clean the apartment and set it back to normal, Tenley offers to stay with me while I call Crew, but I tell her I want privacy so she locks herself in her room to find a new person to add to the documentary.

I walk into my room, close the door, take a deep breath, and FaceTime Crew. He picks up right away. "Hey, Fireball. I was just dreaming of you."

His head is on his pillow. His dirty blond hair tousled. There's a pillow crease on his cheek. The bruising is already fading to a yellowish color on his face. He looks so handsome and he's all mine. I hope this conversation doesn't change that.

"Are you stressing out about the trial tomorrow?"

"I've been anxious," I start and he rubs the sleep from his eyes and focuses on me intently as he sits up.

"I wish I could be there."

"It's okay I told you I can handle this alone," I remind him and take a deep breath. I just have to tell him. "But I decided to help Tenley with some extra interviews for the documentary pitch to keep my mind off of it and... Mallory's brother's new girlfriend was our subject."

"Which brother? Doesn't she have a couple?"

"Emmett. The only one who plays hockey."

Crew nods and rolls his eyes. "Right. The douche who sold out Tate to TMZ."

"He didn't. They thought it was him but it was the other brother," I explain and then shake my head. Stay focused. Clearly, he doesn't know his ex is dating Emmett. "Anyway his new girlfriend... we had no idea but... it's your ex."

He blinks. Furrows his brow. Sits up straighter. "Anne... Anne-Marie is dating Emmett Echolls?"

I nod. Crew says nothing, staring off into space, probably absorbing that information. When he finally looks at me I don't see any jealousy or anger. He looks a little pained, I think, but I get that. A marriage ended. I've looked pained after ending relationships half that committed. "She's gonna ruin his life if he's not careful. Lord knows she tried to ruin mine."

"She may still be trying," I say and his head snaps to attention, his eyes widening.

"What?"

Oh god, I don't know how to have this conversation? I close my eyes. "She said all this stuff about your marriage and you."

"On camera? In front of how many people?"

He's gotten off the bed now, the luxury hotel room is a blur behind him he's moving so quickly. It hits me hard that he hasn't asked what she said. "Yeah. I mean no. Not on film. Not all of it. Tenley called cut as soon as your name came up."

"But she kept talking? Who was in the room? You and Tenley? Was there anyone else?" Crew wants to know. I'm looking at the ceiling of the room now because he must have put down the phone.

"Yeah a couple crew members but Tenley said they all signed NDAs which means—"

"They legally can't talk about anything they hear. Good, I guess, but they still heard her."

"Don't you..." I swallow. My mouth is dry. "Don't you want to know what she said about you?"

The phone moves and then I see his face again. Only I don't recognize it. His jaw is tight, his eyes narrowed and cold, his mouth in a flat, hard line. He looks so mean. "That I cheated. That I forced her into three ways. It's all the same crap she threatened to go to the media with if I didn't pay her more than the prenup had indicated."

"Oh." I want to feel better at this revelation. "So this is her slandering you for money?"

"She got the money. Now she's just slandering me for sport, I guess. But jokes on her. I'll get my dad's lawyer involved again. He won't let her continue to do this," he says firmly, and then he swallows and scrubs his face with his hand, rubbing off the hard, cruel face I didn't recognize. When he looks at me again, I see a glimmer of the Crew I know. The one I've been falling in love with for the past few months.

"So is it all lies? Or is it true but not the way she says it happened?" I bite my lip.

"You know I married young. I told you how hard I worked to stay married even though I knew deep down it was doomed. She asked me to buy her a big stupid house and I did it. She asked me to experiment, sexually, and I did that too."

"So... you guys cheated on each other? Because she wanted you to cheat?" The Crew I know is monogamous and happy about it. I think.

"It wasn't cheating. We opened our marriage," Crew explained. "With ground rules. And she broke those ground rules, not me."

"And there were... three ways?"

He swears, the hardness coming back to his features and his voice. "Is that the part you think is horrible? Or is it the part where she says I had three ways involving men?"

"No. I don't think that's horrible. I think it's horrible she's calling you something you aren't," I don't think I'm handling this right but I don't know what right is here. All I can do is handle it the best I can and I'm trying. "Because she said you were gay and that isn't true because you have feelings for me."

He calms a minute, all the pressure I could see building in

his chest, tightening his muscles, making the vein on the side of his thick neck throb, it all slows. "That's right. I do."

I slowly exhale. "I care about you too Crew. More and more each day."

"I'm not gay."

"Please know if you were I would want you to be. I'd want you to be whoever you truly are and I would be devastated because I'm falling in love with you at a blindingly fast pace, but I wouldn't be devastated that you were gay because there is nothing wrong with being gay. I'd just mourn not being what you're attracted to." I am babbling but I think I make sense. Please may I be making sense?

"I think I've made it abundantly clear that you are exactly what I'm attracted to," Crew replies. "I've even provided photographic evidence today."

I smile softly. He smiles too but it's not the kind he usually gives me. He's not lighting up any rooms today. "But... I have been meaning to tell you that... in the past, I've been with men. And I've liked it. Because I'm bisexual."

I blink. He's staring at me with such a soft, open, vulnerable look. My head is spinning, my heart is aching. "But now you're with me. And only me."

"Yes. And I only want to be with you."

"Okay."

"Okay?"

"Yeah. I've always believed sexuality is a spectrum," I explain but something about this is sitting wrong. Not exactly wrong but... something is still causing an ache in my chest. "I don't care that you're bi, Crew. I care that you didn't tell me until you were forced to."

He doesn't say anything. In fact, he doesn't even look at me through the screen. I have a sudden urge to apologize, say forget it, and just brush this whole thing under the proverbial bed because I'm a people pleaser. And I don't want to lose him. But I'm trying to be stronger, like my mom, and she is the queen of speaking her mind and standing up for her feelings so I will too. "I told you everything about my biggest worries and my secrets. The attack. I didn't want to but I did and I thought we were both sharing. That's a big part of who you are and you kept it from me."

"Because, I told you, I don't trust women."

"I'm not women," I argue. "I'm *your* woman. I've never given you any reason to think I would do anything other than have your back. But you keep lumping me in with someone who wronged you. I can't fix that, Crew. So I think you need to decide whether or not you can really, truly let me in the way I've let you in. Because if you can't... I have to walk away."

"What?"

He sounds angry and shocked. I feel sad and tired and terrified he's going to let me go. But I have to stick to this. I know I do. "So think about it. I'll see you when you get back."

He hangs up before I can and that feels like a very, very bad sign.

Chapter 26

Liv

I hope that the waterproof mascara and concealer I applied works. I really do not want my makeup sliding off my face if I cry today. Everyone will see the bags under my eyes from the sleepless night I just spent tossing in my bed. Now I'm not just worried about facing my attacker, I'm worried about losing my boyfriend. I sigh, take one more look in the mirror, and turn and leave my room.

The trial is supposed to start at nine-thirty. It's barely six thirty as I grab my purse, a jacket, and a good book and leave my apartment. The courthouse is in Santa Monica and the fact is with Los Angeles traffic it might take me over an hour to get there. I'm giving myself three because I can't sleep and I am so anxious I would rather sit there, in the courthouse parking lot, and wait than lie in my bed staring at the ceiling. Tenley offered to go with me, but I refused. Tate offered too. So did Mallory. I'm a little shocked that one, or all, of them, haven't ignored my wishes and shown up to go with me anyway. That's how my family works.

But then I turn the corner of our building to the long row of parking spots tucked under one side of the building and I know exactly why they kept to my wishes. Because my mom is leaning against the hood of the car I share with Tenley, two coffees in her hands.

She puts the coffees down on the car and gives me a smile. "You can totally do this alone. I know that. But you don't have to and that's a luxury I didn't have at your age. From a very young age, I *had* to be strong because I didn't have parents. I promised myself when I had babies they would never have to be strong all alone. They could be strong, and they would be strong, but never alone. So I'm here. I'm sorry."

I lose sight of her through my tears of relief. "Don't be sorry. I love you. I need you."

She rushes to me and wraps her arms around me and I cry into her shoulder like I used to do when I was little and I'd skinned a knee or had my feelings hurt by the class bully. Her hands smooth the back of my hair. "You do not need me, but I got you baby. I will always have you."

"I just talked to you and Dad, in Maine, yesterday after-noon." I sniff my voice trembling. "I even made sure the flights weren't available. How did you get here?"

She holds me tighter. "I'm Callie Caplan-Garrison and nobody stops me. Your brother's team was starting their west coast road trip last night so I hitched a ride to San Francisco and then rented a car and here I am."

"I'm so happy you're here."

"Your dad is here too. He's at our hotel in Santa Monica. One text and he'll join us at the courthouse, but he didn't want to overwhelm you. And he knew there are some things a mama bear can handle." She kisses my forehead and wipes away my tears.

"You can handle anything. You're Callie Caplan-Garrison," I smile through my blubbering. "I really want to be like you, Mom."

"Oh, Olivia." Tears fill her eyes, but she blinks them away. "You are better and more than I could ever hope to be. Now let's get going. I'll drive. Grab your coffee. I have some makeup in my bag so you can touch it up on the way there."

At the beginning of the car ride, I just hold my mom's hand and spill my guts about this attack. She listens quietly, which is odd because my mother is never quiet. When I'm done with the details and all the ugly feelings I had to deal with she lets out a hard breath. "I am so upset I wasn't there for you, Liv."

"I needed to process it on my own," I explain. "I don't regret that part. I also don't regret finally taking everyone's advice and seeing a therapist."

"Everyone?"

"Tenley. Tate. Mallory. Crew. He's the one that finally convinced me," I explain and my stomach swirls with anxiety over my relationship but I push it down. "He told me he wouldn't have made it through his divorce without therapy. What he said made me understand that what I went through, no matter how quick and thankfully without lasting consequences, was still traumatic. It was strong to ask for help, not weak."

"But you still didn't apply that to your parents."

"I told you. That was the first step."

"Well remind me to thank Crew when I see him. How is your boyfriend?" Mom asks and there's excitement in her voice.

"Can we talk about that later?" I ask as I start digging in her bag for some concealer to fix my makeup.

"Umm... okay but that sounds bad."

We're settled in the courthouse parking lot an hour later and the place isn't even opened yet so Mom asks about Crew again. "Remember I'm the cool mom you can tell me anything. If it's a sexy problem, I bet I can help you solve it. An emotional one? I've got you covered there too. Your dad and I did not have an easy start. He was married before me too, remember?"

Right. I often forget that because we're such a well-blended family. I never call Conner my half-brother. He's just my brother, full-stop. "Crew doesn't trust women. That's what he said when we first started dating. And I thought it was a red flag but I... I was crushing too hard to see straight."

"Good D will do that to you."

"Mother!" I let out an exasperated sigh. She grins guiltily and then pretends to zip her lips closed. "And we turned this thing between us into more than a one-night stand. And he encouraged me to open up, about the attack and everything and I felt like I was obviously different. I wasn't a woman he didn't trust. Except last night... I found out that he hasn't told me about a very big part of who he is. And his past."

Mom nods and stares out the window. "Is it something that changes how you feel about him?"

"No."

"Is it something illegal? Would it get him arrested? Would it put you or others in danger?"

"No."

She turns and looks at me, a soft smile crinkling the corners of her eyes that are so similar to mine. "I know you're new to this in a lot of ways, like the sex way."

"Mom, stop."

"But Crew is new to this in some ways too. He was with his ex for a long time. He's never dated divorced. He's probably got scars. This trust thing is valid." She pats my hand. "But two things can be true at once. His feelings can be valid and so can yours, even if they don't match up. If you really feel this is a hurdle you can't get past, then don't get past it. You are young Livvy. You are smart and brave and strong and drop-dead gorgeous. You deserve everything you want from life and from men. Leave him. There'll be someone else."

I yank my head back and glare at her. She's still smiling

sweetly at me, her face a mask of innocence. "Just like that? Just... what? Dump him? Because of a hiccup? Gee, Mom, I thought you understood that there were bumps in the road. I mean Dad didn't give up on you and Uncle Big Bird says you were a total disaster when you and Dad started dating."

Mom laughs. "Oh my God, I expected this reaction but I didn't think you'd hit below the belt. Uncle Big Bird? Are you siding with him? I could list you all the chances he had to beg your Auntie Jessie for but we'd miss this court date and be here in this parking lot all week."

"See, Jessie gave Jordan a bunch of chances and they're happy," I argue. "But you're telling me to just walk out on the first truly happy, intimate experience I've ever had without even letting Crew have a chance to make it right?"

"Yes, I'm saying that, so you'll realize how stupid it would be, freak out on me, and follow your heart on this. Because you already know what it wants." She squeezes my hand again and winks.

"Reverse psychology."

"And you fell for it so quickly!" Mom looks mighty proud of herself.

I see the guards opening up the courthouse and I feel a quiver of panic slide down my spine. "We should go inside."

We both get out of the car and walk toward the building slowly. She holds my hand the whole way. We pass through security and walk down the hall until we find the courtroom number I was given by the District Attorney. We're told to sit on one of the long wooden benches in the hall and wait until the court opens so we do.

It's a long painful wait and I am fighting a losing battle with my anxiety. Finally, the courtroom opens and we file in, but before we can sit down someone calls my name. "Olivia Garrison?" A thin man with a narrow face and tired eyes wearing a brown suit extends his hand. "I'm Milo Suzuki, the state prosecutor for this case. We've had a development I wanted to discuss with you."

"Oh... okay." I swallow. "Can my mom come with me?"

"Of course." He motions for us to slip out of the aisle and we follow him down the hall to a small room with a bleak conference table and no windows. I feel like I'm having an out-of-body experience as he explains that my attacker has opted for a plea deal.

"He'll get sixteen months, and then two years' probation. He'll also have mandatory psychiatric counseling and will enter a substance abuse program while serving his time," he explains, looking proud of himself.

I get it. This is a win for an overworked public defender. But to me, it's not that clear-cut. I want him locked up and the key flushed down the toilet. Mom shakes her head. "Did he tell you why he did this to my daughter? Do we at least get that?"

Mr. Suzuki shrugs. "He's an addict. Painkillers. He was looking for money for a fix. Or for some drugs himself. College kids are often on medication of some sort. And your daughter is tiny and was walking alone. He hasn't said all this, verbatim, but it's been implied. He has a history of petty theft and nothing else so it fits."

"And his likelihood of reoffending?"

"High."

"If he comes after my daughter..."

"He won't be doing that. He won't even remember her name. He probably doesn't now," Mr. Suzuki says, and I hope he's right. "So now you can face him in court and give an impact statement, but his sentence is already fixed. It won't sway a judge or a jury but some victims like to do it to get closure. We welcome that."

"I just want to go home," I say. "I don't need to prove

anything to him, or you, or myself. I just want to forget this man the way he is hopefully forgetting me."

"Well, he won't entirely forget you," Mr. Suzuki says. "His nose never set right after you broke it. He'll have a bump on it that will be a gentle reminder that he picked the wrong woman."

My mom smiles proudly at that. I hook my thumb in her direction. "I get that from her."

We say goodbye to Mr. Suzuki and head back out into the hallway. Now I'm face-to-face with the couple who intervened. They're sitting on the bench where I had been earlier. Their eyes light up when they see me and they smile. My mom drops her arm from my shoulders and rushes to them. "I'm her mom, Callie, I can't ever express my gratitude for what you did to help my baby."

She hugs them both in one giant sweep of her arms. They smile and hug her back and Mrs. Jackson reaches out and rubs my arm. "Are you holding up okay honey?"

"I am. He copped a plea deal."

"We heard. I'm sorry. I wanted the rat bastard in jail for a century," Mr. Jackson says and frowns.

"We got your card," Mrs. Jackson says to me. "It was a very sweet gesture and the flowers were too."

"The least I could do. If you hadn't helped me, I don't know what would have happened next," I tell her.

"We did the right thing. Nothing more," Mr. Jackson says. "I'm glad you're okay. I'm glad this is over."

"Us too," my mom says.

Mrs. Jackson smiles at me. "Maybe we will see you at a Quake game?"

"Quake?" I never told them I was related to a player. Do they know Tate is on the team? Did Google tell them or something?

"Your boyfriend has kindly offered us tickets," Mr. Jackson says, his dark eyes swirling with excitement. "Our grandson is a huge fan and he said we could take him and even meet the team after the game. It's such a generous offer."

"My boyfriend?"

"Yes." Mrs. Jackson motions with a tilt of her head and my eyes drift down the hallway.

Crew is sitting on the last bench, leaning forward, fingers tented between his open knees. I hug Mr. and Mrs. Jackson goodbye and leave my mother to say her goodbyes, and probably thank them another hundred times, and make my way to Crew.

He stands as I get closer. "I know you said you could do this alone. And I know you can, but I needed to be here. I'm sorry."

"You needed to be here in case I couldn't handle it by myself?" I ask.

He looks at me for a very long minute, speechless, just watching me in a way that is breathtaking. Like he's drinking me in. "No Olivia I needed to be here to watch you do it. You are a fucking inspiration and you don't even know it."

He reaches up and cups the side of my face. Shivers spiral down my spine. He tilts his head, and his lips turn up in a soft smile. "I needed to see you be this strong, authentic person who faces her fears head-on so I could remind myself how fucking lucky I am. And scare myself into letting go of the garbage I've gone through before it takes you away from me too."

He kisses me. It's gentle and soft and demure because we are both highly aware of where we are. But the emotions running through us are deep and so real they take my breath away.

"I'll meet you outside Liv." Mom's voice breaks us apart. Her eyes go to Crew. "You're a lucky man."

"I am."

She smiles at him and continues down the hall to the exit.

"How are you even here?" I ask as he slings an arm over my shoulder and pulls me into his side. We start toward the exit too. "You're supposed to be on your way to Vancouver."

"I have to be on a flight in two hours," he admits. "Coach made it happen for me though, when I explained why I needed to be here."

"Thank you."

"Thank you," he replies and stops walking. I turn toward him, the sun kissing both our faces. "For not just dumping my ass."

"I see potential. I'm not ready to let go," I say and wink at him, which makes his eyes go dark because Crew is turned on when I get sassy.

I lean into him, pressing our foreheads together. He cups my face again. "I'm falling fast too, Fireball."

"Don't worry. I've got you. You can trust me," I whisper.

"I know," he replies. "And I do."

He kisses the smile right off my face.

Epilogue

Crew

Six Months Later...

"Wow, this is intense," I note as I walk back into the living room from the kitchen, carrying a tray of relatively healthy food since, thankfully, our season is not over.

Tenley hushes me like noise will somehow throw off her cousin Theo, who is on the ice in the game on my television. The Quake regular season ended last night but Theo's team is playing today and they need to win the game to slide into the last wild card seat in the playoffs, which start in eight days. I invited Tate and, well, everyone, over to watch the game at my place.

I put the plate on the dining room table, my eyes on the TV in the adjoining room. Theo steals the puck from his opponent but whiffs on his shot on net. "Fucking hell, T. Since when do you miss an easy five-hole?" Grady grumbles.

"Something is off with him," Tate observes. "And he can't afford to be off right now."

Liv drops her head into her hands and stifles a groan at her

287

cousins' performance. She's all cute in a pair of jeans and one of my T-shirts. She's barefoot, and her hair is damp from the shower we took together before everyone showed up.

She came to our game last night, in my jersey, and of course, I dragged her home to have her ride my cock while still wearing it, so she doesn't have an alternative besides my clothes this morning. No complaints. She looks perfect. Our eyes meet and she smiles. I smile and wink.

God, I love this woman.

Nash wanders over and grabs some food off the table. "Stress-eating. I totally want Theo to win, because I'd rather face the Quebec Nationals in the final than the Portland Riptide. We perform better against Quebec."

"That's my bro. Over-thinking and over-analyzing like a boss," I smile. "We haven't even started playoffs yet and you're determining who we'll face in the finals."

"Also if you keep stress-eating you'll be too out of shape to play in the finals," Tenley chirps without even turning her head.

I bite back my smile. Nash makes a face at her and even though she isn't looking, she lifts her hand and flips him the bird. I let my smile fly and Olivia rolls her eyes with a grin at their antics. I still haven't told her what Nash confessed in that hotel room months ago, because it's Nash and Tenley's secret to tell. And Nash says the lawyer didn't find any proof they were actually legally married. It seems like maybe they were both just very drunk and no one ever filed the paperwork.

"When does your docu-series start filming and please say it takes you away from Los Angeles," Nash snarks at Tenley.

"I get to spend some of my summer in Canada at your house so buckle up," Tenley replies.

"Really?" I interrupt my eyes darting to my darling girl-friend. "Olivia is spending part of the summer with me, we can all hang when you aren't working."

Olivia claps. "That would be so great!"

"Yeah. Great Woo. Hoo." Nash's tone is as flat as a board.

I chuckle. He glares.

"I don't think they'll do it. Damnit Theo," Tate grumbles watching his cousin as the clock ticks down on the game. He nudges Mallory. "How are you not stressed. It's your brother's team too."

"Because I barely talk to my family and if Emmett makes it to playoffs, and plays you then I have to deal with that troll he's dating even more." My shoulders tense at her words. My ex is still dating Mallory's youngest brother. Right.

"Go Riptide!" Olivia shouts.

Every one of her family members turns to look at her. "I'm sorry, but Theo is young. He'll make it another time. And I don't want to deal with that woman."

"Neither do I," I sigh.

Everyone goes back to the game, as the Riptide gain control of the puck. Conner is flying down the ice but he's checked hard and the ref blows his whistle. I head out onto the deck off the front of the house for some air.

Buying this place in Laurel Canyon was definitely the right move. I absolutely love it here. It's the first place in LA that's felt like home. I take a deep breath and close my eyes, tilting it to the spring sun beaming down through the canopy of palms and Jacarandas. I feel a set of arms circle my waist. Olivia's body leans into my back. "You okay?"

"Yeah. You?"

"Yeah," I feel her lips on the back of my forearm so I turn to face her. Her beautiful dark eyes are clear and bright. "And even if you play Emmett's team in the finals, we'll be fine. I love you."

She's said it before but it never stops amazing me. "I love you too."

I kiss her and I keep kissing her until the patio doors open again and people start wandering out to join us. "Quebec tied, so it's over."

"Huh?" Liv looks confused so Tenley explains.

"They needed to win outright to beat the Riptide for the playoff spot. A tie means the Riptide gets a point so now even if Quebec wins, they can't secure the wild card spot." Tenley says and Olivia looks up at me and I nod.

"Hockey is confusing," Olivia announces. "But yay Conner and hugs to Theo."

"Any more of this crappy beer, Crew?" Tate asks as he and Mallory wander out holding hands.

"I only bought a twelve pack," I confess. "trying to be good with playoffs looming and all."

"I think we need more," Grady replies and turns to Tenley. "Can I borrow your car? I'll head down to the place at the bottom of the street and grab some. Your car is blocking mine on the driveway."

Tenley reaches into the pocket of her cardigan and tosses her cousin the keys.

Two hours later, everyone is tipsy and upbeat. Condolence calls have been made to Theo by every Garrison in the place and once again, I'm amazed at how tight the family is. Nash and I are tight now too. Tighter than we've ever been, which isn't to say we don't bicker. But we're co-captains and we're working together and communicating better than ever before.

"If we really focus, we can beat the Riptide, if they make it that far in their division, which I think they will," Nash tells me. "But we have to really practice our blind passes."

Yeah, we're back to doing that thing the fans and coaches love, where we anticipate where the other will be on the ice and shoot the puck in that direction before the other even gets there. It's put me up in the top three scorers in the league and given Nash the title of most assists.

"We have to get to the end first, Nash," I remind him as Tenley plays a heated game of ping pong on my table at the edge of the patio with Grady. Surprisingly he is not kicking her ass. "It's a long road to the finals, which is the only time we'll play a team from the other division."

"I know but come on, I feel it. Don't you?" he pushes his shoulder into mine as we sit beside each other on the couch. Olivia walks in with a new tray of food she must have prepped in the kitchen.

I shoot her a grateful smile and turn to my brother. "If I say I feel it I jinx it."

"I thought I was the superstitious twin," Nash chuckles. He pauses, sips his beer, and his eyebrows, the same shade as mine, furrow a moment. "You gonna marry this one too?"

"Not right now, no," I reply. "But I hope when I'm ready, she's ready too."

"Good. This is the right call. The right girl," Nash replies. "I'm happy for you."

I'm about to make some snarky remark about how that means we'll be legally tied to Tenley when Olivia holds up a crumpled piece of paper. "Who dropped this?"

"What is it?" Mallory asks.

Olivia unfolds the paper and smooths it out. It looks old and stained and I wonder if it's just garbage that blew in off the street. "A receipt... no a... what? I..."

She pauses pulls her phone out of her pocket and switches on the flashlight. The sun has dipped and the solar lights around the patio aren't that bright. Olivia's head snaps up and she spins to stare at Tenley.

"What?' Tenley asks.

Olivia's head snaps to Nash and then to me before her eyes find the paper again, but Tate is snapping it out of her hand, annoyed with all the suspense. He reads it and his mouth falls open. He looks at his sister. "It's a marriage certificate. For you. And Nash."

"What?" Mallory squeals.

Tenley's face goes pale, and Nash's goes blank like his brain has disconnected. Tate waves it in the air. "Tenley tell me this is a joke. What the fuck?"

"Oh my God!" Tenley lunges and snatches the paper out of Tate's hand.

Nash is on his feet beside me. "You had this? The whole time?"

"It must have been in my sweater pocket. I haven't worn this in forever," Tenley looks like a bear in a trap. Tate snatches the paper back from her and turns to Nash, his eyes narrowed.

"Tell me this fake. A joke."

I step up to stand beside my brother, to have his back if he needs me, and block the punch Tate looks like he wants to throw. "It *might* be."

"I'll call the lawyer," Nash mutters and stalks back into my house. Tate moves to follow, but I hook his arm.

Tenley scurries off after Nash. Tate stares at me. "You knew?"

"Yeah. Sort of."

"Holy shit." Olivia gasps and stares.

Grady puts down his beer and slaps my shoulder. "Great night! The entertainment was top-notch. I'm going to head out. We should do this again sometime."

Mallory tugs on Tate's arm. "Let's go too. We can talk to Ten about this tomorrow."

The next thing I know it's just me and Olivia in the kitchen cleaning up. She's quiet and it doesn't feel like a good quiet. I take a deep breath and finish loading the dishwasher. "So are you mad at me for not telling you about Nash and Tenley?"

She glances up at me as she finishes putting some uneaten fresh veggies back in the fridge. "No. I get that it wasn't your secret to spill. I'm just.... I'm bummed she didn't confide in me."

"I think she just thought if she didn't talk about it, it didn't happen," I explain, relieved that she isn't mad at me. Olivia turns, her back to the countertop and she sighs. I hold her hips in my hands and stand in front of her. "Honestly, I think it['s a fake certificate. Nash hired a lawyer when it happened and she couldn't find any record of the marriage actually being registered."

"When did it happen?"

"In Vegas, on the same trip where we happened."

Olivia laughs her head tipping back, putting her smooth long neck on display so I press my lips to it. Her laughs turn to a sigh and her fingers slip into my hair. "Leave it to Tenley to out-crazy me. I go for a one-night stand. She goes for a marriage."

I kiss her earlobe, her jaw, her cheek. "Hopefully her marriage is as fake as our one-night stand."

"The only fake about that night was my second orgasm."

"Zing!" I say and pull back to look into her eyes which are glimmering with sass. "And also ouch. I'm still embarrassed by that."

"You've more than made up for it," Olivia replies.

"I should probably try again, just to make sure," I lift her ass onto the counter and kiss her, long and slow, letting my tongue explore and play. "I love you."

"I love you too."

"Now take me upstairs or lose me forever," Olivia demands and I chuckle. "My mom made me watch Top Gun."

"I don't remember that line."

"The original, not the new one."

"Oh," I laugh. "Well, it's a good line and who am I to argue?"

I kiss her again before lifting her off the counter and carrying her to my bedroom. I have no idea what is going to happen to my brother. But I do know that he may not know if he's technically married to a Garrison girl, but I'm pretty sure that I will be... one day.

Acknowledgments

I'm writing this on November 6th, 2024 and I will admit, at the moment, I have a migraine and my soul is tired. Making a living this way, as an author, is a gift. Creating loving, witty, strong, and sexy bi characters like Crew is a dream come true. I'll keep writing them regardless of political climate, and I hope you get to keep reading proudly, and that you have easy access to all books in the romance genre.

I had major burnout writing this book this summer so I'm grateful for my writer friends who listened when I complained, who gave helpful tips and encouragement when I needed it. And big hugs to my readers, and bookstagrammers, who ate up all the teasers and told me how excited they were for more Hockey Royalty. You guys gave me the strength I needed to keep the words flowing. Thank you to my husband, as always, for being the biggest cheerleader of my career and of me. Thanks to my mom for always reading.

Major gratitude to my editor Brandi who works with my crazy schedule and delivers on time, every time. I love working with you! Thanks to Jen Obirek and Rosie who beta read and have eagle eyes for little typos. You guys are amazing. Thanks to my agency, Brower Lit.

I want to thank, with all my heart, everyone who has a tired soul, like me, but will continue to fight for human rights and decency... and for characters like Crew to exist without fear or hatred, on pages and, more importantly, in real life.

About the Author

Victoria Denault is an award-winning Canadian romance author. Her book Dauntless won Best Queer Romance in the 2023 Canadian Romance Awards. Victoria writes both MM and MF romance in mostly the sports and small-town genres all with heat, heart and a little snark. She's a nomad at heart and has lived in three different Canadian provinces, as well as California and France. She spends her spare time at the beach, baking, or snuggling her new puppy, Maximus.

For more on her books, and to read free chapters, head to victoriadenault.com